Bethenia grasped a door handle in each hand and thrust open the mahogany carved doors. "Haste!" She stood stock-still at the sight of the cowboy she had thought was out of her life forever.

Bethenia clung to the door as Haste reached for her in two powerful strides. His face was flushed with emotion as he blurted out, "Why did you leave, Bethenia? Run away?"

"Run away?" Bethenia interrupted quickly. "Haste Allen Terrell, I have never run away from anything in my life!"

"Bethenia, you knew I'd be back."

She walked to the bay windows, then turned to face Haste. "No, I didn't."

Haste reached out to her and clutched her hands. "I'm going to tell you something right now, Miss Bethenia Cooper. I've come all the way from Texas to ask you to be my wife and to return to Texas with me. Now, I'm not going to beat around the bush. I just want an answer, one way or another."

"And you expect me to fall in to your arms simply because you came all the way from Texas?" she demanded.

"No, not just that . . . Bethenia, it was if the world had come to a stop," Haste's voice softened. "I knew I would not be able to go on if I didn't find you . . . to tell you—"

"Tell me what, Haste?" Bethenia prompted, looking deeply into his dark eyes.

"That I love you . . . want you . . . need you."

As Haste took Bethenia into his embrace, Aunt Lacey entered the parlor. "Aunt Lacy," Bethenia began. "This is Haste Allen Terrell. He has asked me to marry him."

"And . . .?"

Bethenia turned to Haste. "I'm going to."

SENSUAL AND HEARTWARMING
ARABESQUE ROMANCES FEATURE
AFRICAN-AMERICAN CHARACTERS!

BEGUILED   (0046, $4.99)
by Eboni Snoe

After Raquel agrees to impersonate a missing heiress for
just one night, a daring abduction makes her the captive of
seductive Nate Bowman. Across the exotic Caribbean seas
to the perilous wilds of Central America . . . and into the
savage heart of desire, Nate and Raquel play a dangerous
game. But soon the masquerade will be over. And will they
then lose the one thing that matters most . . . their love?

WHISPERS OF LOVE   (0055, $4.99)
by Shirley Hailstock

Robyn Richards had to fake her own death, change her
identity, and forever forsake her husband Grant, after testi-
fying against a crime syndicate. But, five years later, the
daughter born after her disappearance is in need of help
only Grant can give. Can Robyn maintain her disguise
from the ever present threat of the syndicate — and can she
keep herself from falling in love all over again?

HAPPILY EVER AFTER   (0064, $4.99)
In a week's time, Lauren Taylor fell madly in love with
famed author Cal Samuels and impulsively agreed to be his
wife. But when she abruptly left him, it was for reasons she
dared not express. Five years later, Cal is back, and the
flames of desire are as hot as ever, but, can they start over
again and make it work this time?

JOURNEY'S END

MILDRED RILEY

PINNACLE BOOKS
WINDSOR PUBLISHING CORP.

PINNACLE BOOKS are published by

Windsor Publishing Corp.
850 Third Ave
New York, NY 10022

Second Printing: February 1996

Printed in the United States of America

Chapter One

1875

With courage and determination, Bethenia Cooper clung tenaciously to Jasper's neck. As the gelding moved, she flattened her body along his back to expose as little of herself as possible to the wind. With soft pleas, she urged the animal to go faster. His ears pricked up as he responded to her commands. It was as if he knew she *had* to get away from the Yorkes' homestead.

"Go! Go!" she urged him. "Got to get away from that place! Those awful people," she breathed to herself as she rode through the early morning darkness. Quiet dawn had not yet appeared in the eastern sky. The waning moon hung low on the horizon as Bethenia raced to the place where she hoped to find help.

Since her beloved father's accidental death four months ago—he had not survived a rattlesnake's attack—Bethenia had been forced to endure a life she knew her parents had not planned for her when they left their pitiful log cabin on a scraggly hillside farm in Tennessee.

* * *

The Civil War had left her father's world in ruins. The government, so the reconstructionists said, had promised the freed slaves "forty acres and a mule." But all Lee Cooper had was the small cabin he and his father had put together out of salvaged lumber and whatever else they could find on abandoned farms and plantations.

"Son, sure hope when you and Molly Mae get married, you can make a decent life together. But you know," he warned, "Grover owns the land that this here cabin is on."

"I know, Pa, but old man Grover says it's all right, long 's I help get his tobacco crop in."

"I hate to have you start out beholding to anyone," his father asserted.

Lee could tell by the grim set of his father's proud face that finally to be free was the high point of his father's life.

"I know how you feel, Pa, but we are goin' to have a better life, me and Molly Mae, or I'll die trying," Lee had insisted.

So far, that life had evaded him. His life was sharecropping daily for Ray Grover, whose small acreage could barely support his own wife and family. But Lee did have Jasper.

"Sure, you can have him, if you think you can do anything with him," the Union Cavalry man had said. "Believe he got into some locoweed. Don't have time to wait round here for him to get better. He's yours. Here's a bill of sale, so folk won't think you stole him."

Something in Jasper's large, liquid-brown eyes had appealed to Lee, and by the time he had led the rescued animal away from the stable, a bond had already formed between them.

"Did you know they might have shot you?" Lee had

asked the animal. He could have sworn Jasper nodded in acknowledgment. They had become best friends. Lee had confided to Jasper the frets and worries that he could not share with Molly Mae.

He trudged home, wondering if he ever would be able to reach the goal he had set for himself. Still hot with its angry August blaze, the setting sun beat down on him. His day had been spent eating the dirt stirred up by Jasper's plodding hooves; his night would be spent cajoling and caring for his ailing wife. Never had he thought his life would have turned into one of such bleak despair.

"Daddy!" His daughter came running out of the house when she saw him move past the back door. He grinned at Bethenia, the "light of his life," as his mother put it.

He suddenly felt less weary, less tired, and he no longer felt the sticky sweat that trickled down his face from beneath the tight band of his old hat.

"Watch him, Daddy!" Bethenia warned.

"Oh no, you don't, not this time," Lee said as he ducked away from Jasper's nobby head. It was a game they played every night: the horse tried to knock Lee's hat from his head into the trough. Sometimes Jasper won, especially when Lee was preoccupied with his chores. Lee told Bethenia that, "Sometimes I'd swear old Jasper grins when he wins and my hat gets wet."

"I believe so, too, Daddy. This came today." She handed her father the letter and watched his face as he tore it open.

Dear God, let it be good news, she prayed. When she saw the grin on her father's face, she knew her quick prayer had been answered.

He threw his arm around her shoulders, and they went into the small cabin together.

* * *

"We goin' git a chance at a new life," Lee Cooper told his wife Molly Mae, as he waved the letter he'd received from his brother.

"Conroy's done right well out there in Colorado." Lee continued, "Got himself a big workin' silver mine and a hotel. Wants me to help him run it."

He winced inwardly when he saw the fear cross his wife's face, but he forced positive cheer into his voice as he continued.

"Sure was a good thing for Conroy . . . *us,* too . . . when he left the Union Army and looked for his fortune out west. Now, he's doin' good. Real good."

"But, Lee," Molly Mae whimpered, "I'm afeared o' goin' someplace where I don't know nobody. Somethin' may happen . . . Indians, robbers, don't know what's out there."

"Molly Mae, don't worry so. Got it all figured out. Got two horses, Jasper and the mare, and I fixed up a nice buckboard. Found out that Sam Yorke, you know, the blacksmith, is headin' west with a bunch o' settlers, and I aim for us—you, me, and Bethenia—to be with them."

Bethenia's bare feet slid noiselessly over the floor as she backed out of the kitchen. She would not embarrass her father, not now. So, she waited in the dark hall until she heard his chair scrape along the floor. Then, she heard water splash from the bucket into the porcelain bowl as he washed his face.

"Morning, Pa." Bethenia made her voice as cheerful as possible. Her father turned to face her, his skin still moist from the water. She saw the redness in his eyes.

A sense of helplessness filled her. This feeling frightened her, and her knees trembled as she had stood in the early morning light, hidden behind her father's chair. In his grief, he had not heard her come into the kitchen. Bewildered, she had watched his shoulders shake— those shoulders that she had known to be stalwart, sturdy, and strong. Now, she had seen them shudder in despair.

Fearing she would not be able to maintain her own sense of balance, Bethenia chose not to focus on her father's face. She knew her father was trying to control his emotions when she saw a forced smile break across his face.

"Bethie, you're up early."

"I'm excited 'bout the trip. Want to start packin'."

"Not takin' much. Only what we got to have—frypan, pots, bedclothes—got to travel light. You got somethin' special?"

"Jasper. The quilt Momma made when I was born."

"Well," he smiled at his only child. "I'd say that was important."

Bethenia knew that it was her mother's strange illness that tore at him, that bowed her father's shoulders, and caused the redness in his eyes. The insidious malady that stole his lover from him and robbed his child of a mother. A silent understanding between them filled the small kitchen. Her father did not have to speak, but he did.

"Bethie."

"Yes, Pa?"

"Do whatever you can to help your mother. I promise I'll make it up to you."

Again, his eyes filled, and he pulled his daughter close. He kissed her cheek, a rare display of affection, and Bethenia was startled by the scratchy, brittle roughness of his day-old beard.

The tearful good-bys had been said, and a dozen black families traveling in Sam Yorke's wagon train headed for what they dreamed would be a new life with no more taskmasters who tried to keep them as slaves, denying them their freedom even after the war.

"Goin' to the promis' lan'," they exulted as worn, hardworking farmers and their equally hardworking wives joined together in their trek to the golden fields of the beckoning West.

Memphis, the first good-sized city they approached, disappointed them with its dusty, crowded streets that bustled with cowboys, miners, prospectors, salesmen, and other adventurers out to succeed after the war. Everyone, it seemed, was searching for their own homestead, their own "forty acres," and a future with silver and gold.

The great muddy Mississippi River daunted them even more, but Sam Yorke, the wagon boss, herded the small caravan aboard the ferry that took them from their native Tennessee into Arkansas. Now, they thought, "We's on our way!"

"Lee, please take me home. Take me back, please, Lee," Molly Mae tearfully begged her distraught husband. He tried to reassure her with tales of their new life.

With her hair wildly uncombed, and her clothing stained, she refused to wash up or eat; she would only cower like a twisted doll in the darkness of the covered wagon. The other women in the wagon train tried to help, tried to encourage her with hopeful words.

"Molly Mae, why are you carryin' on so? You know

your husband is doin' his best to find a better life for you and Bethenia."

She would only stare at the women, pick at her hair and clothing, and constantly whimper, "Home, want to go home."

The women shook their heads and gave up. They had problems of their own. A wagon train required a great deal of work and attention; they had none to waste.

One morning after they had been on the trail for almost a week, Lee was handling the reins when he heard his wife scream. He turned to see her bolt suddenly from the back of the wagon to the front. Startled, he grasped her by her waist before she could propel herself beneath the thundering hooves of the horses.

"Oh, Molly Mae." Lee held his quivering wife in his arms. He trembled as much as she did. The thought of her falling and being crushed was more than he could bear. He had no alternative. He tied her to the buckboard, tears streaming down his face.

"Forgive me, Molly Mae, I have to do this. I love you too much to let you hurt yourself."

Between him and his young daughter, they did their best to take care of her.

"One night, in a brief, fleeting moment of clarity, Molly Mae called Bethenia to her side.

"Don't disappoint your daddy like I did. He's a good man, and he deserves better than what I gave him."

A few nights later, she managed somehow to free herself and screaming wildly ran down the rocky slope from the mountain road on which they were traveling.

Lee Cooper wept as he cradled her broken body in his arms. She was buried at the foot of the slope where her husband had found her.

* * *

The fingers of dawn finally streaked and glimmered with a pearl-like iridescence as Bethenia moved toward her destination. Jasper, the gelding, the old mare, and the buckboard were all that the orphaned girl had. Sam Yorke and his wife Hester had assumed responsibility for her welfare.

She had other plans. She *would* find her way, somehow, to her uncle Conroy Cooper. She remembered her father's last words before the rattlesnake's poison ended his life.

He had tried to warn his daughter of the dangers ahead and sought to bolster her confidence in herself.

"Honey," his voice was hoarse and raspy. The poison that raced through his blood had weakened him. His foot, swollen and blackened by the venomous bite, had been propped up on a pillow. Pain was evident in her father's face. Tears streamed down her own face as she leaned closer so as to hear her father's weak voice.

"Daddy, don't leave me! Don't die!" Her tear-streaked face was close to his as she wept.

"Honey, take care of yourself." He struggled to pull out the letter he had received weeks ago from his brother—the letter that had given him such high hopes.

"Here, take this to your uncle in Colorado. Tell him who you are and tell him I tried . . . to git to him." He thrust the letter into her trembling hands.

By the time her father was buried in the scrabble poor cemetery for the transient people on the trail, Bethenia knew that her future depended on her own strength and determination.

Eighteen years old, her athletic tomboylike figure had given way to the ripening curves of a young woman. More than one of the men on the trail had noticed the blossoming loveliness of her softly rounded bosom and enticing limbs. Her brown skin was flawlessly clear, and

her dark, wide-set eyes looked at the world with startling clarity. Thick, dark braids wreathed her face.

The women had noticed Bethenia as well. Together,
they wondered what it would mean to have an unat-
tached single woman on the trail. More than one sighed
with relief when Sam Yorke and his wife mentioned that
they had decided to settle in Oklahoma territory and as
Bethenia's guardians, she would stay with them.

One evening from the back kitchen window of the
Yorkes' homestead, Bethenia had glimpsed a tall,
nutbrown complected cowboy who had brought in a
wagon for repair. He had hailed the blacksmith from the
yard. Who was he?

"Needs the springs fixed. Can you do it right way?"
Bethenia had heard a deep, crisp, authoritative voice in-
quire of Sam Yorke. Could this strange cowboy be the
answer to her father's admonition that she had heard so
often in her mind? "Git to your uncle, somehow!"

Bethenia had shaken the dishwater from her hands,
dried them on the towel, and before Hester Yorke could
demand that she start another odious task, she had
called out to the stern, cold woman, "Goin' to slop the
pigs, ma'am."

She had known that she'd have an opportunity to
wander by the blacksmith's shop. She had to learn all
she could about that cowboy. Maybe he could help her.
Bethenia hated the Yorkes and her few weeks in their
care were hellish. The woman in the front room of the
sod house had been taking her ease while Bethenia
worked. Hester Yorke had not become the surrogate
mother and friend she'd have others believe, but instead
she was a malicious termagant who treated Bethenia as
a hired hand. While her husband Sam Yorke had not

been physically abusive, he had made Bethenia uncomfortable with his suggestive remarks and unwanted advances.

"Don't you think you ought to give your uncle Sam a good-night kiss," he'd whisper slyly, when his wife was out of earshot.

His beefy, corpulent body, topped by an overly-large head, and his hamlike hands had forced an uneasy dread in Bethenia. She had known if he ever came too close to her she'd have to fight ... and probably lose. Her common sense had told her she would be better off somewhere else—and the sooner the better.

She had gone through the backyard, past the cornfields to the hogpen. She had fed the hungry animals the table scraps and the cornhusks from the day's work of canning corn. Then, quickly, furtively, she had doubled back to the blacksmith's shop on the other side of the cornfield where Sam Yorke worked his trade as a smithy.

The firelight from the hot forge had reflected on Bethenia's anxious face as she peered through the window. He had been standing there, watching Sam Yorke work. He had been tall and lean, and Bethenia had seen the powerful muscles of his thighs straining against the leather-fringed chaps he wore. He had seemed to have a lanky grace, and long, wavy black hair fell to his shoulders and framed his satiny brown face. He had pushed his sombrero far back on his head, its leather string dangling around his chin. Bethenia had seen honesty and caring in the cowboy's face as he had leaned toward Sam Yorke to discuss the repair of the wagon.

"Got to make New Mexico territory before the end of the month," he had told the curious smithy. "Can't do it with a broken-down chuck wagon. Most important part of our wagon train."

"Headin' furtha' west, are you?" Sam Yorke had wanted to know. "We got as far as this place, Oklahoma, and decided to stay. Couldn't seem to make it no furtha'."

"Yes, sir. We got twenty-five-hundred head of cattle to get to Wyoming. Outfit up there bought them from my boss Evan Connolly. By the way, my name is Haste Allen Terrell. Friends call me Hat."

He had offered his hand to Sam Yorke and added, "I'm the trail boss."

"You the trail boss?" Sam Yorke had questioned.

"Yep, first Negro one Evan Connolly ever hired, and I aim to do a first-rate job for him. Seein' as how he trusts me, can't do nothing else. Now, can you fix this wagon?"

When Sam Yorke had grasped the young cowboy's hand he had sized up his customer right away. He hadn't thought it would be wise to do a poor job for this young man.

Sam had strong hands from years of working the hot forge with hammer and anvil, but Hat Terrell's hands had been equally as strong and sinewy from years in the saddle, roping, bulldogging, and handling guns—and men. Sam had sensed unmistakable strength. He had recognized pride and determination as well. He had bent to his task; his foot had pumped the bellows as he flamed his fire to white heat, determined and proud to do a good job for another colored man who was trying to succeed.

As Bethenia had watched and listened from her hidden spot, a plan had begun to form in her mind. If Haste Terrell was on his way to Wyoming, he would be using the Goodnight-Loving cattle trail that goes into Colorado. So would she.

Chapter Two

Haste remembered in vivid detail the torn blue sleeve, the rusty streaks of dried blood caked on the soldier's pale face, and the coarse, whispered, dry rattle of the young man's voice.

"Boy, come here. I need help, help. . . ."

The voice died away, and the Union soldier nearly collapsed at the twelve-year-old's feet. Haste had moved quickly. He knew that anyone in a blue uniform found in his home state of Georgia was to be turned over to the authorities. The Northern Army had just marched through Georgia, and life there would never be the same again.

Lieutenant Everett Jamison had had little experience with people of color. There were times when he was growing up in Vermont that he had played with some of the French Canadian children whose parents had migrated to find farm work. He had also known some of the Abenaki Indians who traded at the general store, but he had seen very few colored people. When he went into the army, he was surprised when he ran into a Negro regiment from Massachusetts. Now, he found himself wounded and separated from his men, hiding in a hayloft, dependent on a twelve-year-old Negro lad for survival.

"Name's Everett Jamison, what's yours?" he asked. He winced as Haste pulled the blood-soaked sleeve from his wounded arm. He could tell the lad was efficient and confident by the way he tackled the problem at hand. Haste went about his task, cleaning the wound with water he'd fetched from the well and applying clean cloths to the injury. Could have been an everyday occurrence.

"My name is Haste Allen Terrell. Folks mostly call me Hat," the youngster said, as he helped the lieutenant into a sling.

"Well, Hat, I thank you for your kind assistance. The way I was bleeding from this bad slash from my enemy's saber, I might have been done in for sure if you hadn't showed up when you did."

"Yes, sir, guess it was a good thing."

Haste's dark eyes searched the stranger's face, took in every detail, and he decided that it had been the right thing to help the man ... even if he was a Union soldier. The man would have to be kept hidden, though. Haste noted particularly the friendly blue eyes, the bristle of reddish-brown hair as well as the congenial smile of the stranger. Always curious and inquisitive, Haste saw the intruder as a welcome excitement in his life.

For his part, Everett Jamison thanked his lucky stars that his young rescuer was a calm, capable young lad, whose dark eyes missed little and whose practical nature and native intelligence had led the boy to assist him.

After caring for the wounds, Haste had helped the injured soldier hide in the musty, dark hayloft and had brought what food he could forage from the family's meager supply (he had told his mother he needed bait for fishing). But when he came home, day after fruitless day with no fish, she warned him, "Not givin' you any more my biscuits if you can't do better than come home empty-handed."

For almost a month that summer, Haste took care of Everett Jamison.

"Can you read?" Everett Jamison had asked Haste one day.

"No, sir. Never bin to school."

"Not even a little?"

"Well, my pa can read some . . . told me my letters and numbers."

"Have to repay you for helping me. Start right now. Hand me that stick." And the young soldier traced letters on the barn's dirt floor.

Haste was a good student, and his new friend encouraged him. Everett fired Haste's imagination with stories about the green mountains of his home state, about snowstorms, blizzards, and the verdant fields of the Vermont countryside. He told Haste about the bloody battles of the war, watching the boy's eyes widen as he glimpsed an unknown world.

It was over too soon. Early one morning, Haste's mother watched her son move furtively toward the barn. Haste was about to put his foot on the bottom rung of the ladder when an unexpected flood of morning sunlight covered the interior of the barn.

"Boy, what are you up to?" His mother's voice trapped him where he stood, transfixed, one foot on the ladder and his left hand raised to ascend.

"What you fixin' to do with that food you took from the table?"

Haste looked at his mother and then up to the loft, speechless.

"Whoever you are up there, might as well come on down, cause I ain't leavin' till you do."

Lieutenant Jamison looked down from the hayloft to see a large, brown-skinned woman wearing a voluminous apron over her ample waist. With hands akimbo on her hips, her direct attention was focused on him. He knew he'd have to respond appropriately or face whatever might come his way.

Hat stood beside his mother, his open expression said, I tried, but. . . .

"Lieutenant Everett Jamison, ma'am. At your service, ma'am," he called down.

"Git down from up there!" Mrs. Terrell ordered. "Don't need no service. You got to leave fore the Confederates find you here, that's what!"

Mrs. Terrell watched as the young soldier climbed down the ladder. He looked directly at the woman, then bowed low before her.

"I'm obliged for the care your son gave me, ma'am. If it hadn't been for him, I would have died, bled to death, surely."

"Haste was always a smart boy," Mrs. Terrell responded, giving a loving gaze to her son. "Can always depend on him. Now, let's get you some food packed, so you can be on your way. Ain't got much, but we share."

"Yes, ma'am. Thank you, ma'am."

Everett Jamison soon limped his way out of the Terrells' dusty yard with both mother and son watching him. He turned at the road for one final salute. Then, he was gone.

Haste's father Anson Terrell had vowed some day to be free. He had worked hard as a cooper, making wooden tubs and barrels. Every penny he had earned he saved toward buying his freedom. When he had finally succeeded in doing so, he told his wife that he *had* to leave home to fight for the Union Army.

"Men from all over coming to fight for freedom for everybody. Least I can do is to try to help," he had told her. "I'll be back directly, Haste," he had told his eldest child. "Help your momma with the children till I get back."

They never had seen him again. In November of that year, Anson Terrell had been killed during Sherman's "march to the sea." Haste's mother had received the news with stoic calm.

"Well, Anson left here to die for what he believed. Just one of many, I guess" had been all she would say. She never had let her sorrow show.

The responsibility of the family had fallen on Haste's young shoulders. He had done all the chores his mother required of him without complaining.

It was after Lieutenant Jamison had gone that Haste began to become restless. Would he ever see green mountains, the roaring oceans, the mighty rivers that the lieutenant had told him about? He ached to see a wider world, meet people like the Frenchies, the Canadians, the Indians that he heard were all over the United States.

Haste's imagination had been fired as well by his friend's stories of the loyal comradeship of military life.

"Hat," Lieutenant Jamison had explained, "when you've been with your comrades in battle, when you've fought side by side, you have made a friend, a buddy, for life. I can't tell you how it is; you have to experience it. But I can tell you, son, my buddies will be glad to see me get back to camp. I owe my life to you, son. I'll never forget you, Hat. Here, take this."

He had handed Haste a uniform patch with the Green Mountain insignia on it.

Haste had tucked it into his pant pocket, stepped back, and had given the lieutenant a smart salute.

"Well, sir, guess I taught you well." The soldier had grinned as he returned the gesture. "You'd make a fine soldier just like your father was, I'm sure." He remembered Haste's tale about his father and his fight for freedom.

"Sorry, Hat, that I never met him, but I know one thing. I'm sure he was proud of you, to leave you in charge of the family like he did. Mighty proud."

The war was finally over. Haste was sixteen and even more restless. He approached his mother one evening after supper.

"Ma, I want to leave home."

His mother rocked silently in her rocker for a few moments, then her face crumpled into a wreath of sorrow that tore at Haste, and he swallowed hard to keep the tears from his own eyes.

Finally, his mother spoke. "I know son. I'd be a mighty selfish woman to try to hold you. You have your own life to live. May as well tear my heart out from my body, but I know you got to go. Find your way in the world. And remember to be a good man. I love you, son."

So, Haste left home with a bag his mother packed for him and a few dollars, walking westward with nothing more than a willingness to work, a desire for adventure, and the Green Mountain insignia in his pocket.

* * *

Haste walked almost ten miles the first day. The freedom he felt was exhilarating. He missed his brothers and sisters, but the excitement of this new adventure of being on his own dulled any momentary sadness. The food his mother had packed for him, fried chicken, biscuits, and sweet potato pie, was gone by the end of the second day. He was more than twenty-five miles from home.

Farms and plantations were some distance apart, but for a few chores, cutting wood or hauling logs, he could beg a meal or two. He was not alone. The road traffic was substantial. He met many ex-slaves heading west, a few Indians moving to other Indian territories, as well as drifters, ex-soldiers, con artists, carpetbaggers—all people displaced by the war and untoward circumstances. Haste was intrigued by their stories, but to find food and shelter, he was better off alone. He learned something new every day.

He had been on the road for almost a week and had crossed over into Alabama, cotton country. He reached a cotton plantation. The field was crowded with cotton pickers—men, women, and children. Their bodies moved rhythmically, bending, reaching, and plucking the white balls, stuffing them into tubular bags tied to their waists.

A man on horseback saw Haste walking along and approaching him, called out with a loud yell. "Hey, boy, want to work? Pick cotton?"

Haste knew little about picking cotton, but he could use the money. He also wanted a place to sleep. He ached for a good night's rest, but most of all, he wanted a horse. He was tired of walking, and he wanted to move faster.

Anson Terrell once had told his son, "Hat, it might take you years to do it, but as soon as you can, buy yourself a horse. Save every penny you can come by, cause when you get a horse, not only can you ride, but sitting up on that horse, people will have to look up to you."

Haste's hesitation intrigued the overseer. He had noticed the wide shoulders, the strong back, and the muscular legs of the young man as well as his independence. He nudged his horse to keep pace with Haste.

"Give you ten cents a bale and three meals a day," he offered. Haste shook his head.

"Twenty cents a bale, a place to sleep, and I won't leave till your field is picked clean," Haste countered. If he could earn twenty-five dollars, that would be enough for a good mare.

The overseer grunted and spit out a dark stream of tobacco juice before agreeing. "You drive a hard bargain, but since you promise to stay, it's a deal. What's your name?"

"Haste Allen Terrell. Folk call me Hat."

"Well, Hat, you just mosey on over to that there shack, get youself a burlap bag and start pickin'."

There were several families who worked together in the field. The men showed Haste how to pick the balls of cotton without straining, and when mealtime came, the families shared with Haste.

Mr. Peterson, a dark-skinned man who reminded Haste of his father, asked him where he was headed. The Petersons had invited him for dinner.

"Don't rightly know," Haste told him, as he munched gratefully on a chicken leg given to him by Mrs. Peterson.

"Well, how will you know when you get there if you don't know where you're goin'?" Mr. Peterson said with a barely hidden smile.

Haste chewed thoughtfully and swallowed some lemonade before answering. "If it feels right, then I'll stay and make the best of it."

"Makes sense, eh, Miriam?"

"Could be," his wife said, "long 's *you* don't git no travelin' ideas. Got enough to do right here with your own family."

Later that evening, after everyone had gone home from the field, Haste went to the nearby brook to bathe. After he had washed the dirt and grime from his body, he washed his clothes and dressed in clean pants and a shirt from his knapsack. He would sleep almost fully dressed, removing only his shoes. His clothing, freshly washed, would be dry by morning.

On his way to the shed, he wandered by the stables to look at the horses. He had a turnip and some carrots he'd pilfered from the garden. He fed the vegetables to one of the horses, a handsome chestnut. What he wouldn't do for that horse, he mused. The horse ate eagerly from his hand. Satisfied that he had made a friend, he went to the shed and soon fell asleep on a pallet on the floor.

All the cotton had been picked by the middle of Haste's second week. He went to collect his pay.

"Here you are, Hat," the man said. "Figure I owe you a little over fifteen dollars, minus, of course, what you owe me for room and board. Your pay comes to ten dollars."

Ten dollars! Haste felt a surge of anger well up within himself. He had counted the bales of cotton he'd picked daily and had estimated that he had earned at least twenty-five dollars. He had not expected to pay for sleeping in the shed, and he'd not received any meals from the overseer, only an occasional dipper of water.

Now, he had little to show for his ten days of work. He took the money without a word and walked over to say good-by to his newly found friends. He thanked them for their kindness.

"Anytime, Hat," Mr. Peterson said. "Anytime you come back around these parts, Miriam and me will be right here. Be glad to see you."

"What happens now," Haste asked, "to the cotton?"

"They goin' to take the cotton to the cotton gin, git the seeds out, and load it on barges to go down river."

"Overseer does that, too? Goes with the cotton down river?" Haste's eyes lit up.

"Yep, part of his job to see that the cotton gits to the gin and then down river to the harbor where the big boats take it north. What you plan on doing?"

"I believe I'm going to see that part of the country. Expect to leave early evening. Too hot to walk in the daytime."

Sometime during the night a horse was taken from the stables. There was a note pinned to the wall with ten dollars tacked underneath it.

"You owed me twenty-five dollars. Here is the ten dollars you gave me. I took the chestnut mare. So, we are even—Haste Allen Terrell."

From Alabama's red dirt to Louisiana's bayous, where Haste learned to eat gumbo, crayfish, and beans and rice, to the wide Texas fields, both Haste and his friend, the chestnut mare, kept on the alert for thieves and cut-throats.

One night, just after crossing the Texas border, Haste hunkered down in a wooded area near a stream. He always tried to find water and sweet grass for his chestnut mare he named Lady Belle. Before he took care of his own needs, he took care of his horse. She seemed to appreciate his consideration and tried to please him.

"Lady Belle, you and me are going to have a good rest tonight, cause tomorrow I hope we hit one of them forts people were talking about in Shreveport. Seems like now the war is over, President Johnson wants to start up some cavalry troops from what that Union recruiter said back there. Something about needing soldiers to move the Indians back in their territories."

Haste talked to the horse as if the mare could understand him. He was almost sure she did, the way she would nod her head and look at him with large brown, liquid eyes.

"Of course," he continued to tell his horse, "I can't say that I hold with moving the Indians off their land, but I guess that's up to the government. From what Lieutenant Jamison used to tell me, when you get in the military you keep your thoughts to yourself and do as you're told. My daddy loved the military and this country and died fighting for it. I want to carry on in his footsteps. You understand that, don't you?"

Lady Belle nodded her head as if in agreement. Haste loved the way her coat gleamed when he brushed and curried her. He enjoyed the feel of the strong muscles under her velvet hide.

He almost lost her that night. After completing his chores, he ate some hardtack, washed it down with coffee, and spread his bedroll very close to a stand of trees. He had staked his horse nearby. Tired, he soon fell asleep.

The faint sound that he heard was Lady Belle's soft snicker. Haste bolted upright at once, flung his bedroll to one side and reached for his gun. Back in Louisiana, he had received a bottle of whiskey from a peddler who had a bad foot and needed a ride. Haste did not drink and had traded the whiskey for a gun. He had never realized he might need the weapon until this moment. Now, he was glad he had it and even happier that he'd been shooting at targets with it.

In the darkness, he saw two men moving toward Lady Belle, whose nervousness was revealed by her throaty rumble and snickering.

Haste fired immediately, hitting one of the intruders in the leg. The man let out a bellow of pain, and his companion dragged him into the brush.

Haste wondered if the men had been following him? Did they know he was alone? It was evident they were horse thieves. But, he thought with a chuckle, in the eyes of the law.

"Well, old girl," Haste told the quivering, tense animal, "this is it. Better be moving on. We're not stoppin' till we reach Fort Stark, Texas, to enlist in the cavalry. What was it the recruiter said, 'Twelve dollars a month, uniform, food.' Maybe, Lady Belle, they'll take even you in the army." He patted her gently on the nose as he drew the bridle over her head. In the dark of night, he was on his way to a new life.

He was only seventeen by the time he joined up, but Haste found himself in the company of Negro men eager to prove themselves. They wanted to find a better life after the Civil War.

The Civil War had interrupted the opening of the West, and the various Indian tribes had taken advantage of the nation's preoccupation with the war to reclaim their lands. Now that peace was at hand, what to do with the Negro men who had joined the Union Army? General Grant decided to organize a regiment of Negro

cavalry, the Ninth and the Tenth, and send them to deal
with the hostile Comanche.

The marauding Comanche had swooped down on Fort
Balance, stolen many horses, and raided the post's com-
missary of whiskey and guns. To make the situation
even more reprehensible, the week before, they had attacked a wagon train and scalped and killed several
members of the party. In their anger, they had burned
down a mail station about fifty miles north of Fort Balance.

Peaceful measures by the Indian agent had failed to
get the Indians to return to their territories. Every attempt to do so had been resisted by the warring, angry
tribe.

Haste's Company E, plus Company F and L all of the
Tenth, were dispatched by Colonel Wooster to find the
trail and bring the culprits to justice. Haste was determined to succeed.

Haste was a quick learner, and his abilities had not
gone unnoticed. He rose from private to sergeant in
three years. Now, at twenty, he led his men toward the
Comanche. He was in charge of Company E.

As he and his men crawled through the Texas brush,
Haste could hear the Comanches on the rise ahead—
taunting, jeering, screaming their war cries as the troops
tried to rout them from their advantageous position.

It was getting close to dusk, so Haste told the troopers, "We'll back off two miles north, and they will think
we've given up. We'll bivouac, and at first light, we'll
go around the mesa and hit them from the rear."

Corporal Al Page walked over to Haste, and the two
men hunkered down, the corporal's face creased with
worry lines.

"Sergeant, the mens is skeered. Talk is them Indians ain't goin' let up. We goin' die here."

"Keep them busy, Corporal, so's they don't have time to be afraid. You know we can't finish Fort Washinor if there's constant threat of Indians. Have them put the horses into the center of the field in a corral and start the others digging a trench around the edge. We ain't going to die here! Station the men in the trenches every ten feet with their carbines at ready. Change the guard every two hours. Now, find Private Ben Porter, and send him to me. Don't worry, Corporal, we're getting out of this, never fear." He grinned at the worried soldier. Haste had some good men, and he knew it. Corporal Page was one of them.

Private Benjamin Porter was another. He was a light-hearted recruit with an ability to make jokes, cheering the troops with his antics and good humor. Haste gave him his assignment.

"Private, you go to every man and tell him that I say there's only one way out of this fix. That's to fight those damn Indians with every ounce of spirit and know-how they got. And if they ain't got any, tell them to come see me, and I'll see that they get some, with a good swift kick up their behinds! Colonel Wooster gave us a job to do, and we're goin' to do it!"

"Yes, sir." Private Porter loved the military and was happy to be singled out.

No fires were allowed that evening, and the men had to settle for hardtack and cold coffee.

Haste sent for two more of his men. "I want you, John Roy, and you, Isaiah Jeffrey, to scout that rise as close as you can. See if you can figure out how many Indians are up there and how many mules, horses they've got." His face took on a sober attitude as he warned the men, "For God's sake, don't expose yourselves. Know it's dusk now, but try to get back before dark. Report to me."

"Hey, Sarge," John Roy said, with a wry grin on his young face, "my momma didn't raise no fools. Don't worry 'bout me bein' keerful. I ain't 'bout to expose this body o' mine. It's all I got!"

Haste nodded, "You're too good a man, John Roy, and I don't want to lose you. Just don't be foolhardy. Do your scouting and get back safe. Can't afford to lose another man."

It worried Haste that the company had already lost a number of men: some to cholera, some to dysentery, many had been sent to the hospital for treatment of their war wounds.

Conditions had been less than ideal. It was almost as if Washington had abandoned them. Bad food, sour bread, moldy bacon, and hard canned peas did not make for nutritious meals.

"Sir," Haste had said, as he confronted his colonel one day, "it's bad enough that our horses are dying almost as soon as a soldier puts a leg over the saddle and that our uniforms are in tatters. Some of the men have no boots, have only the moccasins they've cadged from dead Indians. My men aren't complaining, mind you, but—"

"I know, Sergeant, I know," Colonel Wooster had broken in. "I intend to send a dispatch to headquarters immediately for more supplies."

Haste had been aware that besides the problems he had listed, the colonel had an even more pressing concern. The Mexican government had denounced the officials in Washington, D.C. for allowing the troops to follow the Indians when they crossed the Rio Grande into Mexico. As the colonel had explained to Haste, "Washington says we can cross the Rio Grande only if we are in 'hot pursuit' of the enemy. I say damn the Mexican government anyway, Terrell, and Washington, too, for not understanding our situation."

Roy and Jeffrey reported to Haste later that evening that they had skirted the edge of the rise for about five miles before they reached an open valley that revealed a little-used trail on the other side. The country was rugged, broken, and wild. There was a dryness to the soil that rose from their moving feet like ashes from a dead fire. Clumps of strangely formed cactus trees loomed in the gathering darkness. Huge rocks balanced around them like brooding giants. "Man, it was spooky out there," Roy said, "but we kept close to the ground and kept on searching."

"Almost walked into they camp!" Jeffrey broke into Roy's report. "Come up on it suddenlike, behind almost two-hundred yards of them big rocks!"

"And," Haste asked, pressing for more information, "what did you find?"

" 'Bout fifty lodges, the horses they stole, plus a good number of cattle that I guess they rustled from the ranchers."

The company attacked before dawn streaked the morning sky. They moved in a silent convoy toward the sleeping enemy. The troopers charged with vigor and zeal, and soon, in a matter of a few brief minutes, it was over. Some of the Comanche leaders fled, but others were captured. The men rounded up all the animals and their captives, and they headed back to Fort Washinor to continue preparing the fort.

Weary and worn, the men nevertheless were elated because they had successfully completed their mission.

"Sarge!" Corporal Al Page called out.

"What is it, Corporal?" Haste turned to smile at the cavalry veteran who had ridden up beside him.

Al Page and Haste had formed a good relationship starting with the first few days of Haste's recruitment. At that time, the officer of the day, Jonah Stephens, had just denied the young Haste's request to keep Lady Belle with him on the post. Haste remembered it like yesterday.

"It's not that she's not a fine animal, but she is a rather old mare, set in her ways now, and she is too old to be trained in cavalry techniques. I'm afraid you'll have to sell her . . . or give her away," the officer had explained.

"Couldn't sell her, sir. She's like family to me. We've been through a lot. I'd rather . . . give her away, sir."

"I know about family." Stephen's face had brightened with a sudden thought. "I think my wife could take a liking to her . . . Lady Belle, you say her name is . . . if she's as gentle as you say. Some of the officers' wives have formed a riding club, and she needs a mount—"

"Why, yes, sir," Haste swallowed the pain at losing his horse. "I'd like to know someone really wanted Lady Belle."

"Good. I'll have her moved to the officers' stable. But I'll give word that you can visit—"

"No, thanks, sir. I'll say my good-by to her, and . . . well, thank you, sir."

He had saluted the officer and was dismissed.

Blindly, Haste had stumbled down the steps of the building and almost had knocked over Al Page, a thick-set, powerfully built, brown-skinned soldier, who was about six feet tall and whose bowed legs marked him as a cowboy.

"Whoa, there, git into trouble walking into folk like that."

Haste had mumbled an apology to his friend, but before he could move another step, a large brown hand had grabbed his arm in a viselike grip and spun him around. Haste had looked down at the largest pair of hands he'd ever seen.

"Son, you look like you just lost your best friend."

The soldier's grip on Haste's arm had been firm. His hands had been made strong and callused by years of roping, branding, and handling steers and broncos. But the voice had been warm and friendly. Haste had seen real concern in the man's eyes.

"She was my best friend."

"A woman, son? You're too young to be messin' with women."

"Not a woman . . . my horse Lady Belle."

Al Page had responded, "Now *that* I can understand."

From that day, the veteran cavalry man had taken Haste under his tutelage. When Haste had risen to sergeant, no man in the outfit was prouder than Al Page.

Al Page had been born a slave, but when the family who owned his family had moved from Mississippi to Texas after the war, he had been thrown into the western world of steers and horses. He had grown up learning to rope, to ride, and to handle steers. He had seen his first cowboys, Mexican vaqueros, and they had delighted in teaching the apt pupil the skills they knew. He loved horses and had broken many mustangs, so he was proud to join the cavalry. His knowledge of the animals was quickly noticed, and he was promoted to corporal.

Now, memories fading, Haste looked at the corporal, aware of the question in his mind.

"Surprised, weren't you, Corporal. Our plan worked."

"I could never doubt you, Sarge. You're smarter than a whip."

They rode in silence, their horses moved in unison. Haste squinted in the brilliant sunlight.

"Should be back at Fort Balance before nightfall," he said to his corporal.

"Hope we git a chance to rest some. Been out a long time. Be happy to git off horseback for a while—"

"Don't be too sure, Corporal. Like I said, in the army, you never sleep."

"Sergeant Haste Terrell reporting to Colonel Wooster," Haste informed the officer of the day on duty at the colonel's office. He gave the officer a brisk salute and received a halfhearted gesture in reply. The offhand flick was all that he'd expected.

"Have you a written report, Sergeant? Hand it over, and I'll see that it gets to the colonel's desk." The implication in his voice was that this Negro soldier could not read or write.

"Yes, sir, I have, sir!"

The officer reached for the folder that Haste carried under his arm.

"Begging your pardon, sir, but when Colonel Wooster sent me out on this detail, he told me he wanted an oral report, a direct briefing, and I'm prepared to do that, *sir!*"

Haste was not surprised at the sarcastic, hostile tone that he heard when the officer drawled, "So, you're one of our smart Nigra soldiers, eh?"

"Only following orders, *sir!*"

Angrily, the officer whirled around and knocked on the colonel's office door. He left Haste standing at attention while he entered and informed his superior that a Sergeant Terrell, one of the buffalo soldiers, was outside.

Haste wasn't surprised by the attitude of the officer and had realized not long after he had joined the calvary that many of his commanding officers were resentful of their assignments to lead colored men. When he had first arrived, he had overheard one officer tell another, "I deplore the idea of serving with Negro troops. I'm going to resign my commission."

His companion had agreed. "How can we move into untried, uncharted areas with raw, uneducated ex-slaves who cannot read or write and still be expected to have a first-rate military success. How can we have a decent army?"

Haste had listened to the exchange made in his presence as if he lacked the intelligence to understand. He had thought all we need is a chance. He had walked back to his barracks, which had been not much more comfortable than a chicken house. Give us the tools, he almost had said aloud, we can do the work.

Summoned, the colonel strode from his office to greet Haste. "At ease, Sergeant. Come right in!"

Inside, Colonel Wooster offered Haste a seat. "Glad you're back. I'm anxious to hear your report."

"Yes, sir, Colonel. As you probably know, after our battle with the Comanche, we had to do quite a bit of work preparing the new camp, Fort Washinor. We had to put up several buildings—houses, barns, stables— build new roads and a bridge across the Washinor River that makes getting supplies to the fort much easier. However, this fort is near the Indian Territory, and we've had attacks by the Comanche and other tribes that live there. They are very resistant."

"So, you say the Indians are not cooperating?"

"Not very much, sir. As soon as we got the bridge up, it was nearly destroyed by a band of renegade Indians led by Moon Dog. Luckily, we had a detachment at the bridge that was able to repel the attack. In fact, we left one there to guard it."

"And you haven't been able to bring in this Moon Dog?"

"Not yet, sir. He belongs to the Arapaho tribe, I believe."

"I thought the government had an understanding with the Arapaho chief, Chief Wolf Bear. Wasn't he one of the chiefs who met at Medicine Lodge Creek and agreed to go to their territories?"

"Don't know about that, sir, perhaps this Moon Dog is one of the young men in the tribe who doesn't want to go back to their territories."

"Sounds like that's it. Anything else, Sergeant?"

"Our latest real skirmish was with the Comanche. We destroyed their lodges, brought back some of them whom we captured, and we rounded up about fifty stolen horses that we are returning with a few head of cattle."

"Good work, Sergeant. I'll see that this report is included in your file. And, Sergeant, I hate to do this to you, but I'm afraid you'll have to go out again as soon as possible."

He searched through some papers on his desk.

"Here are your new orders. Seems there's been a great deal of trouble at Fort Quimby, in the northwest part of the state. Some outlaws are stealing cattle and horses from the new settlers and homesteaders. And the population is clamoring for army protection. Now, I've set aside some of the best horses I have, from a mighty poor lot, I might add. Most of the animals the government sends us are old, useless ones that nobody else wants," he sighed, "but I've give you and your men the best."

"Yes, sir!"

"So, here are your orders. Understand that this is a gang of about eight men you'll be going after who are disrupting the lives of American citizens. Bring them in. Good luck!"

Haste saluted and left his report on the colonel's desk.

He saluted the officer of the day and went out to find the men he needed for the new task. He rounded up Corporal Al Page, Privates Ben Porter, John Roy, and Isaiah Jeffrey, and some of the other men whom he knew were willing to go. He did not ask for volunteers, preferring to take men he knew.

"Mount up, men," he told them, when all was ready. Horses had been saddled, supplies and ammunition had been secured with blanket rolls and ponchos. In addition, four barrels of water carried by two mules were added to the company. They marched, three abreast, nine men plus two more men leading the pack animals.

"Orders cut to go to Fort Quimby. Got a job to do there, brief you on the way," Haste told them.

The men moved into position and started out at a fair pace to try to reach Fort Quimby before dark. It lay about sixty miles away.

"Sergeant," John Roy complained, "it don't seem fair, just got back from the field, and we's goin' out again. Hardly had time to take a bath and change my drawers—"

"Listen up, John Roy, you're in the army now and you *take* orders. Officer gives them, and you follow, that's all there is to it."

Haste understood the weariness that the young man felt, because he felt the same way. But in the army, you didn't ask. You acted.

"Never mind, John Roy, this is a whole sight better than what there was for us after the war. What else was there for us but the army?" Haste tried to sound encouraging.

Haste observed his men; they were really his closest friends. He knew down deep they were proud to be troopers, despite their complaints. They wore blue heavy woolen trousers with a yellow-gold stripe down the leg and a blue woolen shirt topped by a yellow neckerchief. Most of them wore boots which they kept highly polished, despite having to ride dusty trails. Some others wore moccasins or broken-down brogans that they had managed to filch from someone else, either as a result of a card game or the unfortunate demise of the shoes' prior owner.

When they rode out again that day, the sky radiated a blue so brilliant it almost brought pain to the men's eyes. Most of them had pulled their wide-brimmed hats over their eyes for protection. A few puffy wisps of cottonlike clouds moved lazily along the horizon which, to Haste, only magnified the immensity of the sky. He reflected to himself that a peaceful day like this may well turn out to be a fateful one—one that could change them all. He silently said a prayer that he would be equal to the assignment and return with his men to Fort Balance and safety.

Isaiah Jeffrey rode up to join him and Al Page. Haste was fond of the nineteen-year-old lad who was not only one of the youngest members of the company, but one of the most zealous and enthusiastic. Always willing to do the job, he never appeared to doubt his ability to prove equal to the task.

"Isaiah!" Haste gave the soldier a cheerful greeting.

"Sir!" The response was quick and sharp.

"How you coming on?"

"Fine, I think, sir! Where we off to now, sir!"

"Like I just told Corporal Page, we are being sent out to Fort Quimby to round up a gang threatening the settlers and homesteaders out that way."

"Uh-huh."

Haste noted the scowl on Ike's face.

"What's wrong, Ike? You're most always ready for a new adventure. What's the matter?"

"Why, nuthin', sir," Isaiah mumbled, as he skillfully managed his horse that had shied from a sudden, buoyant tumbleweed.

However, his face seemed almost to crumple like a mask made of papier-mâché.

"What you mean *'nuthin'?*"

Haste maintained his horse's gait in the same rhythmic pattern as Ike's horse. Both animals' heads and necks moved in unison like twin semaphores.

"Well, got a real bad letter from home," Isaiah stuttered. "Bad letter."

"Home? Don't you come from Georgia, same as me?"

'Right, sir."

"So, what is the bad news from home?"

"Folk gittin' shot up and killed—"

"What?"

"That's right. My sister wrote me—say my daddy, he's . . . *was* a Baptist preacher back home. He and some of the church folk was shot and killed at the church picnic. Some mob come upon them and said Negroes didn't have no business congregatin' unless they got *permission.* My sister said five was killed outright and some others wounded. My daddy was one of them killed."

"Ike, I'm sorry for your loss. That's a terrible thing to have happen to your father. They know who did it?"

"Merlene, that's my sister, said they know but ain't nuthin' goin' be done 'bout it."

Ike's eyes were shiny with unshed tears as he looked at Haste. There was a slight tremor in his voice.

"You know, Sarge, maybe you should o' picked someone else for this detail. Don't right see how I can go to take care of white settlers when I know what their kind doin' to *my* folk. I'm thinkin' on goin' back home, leavin' this here army."

Haste paused a moment before he spoke. "Can't blame you for thinking like that, Ike, but if you desert, you will be putting a black mark against your name. I never knew your daddy, but I know he wouldn't want that for you. You're mad now, got a right to be, wouldn't be human if you wasn't, but—"

"Why should I care 'bout protectin' folk that don't give a shit 'bout me or mine?"

Haste heard the anguish in the youngster's voice.

"Cause that's the only way to prove that you're a man, equal to any of them ... better than them," Haste insisted. "Able to put your own feelings to one side and do the job you have to do. We're buffalo soldiers, and that means we're tough, strong, and stubborn just like that old bison the Indians named us for."

Haste could not be sure he had convinced Isaiah not to bolt. He stared at the boy's brown capable hands—strong, sensitive hands that held the reins firmly and guided his horse. He looked again at the young man's face, once bright and cheerful, this day drawn and perturbed. He wondered what the future held for Ike and others like him? He knew what *he* wanted most of all—a loving wife and a family of his own. Was such a thing even likely for a trooper of the Tenth Cavalry? As he and the company rode to their uncertain future, he vowed to keep his dream alive. It was all he had to sustain him in these uncertain times. Would it be enough for the days and months ahead?

Colonel Wooster's message to his general made a distinct appeal for the buffalo soldiers who had performed so admirably. His message was brief.

Under trying conditions these soldiers are committed to their assignment to seek out, overcome, and return the Indians to their territories. However, to succeed, healthy horses, better provisions, and proper uniforms and equipment are imperative.

Colonel Wooster did not need to ask for ammunition. That was always supplied. Springfield rifles, carbines, Colt 45s, Gatling guns, and cannons were available. The items he did not ask for were heart and willingness to serve. He knew his men had more than a sufficient amount of these traits. He would have been delighted if his white officers had a fraction of the troopers' zeal and fight.

Chapter Three

Haste had been extremely frustrated when the all-important chuck wagon had broken down. He was anxious to lead the herd and his eleven men, eight cowboys, and two lowly wranglers, plus the all-important cook, to the next camp. It was a long trail to Cheyenne.

His military service in the cavalry was over after ten years service. All he really knew how to do was to deal with horses and how to lead men, and his men were loyal to him.

"No man can do better than work with Hat Terrell," his men would say. "Depend on Hat. He's the last man to let you down."

Such loyalty had been forged by the legends that surrounded him: how he had saved one soldier's life in the fierce battle at Monson's Falls during the Texans wars with the Indians, how he had ridden into a town square, and had single-handedly rescued a buffalo soldier who was about to be hung for a crime which he did not commit. Hat's reputation was that of a fair, courageous man who often slept with his boots on and his gun handy. His boss, Evan Connolly, would say, "I trust him more than any other man I know . . . of any race. I would go to the ends of the earth with Hat." Connolly felt, too, that Haste Terrell learned how to handle men from his cavalry experience.

Haste recognized their abilities as well as their faults, but somehow was able to extract the best from each one of them. It did not matter who, a white Southerner, a Mexican, an Indian, or a recently freed Negro. Haste himself set the example. He never expected more from his men than he was willing to give himself. He would stay upright in a saddle in a blinding snowstorm or pounding thunderstorm for as long as it took to guard and care for the cattle. He fought wolves, hunted wild mustangs, put out brush fires, and turned many a stampeding herd back to safety. He and his horse worked as one being as he went about his many tasks as trail boss. Like the captain of a ship, his word was law, but he administered it fairly and without prior judgment.

"Yo!" he called to two men who rode, on point, near the lead cattle to keep them in the right direction. "Got to make fifteen more miles fore we camp for the night."

"Right, Hat," they agreed as Hat swung by them.

"Checkin' the men on the swing side—better not have any stragglers—ain't got time to search them out, and I aim to get back to the two men ridin' 'drag.' Seems to me they're strung out furtha' than I want. Got to bring the rear up close."

It took some time to get to the rear of the plodding, bellowing herd, and Haste found his last two men, the newest and therefore on the lowest rung of the team, "eating the dust," as it was called. The dust and dirt raised by ten thousand lumbering hooves of cattle covered everything but the men's eyes. Dirt-rimmed, they hailed their boss, happy that they had not been forgotten.

"Yo, Hat!"

Hat grinned at them sympathetically and shook his head as he wheeled his horse beside one of them.

"Gene, go on over to the river and get cleaned up. I'll stay here, then old Bill here can get a break. You two look like a pair of muddy polecats," he said grinning.

Gene let out a screaming rebel yell, turned his horse toward the riverbank, and swam, dusty clothing and all, into the welcoming cool water. The horse seemed to enjoy it as much as he did.

As soon as both "drag men" were refreshed and back to their posts, Haste, satisfied that both wranglers and all of his riders were keeping to their assignments, turned his horse back to the head of the herd.

Five miles long and almost a mile wide, the bunched animals moved sporadically, forced into a milling, bawling herd of dumb beasts. The men who pushed them forward cajoled, "Git on up there, old man" and "Don't stop movin', movin', movin'." Or with strident calls like, "Hee-haw," they encouraged the ponderous long-horned steers toward their destination. The steers weighed about 2,100 pounds, were each five feet nine inches tall, and had a horn spread of eight feet. Like a stubborn, twisting, angry horde, the animals jostled one another for leadership. Those in the back endeavored to reach the front of the herd. Soon, they, too, tired of leading, and another group would take their place. The lead was constantly changing.

Haste and his men were ever on the alert for any old domineering, mossy-horned steers who would sometimes try to lead the younger steers astray. The old steers would try to entice the herd into thick brush or down a rocky ravine. The point men had to be aware of any stubborn old-timer determined to go wherever he wanted.

It was getting close to late afternoon and the camp

would be reached soon. Haste rode wide, away from the herd, so he wouldn't disturb their walking rhythm or set off a stampede. Just a glint of a silver spur or the sudden movement of a horse could provoke this, the most dreaded occurrence of a cattle drive. Haste had vivid memories of his friend falling before the frenzied herd, and when it was over, nothing had remained of Leddy and his horse but a bit of cloth and a few leather scraps from the saddle. It had been a horrible death.

Haste rode past the herd to reach the cook and the chuck wagon. Sent out ahead of the cattle drive, it moved faster with only two horses and the wagon. He knew his old cavalry buddy, "Cook" Al Page, would be set up and ready to feed the men their evening meal— the highlight of any working cowboy's day.

Old Al Page, Cook, who was about ten years older than Hat, had done it all: busted broncos, rounded up wild mustangs, and driven cattle all over from Mexico to Montana. His well-known ability to pick up any language made him invaluable in dealing with the Indians. He had even lived with the Shoshone for some years after leaving the service. Now, broken somewhat in body from too many long, hard rides, Haste was delighted to have Al Page as cook of his outfit. It had made it easy for Haste to recruit men for the drive when they learned that Cook Page was in charge of the grub.

"Oh, man, I'm with you if he's in charge! He cooks the best barbecued buffalo ribs I ever tasted," one of them rejoiced.

Al Page was a big man, and much of his weight had gathered around his middle. Nonetheless, he could move with agility when he had to do so, especially when he was master of his domain, the chuck wagon. He would not allow any man or beast to interfere with what he considered his work—the most important job in the drive, except, perhaps, for Hat's job as trail boss. He knew good food and plenty of it was essential if the men were going to be able to do their work and complete a successful drive.

When Cook clanged the bell and cried out, "Come and git it while it's hot and juicy," every cowboy moved to the chuck wagon, tin plate and cup in hand.

Cook had just completed his preparations for the evening meal. The stew was bubbling in a huge pot, and the barbecued ribs were succulent and juicy, resting in a flat pan at the back of the open fire. Hot biscuits and a large pot of coffee were ready for the eternally hungry crew who would ride in at any moment. A few nights back, one cowboy had told Al Page, "Cook, I'm as hungry as a tiger with a stone-blasted headache! Where's the grub?"

As he worked, Al Page suddenly became aware of thundering hooves bearing down. Now, he thought, what fool cowboy is that? Know they aren't supposed to ride into camp wild like that. Against camp rules—could start a stampede or somethin', besides raising a pile of dust.

He whirled around, ready to lace into the thoughtless cowboy. A muscle twitched in his jaw as he opened and closed it spasmodically. His eyes widened.

"What in tarnation? Who are you?" he sputtered as the slight figure of a young woman almost fell at his feet when she pulled the sweat-flecked horse to a halt.

"Where is he? Where is he?" she panted.

"Where's who?"

"Haste, my husband, where is he?" Bethenia looked around frantically. "Isn't he here?"

"Woman, what you talkin' 'bout?"

Before Bethenia could explain, Cook saw Haste riding toward the camp.

With his characteristic cowboy's bowlegged trot,

Cook hurried to meet Haste as he rode up. His apron was bunched up in both hands so as not to impede his progress.

"Hat! Hat!" His voice was almost breathless. "A woman just rode in here,' he gasped. "Says she's your wife!"

Hurriedly, Haste dismounted and quickly assessed the scene before him. He saw the worried, anxious look on the other man's face, his shaking finger pointed at a small, bedraggled young woman. *Who was she?*

"Damn, Cook! You must be loco! Never saw that woman fore in my life! Dammit, man, how'd she git here?"

"On that there gelding. She was plumb wore out."

Haste wasted no time. "Well, miss," he took off his sombrero and slapped it sharply on his thigh. His voice was steady and controlled. "I don't know who the hell you are, or what the hell you want, but you've got some explaining to do, to my satisfaction, startin' with the biggest, sorriest lie you ever told. I don't have a wife."

Bethenia saw dark anger in Haste's eyes as well as the hot flush that swept to the surface of his nutbrown skin. She recognized the strength that she had witnessed the night before when she had seen Sam Yorke wince at the cowboy's handshake. He was very tall and muscular, and she felt that this was one man who never made a purposeless movement. His long dark hair curled to his shoulders, and his red bandanna streaked with sweat qualified him as a working cowman. He waited impatiently. Somehow, Bethenia knew she had to speak carefully to convince this rugged outdoor individual that she deserved his help. She regretted the falsehood she had told, but she was desperate. She hoped that the man she had to persuade to help her could be stern without being mean, honest without being saintly, and that his ability to deal with people would be extended fairly to her, an unknown woman.

Haste stared at the young woman who dared claim to be his wife. She was a good-looking one, he'd give her that. Her skin was the color of warm toast with a light blush seeping beneath its translucent texture. She was slender, but well-formed. Even though she wore a man's pants under a rough woolen skirt, the aura of soft femininity was apparent. Her dark hair was almost covered by a coarse osnaburg bonnet, but a few curls matted with perspiration framed her large, innocent brown eyes. As she faced her adversary, she made a valiant attempt to maintain eye contact. She's got some spunk, got to give her that, Haste admitted to himself, begrudgingly.

"Well, speak up, dammit! Haven't got all day." He was surprised as well by the passionate response of his own body as he waited for her answer. He felt sudden, unexpected heat in his loins. There was a tightening of his stomach muscles as if he had to ward off an unseen blow. He didn't even realize that he was holding his breath, trying to resist the crazy impulse to grab the woman and hold her close. Damn! He didn't even know her name. How come he felt so drawn to her, a perfect stranger?

"My name is Bethenia Cooper, and I saw you last night when you came to Sam Yorke's place to get your wagon fixed."

Bethenia swallowed hard and plunged forward in her explanations. "I overheard you tell him you were leading a cattle drive to Wyoming, and I . . . I want to go with you as far as my uncle's place in Colorado."

"Absolutely not!" Haste barked. "You must be crazy!"

Bethenia kept on talking. She saw Haste shake his

head in continuous denial, but she persisted, never taking her eyes from his face.

"My parents and I are from Tennessee . . . on our way to my uncle's silver mine and hotel, but, well . . ." She hesitated, her voice grew coarse with the dark memories of her parents' deaths, but she stumbled on. "My folk are gone, and the Yorkes, the people who took me in, decided to homestead here in Oklahoma, Mr.—"

"Terrell, Haste Allen Terrell, ma'am." He bowed, mockingly.

"Well, Mr. Terrell, somehow I've got to get to my kin, and I did eavesdrop last night when you were getting your wagon fixed . . . knew I'd never get away from the Yorkes if they knew I was thinking of leavin', so I just followed your trail. Told . . . told the cook I was the trail boss's wife so he would let me stay . . . not run me off. I've *got* to get to my uncle."

Haste exhaled deeply, his face flushed with anger. He shook his head repeatedly. "No way, miss, that you can stay with *this* cattle drive. No place for a woman, especially one that lies to get what she wants. Oh, no, miss, I've got over two-thousand head of cattle, a bunch of wild, rough cowboys to manage, and a big responsibility to git my job done right and on time. So, you git right back up on that there horse of yours and go back where you came from."

Haste had his hands full, and the last thing he wanted was the certain distraction of a woman on the trail. After the cattle were delivered, the crew would be paid, would disperse to go their separate ways to meet later back at the home ranch for another drive. Only Cook and Haste as regular employees would return directly to the ranch in Texas. But, first, Haste had to set out on his second assignment. Cook would return alone with the chuck wagon. The last thing Haste wanted was the care and disruption that a single female would bring to his longstanding cohesive crew.

Bethenia, uncomfortable with the cold reception she had received thus far, tried to convince Haste. "Mr. Terrell, I don't want anything. I can work—"

"Work! What kind of work can a woman do on a cattle drive! You're out of your mind. Loco! A woman on the trail is like having a woman on a ship! Bad luck!" Haste pulled his hat down over his eyes and started to turn away from Bethenia.

"My uncle will pay you for your troubles, I'm sure—" she tried again.

Haste's face turned almost blood-red with his increasing anger. "What makes you think that all I've got to do is to wet-nurse you to Colorado, miss? Do you know what a problem you'll be when my men find you here?"

"That's why," Bethenia choked, "I said I was your wife."

"Oh, no, none of that! Just go back where you came from."

"Never!" Bethenia spat out. She stamped her foot for emphasis. "I'll find my way to my uncle in Colorado or die trying. I'll *never* go back to those people! My daddy said on his deathbed to go find my uncle, and that's what I'm goin' to do, with or without your help."

She turned on her heel and started to get on her horse.

"Wait!" The cook who had watched the whole episode finally found his voice. He looked directly at Haste.

"Why you messin' with my *niece* like that? She come all this way to find her uncle Alphonso, her dead mother's brother, and you fixin' to turn her back?"

The questioning look he gave Haste offered an indisputable answer, and he knew it. Al Page was aware that he was the only man in the whole outfit that ranked anywhere near the trail boss in authority. Brazenly, he made his final argument in Bethenia's favor.

"Ain't *no* man big enough in this outfit to cross me, you hear?"

Haste shook his head, aware that Cook could never turn his back on any helpless creature, especially a woman.

"Right, Cook, no man can dispute *you*, especially being you're the man who feeds us and my friend, let's get this straight. You and I go back a ways, and I know as the cook you are about the most important man in this outfit. So, if *you* say this girl is your 'niece,' " he threw a look to Bethenia, "guess I *have* to believe you, but you're going to be responsible for her, that's all! Got enough problems of my own, and you know, come hell or high water, I intend to get this bunch of cattle to Wyoming." As his face reddened with concern, Haste remounted his horse and looked down at the pair who were making his life more stressful. He tugged on the horse's reins before he turned away.

"One more thing. Keep your 'niece' out of my way. Don't want to see her, be bothered by her, and if you have trouble with her, you deal with it. Don't come hightailing it to me. Can't help you!"

He tipped his wide hat in a brief salute to Bethenia, who looked from one man's face to the other as it became clear to her that she had a reprieve. She stood still to keep her knees from shaking.

"Glad to make your acquaintance, miss. Be nice to have someone to help your uncle with the cooking." Haste's voice was dry with sarcasm.

To Cook he said, "Hope *you* know what you're doin', you old goat." With ease born of a life in the saddle, he rode back to the herd.

Alphonso Page squinted into the sun as he watched

the boss he had impulsively defied disappear into the distance where the cattle could be heard making their way toward the evening camp.

He looked at Bethenia and saw her eyes widen with apprehension.

Bethenia drew a deep breath, aware that, unbelievably, she had received permission to stay with the cattle drive. She knew, too, that she would be forever grateful for the first friend she'd made since her father's death.

"Thank you," she whispered softly to Al Page.

"Don't worry, child, Uncle Al will take good care o' you and see that you gits where you want to go. Now, let's take care of your horse."

Bethenia wondered if the man was right . . . and if she could trust him. As for Haste Terrell, she vowed she'd never ask him for anything. She'd stay out of his way. She vowed to be as independent and self-sufficient as she could be. She realized it would not be easy. She sighed, but there was nothing else she could do. She had to get to Colorado.

Chapter Four

Despite her unhappy, sobering childhood, Bethenia
could never have known how hard life on a cattle drive
could be. Long, scorching hot days in the saddle. She
had refused to be seen as weak and settle for the unfor-
giving seat in the front of the chuck wagon. Bad
enough, she thought, that she slept there under the
cooney, a loose hanging piece of cowhide tied by the
four corners that stretched beneath the wagon. Usually,
Cook kept woodchips for starting fires there, but as he
told Bethenia, "You'll be off the ground . . . almost like
bein' in a hammock . . . be comfortable with blankets
and quilts."

But the worst was the longing for a bath. Each evening, she tried to wash up and shake the dust from her
clothing, but that only helped a little.

When she had run away from the Yorkes' place, she
brought her uncle's letter to her father, one calico dress,
an old flannel shirt, woolen pants of her father's, and
her mother's tortoise comb and bristle hairbrush. When
I get to my uncle's, she thought, I'll get some new
clothes, and I can look like a girl again. She would not
complain, even though there were times when she wondered if she had made the proper decision after all.

Quickly, she brushed such thoughts aside and tried to view each new sunrise as bringing her nearer to her goal. Somehow, each passing day made her feel physically stronger and more alert.

One day, she had been helping Cook get some vegetables ready for a stew. She had proved to be a hard-working assistant, and she had sense enough to realize that he was the boss. The men in the crew had understood that as well. They had known she was not to be bothered.

Sitting around the fire one night, the discussion had naturally drifted to Bethenia's presence.

"Ain't never been on a trail with a female fore," one of the young men had observed.

"If you got any sense, you better believe you ain't on one now. Better steer mighty clear of Al Page's relative if you want to stay healthy," his companion had remarked. "I believe your life could be cut short if you tried to get close to her. As for me, I'd like to live a little longer."

Al Page had kept alert to the men. He had advised Bethenia to be friendly with all, but not to get too close to any in particular.

"Treat them all as if they were just like brothers," he had told her. "Any of them bother you, let me know."

Bethenia had followed his advice. The men had greeted her each morning with "Howdy, ma'am," and had accepted the fact that she was not only the cook's niece, but his helper. She had wondered how Haste felt about her presence. He had greeted her each day with the same salutation as the men had done and had accepted his plate from her, but beyond that, seemed almost unaware of her presence.

* * *

"Guess you wonder sometimes about Haste," Cook told Bethenia one night. "Why he acts the way he does—"

"Must have his reasons, I expect," she said.

"Well, he does. Hat spent years in the cavalry. Rode all over Texas with the Tenth. I was with him, too. And when he was mustered out—he went back to his mama, but farmin' didn't suit him. After bein' on horseback so much, ridin' and fightin' the Indians and renegades, farm life was too dull."

"So, that's when he started ridin' the range?"

"Yep. Damn straight. Went over to Mexico, worked with them vaqueros, they call them, learned all the tricks of ropin', ridin', worked hisself up from wrangler to cowboy. Then, Mr. Connolly got word of him and saw how he could handle men and horses and cattle, asked him to come work for him."

"You were with him in the cavalry?"

"Right. He was my sergeant. Ain't nuthin' I won't do for Haste. Nuthin'!"

They had peeled almost four quarts of potatoes and carrots. Onions were still to be chopped when the cook again turned to Bethenia.

"Know how to shoot a gun, gal?"

"Oh, yes. My daddy used to take me hunting for possom, coon, rabbit . . . want me to show you?"

She grinned at the man she was beginning to view as a real friend. Even with her very limited experience with the opposite sex, she responded to his rough kindness.

"Let's git these taters and carrots on the fire, then you can show me your stuff."

While the vegetables were simmering, Al took Bethenia a safe distance away from the camp. In the field, he marked some targets. He placed empty bean cans upright on stumps and marked several tree trunks with charcoal.

Bethenia hit most of the targets with ease. Al was impressed.

"By damn, you did all right," he told her. "I'm mighty proud of you."

"Told you my daddy taught me," she said grinning.

"You were right," Al responded. "Taught you good."

Unexpectedly, for Cook, this young woman who had wandered into his crude bachelor life was becoming for him the daughter he had never had. His female contacts had been limited to women as rough as he was. In Bethenia, he saw determination and grit, and he admired those qualities in her. However, he could never find the words to express his admiration. Instead, he showed his feelings by the way he treated her.

Now, he was worried. Soon, they would be in Indian country, and he was well aware of what could happen. He decided he'd better talk to Haste. Wouldn't hurt to have another opinion on the problems he faced, even though Haste had warned him to solve them by himself.

That night the cattle were settled, and the wranglers hobbled the string of the crew's twenty horses. The watch was posted for the next four hours. Not only did the watch have to be certain that the animals didn't stray, but they had to guard against thieving rustlers as well as marauding Indians who, to replenish their own stock, didn't mind stealing a horse or two.

Cook rolled a cigarette and handed it to Haste. Then, he rolled his own, lighted both, and took a deep, satisfying breath before he said what was on his mind. "Kind o' worried 'bout Bethenia, Hat, now that we're comin' to Indian country."

"Yeah, kind o' thought you might be," Haste concurred. "How you figuring on protecting her?"

"Well, believe it or not, she's pretty good with a shotgun. Showed me this afternoon. Got a good eye and a steady hand," Cook went on. "Aim to give her some practice with a pistol so she can have it handy ... in case," he added.

"Glad to know she's used to guns," Haste offered. "Could be she may need to use one sometime."

Haste drew on his cigarette and spit out a shred of tobacco before he answered. Since Bethenia had been with the cattle drive, he had had little to do with her beyond an occasional "good morning" or "good evening," but he was very much aware of her presence.

He seemed to always be aware of her whereabouts as she moved about sharing daily chatter with the men. They responded to her inquiries about their days on the trail. She treated all the men with the same smile, the same friendly attitude, yet he found himself jealous of her warmth and friendliness toward his men. He admitted to himself that he, too, looked forward to seeing her lovely smile at the end of the day when she handed him his plate of food.

"I've got a derringer. It's small ... full-length it's 'bout four and a half inches. Think she could handle that?" Haste asked Cook. "It weighs 'bout eleven ounces, single-action, but its forty-one slug can do plenty of damage."

"Don't know why not. I already told her we'd be comin' to Indian country. Told her she'd have to cut her hair short and keep on wearin' pants. She could probably keep the gun in her pant waistband."

"Nah, got a holster to go with it," Haste said. "I'll get it cleaned up and ready, then you can help her try it out."

"Good thing she knows how to ride, eh, Hat? You

seen her with that gelding, Jasper? He looks like he knows what she wants before she asks him."

"I've noticed, Cook, I've noticed."

Indeed, Haste had noticed the very practical, calm, self-assured manner Bethenia showed. She never seemed scared or unsure of herself. She treated every cowboy, even the lowest wrangler, with respect. She didn't appear to be aware of it, but with one or two exceptions, she had somehow encouraged this league of men to respect her. Haste knew also that most of the men would protect her. He had heard it in their voices when they spoke of "Cook's niece." Most of them knew, too, that to cross the cook would be as risky as trying to braid a mule's tail. There were two men, the white Southerners, who had been in the rebel army, whom Haste kept his eye on. They might spell trouble, he thought.

"She ever tell you, Al, why she left the Yorkes?"

"From what she said, and I believe her, the old lady treated her like a slave. Made her work all day. Said she didn't mind doin' her share, but every day it was 'sun to sun.' And, she says, she was scared to death of that big blacksmith. Acted like he owned her, like she owed *him* favors for takin' her in after her folk died. Tried to entice her to kiss him, makin' remarks and such!"

The two men continued to smoke in companionable silence.

"We sure did go down many a lonesome trail in them days, Haste."

Cook and Haste talked often of their military days in Texas and the New Mexico Territory.

"I never believed we'd see the day when that country would be civilized," Haste said. "But you know, Cook, I never blamed the Indians. They tried their damnedest to hold on to what was theirs."

"I know, Haste, and even them callin' us buffalo soldiers didn't bother me cause I knew how much they
loved and respected that animal."

Haste spoke slowly. "The Utes are part of the
Shoshani tribe and the next nine-hundred miles will
bring us into Ute country. Can you deal with them, Al?
Lived with them Shoshani for a while, didn't you?"

"Two years, near 'bout. Know somethin' 'bout them
mountains, too. Best we try to get there before that
Keewadin wind. Indians say that 'northwest wind sure
to bring winter and plenty snow to the prairies.' "

"Yeah, I heard that sometimes the snow can be real
bad, up to twenty-five feet in places."

"That gives you plenty to fret 'bout, Haste. Bad
weather, Indians *and* gettin' through them mountain
passes."

"I know," Haste said thoughtfully as he drew on his
cigarette, noting that Al did not place Bethenia in the
list of his worries.

There was silence for awhile, then Al Page spoke
again. "When I was up there with the Indians, the Ute
were real angry, but I guess since then they have quieted
down some. Still, you gotta be careful. Old Chief Buffalo Bear was a fair man, but he could be dead by now
... don't know who the leader is now or what he's like.
Sure hope it's not his son, Snakeface. He was mean as
a kid."

"Be glad, Al, when we get to that place in Colorado
and drop Bethenia off at her uncle's."

Haste grinned at his friend and said quietly, "Probably give you a reward."

"Me? Don't want no reward, Hat, and you know that.
Satisfied to see her safe and sound, that's all."

Despite the baggy pants and oversized flannel shirts
that Bethenia wore, her loveliness was not hidden. Haste

was becoming increasingly aware that he had to be concerned for her safety, now that they were moving into Indian territory.

They had completed the evening meal. She was storing Cook's pots and pans in the chuck wagon, all cleaned and ready for the next day's meals. Haste cleared his throat as he approached Bethenia. She looked at Haste expectantly and she saw concern in his face.

"Don't want to alarm you, but we're moving into the country where there are some treacherous Indians. Besides that, we know there are plenty of rustlers, highway robbers, and tough men in these parts, especially as we get close to Denver, where you say your uncle lives. So, be alert at all times. . . ."

Bethenia's eyes flashed back at Haste. *What did he mean, "where you say your uncle lives?"*

"Are you casting doubts as to what I said?" she challenged him. "My uncle *does* lives in Denver. Why should I lie about that?"

The moment the words left her lips she regretted having said them. Hadn't she lied, said she was his wife, to be accepted on the trail? She wanted to bite her tongue. She looked at Haste to assess his reaction to her outburst. His mind must have been on something else, her personal safety perhaps. It was as if he hadn't heard what she said. Lost in his thoughts, he made no further comment.

His thoughts surprised him. If ever he married, he'd want a strong woman like the woman riding the herd. He shook his head to dislodge such foolish thinking. There was no time or place for a woman in his life, not even one as lovely as Bethenia Cooper. His job was to get the drive finished, move to his next assignment, the capture of the Ward brothers.

He gave a heavy sigh when he thought about his next assignment. The Ward brothers. No one else on the trail knew about his position as a Pinkerton Detective; it was a fact that had to remain hidden for he may end not only his cover but his life. The Ward brothers were some of the West's most notorious criminals, men that knew no value for property or human life. They left a bloody trail wherever they went.

Haste was assigned the mission because he had tangled with Frank Ward before, when he was in the military. Since then, Frank and he had become bitter enemies. Haste wanted to finally put Frank and Henry Ward in jail for good.

Until then, he had to get the cattle through and protect Bethenia Cooper from whatever may come their way.

He walked over to speak to Cook. Cook's question was on his face. "Did you tell Bethenia she'd need to be careful, Haste? Think she understands?" Cook asked.

"Seems so. All she worries about is getting to her uncle. That's what's on her mind. Have to admire that."

"Right," Cook agreed. "Girl knows what she wants, seems bound to get it."

"Uh-huh," Haste agreed. "It's a good night for sleeping, Cook," he said as he looked up at the brilliant stars that twinkled in the black velvet sky. "Get some rest, sun will be up fore we know it."

"Right, Hat. Night. Goin' sit here for a few more minutes and listen to that lonesome cowboy out there singin' to the herd. Bart really knows how to settle them down, don't he, Hat?"

"Surely does. That boy's got a good voice. See you in the morning, Cook."

Al Page did not envy Hat his job. The next few weeks could be the most treacherous of all—mountains to cross, Indians who might challenge the drive, and fickle weather. Any, or all three, could prove fatal. Combine all of that with the presence of a beautiful young woman and anything could happen. Anytime.

A few minutes later, when he had settled down on his bedroll, Al heard the quiet, reedy strains of a harmonica accompanying the young cowboy. Now, Cook knew that Hat was truly concerned. *Oh, God, when he plays that mouth organ, he's got somethin' on his mind.* Cook remembered how on many nights before a cavalry battle the sound of Hat's mouth organ meant he was worrying over a problem. But he was sure to settle it, one way or the other. Always, the next morning he was ready.

Chapter Five

As usual, Bethenia got up early, when the first streaks of rose-colored sunlight streamed across the molten-gray horizon. This was her favorite time of day; the air was peaceful and still, and only a few lingering hawks wheeled in the sky as they searched the ground below for mice and chipmunks. The delightful freshness of a new day reinforced her constant optimism. She embraced the day's challenge with her strong belief in herself. "If it is to be, it's up to me" was the motto she lived by. Many times she thought of her father's favorite, "Those who fail to plan, plan to fail." Bethenia was determined always to do the best she could for herself and not fail.

Cook Al Page, "Uncle Al" as she called him, had warned her of the perils that might be waiting for them as they passed through hostile Indian territory.

"Sometimes," he had told her, "they'll be satisfied with a steer or two that they butcher and eat . . . other times they want more, horses, saddles, guns, even I've known them to ask for my stew pots fore they'll let us pass through. Never know," he had added thoughtfully. "So, keep your gun by your side, day and night. Keep it in your pants pocket, somewhere's you can git to it in a hurry if needs be."

Bethenia had listened carefully to his warning, but her mind was on her work as she stirred the gray embers of the fire, adding fresh woodchips that would kindle hotter flames, pouring fresh water into the large coffee pot, and relishing the early morning duties Uncle Al had assigned to her.

She did not notice the small group of Indians who stood quietly watching her from behind the hill, but a sudden, prickling sensation of awareness crept over her just as she heard the unmistakable yell of the painted men who swept down the hill toward her.

A young Indian was almost upon her, his face garishly painted with red and black streaks. Bethenia gasped, fear clutching her throat, but she fired quickly and watched in horror as the Indian screamed in pain and fell, holding his leg.

As Bethenia instinctively backed away from the onslaught, she heard the sound of someone running toward her. She caught a glimpse of Haste. He yelled, "Git down on the ground! Down!"

She did as he had commanded and saw him move forward with both of his guns drawn, hitting two more of the intruders. Then, it seemed the whole camp was awake, with several of the men mounted and in pursuit of the fleeing Indians who quickly had given up and disappeared over the crest of the hill.

Haste turned to face Bethenia. She was surprised to see the concern on his face. "Are you hurt?" he asked.

"I'm fine, but the Indian I shot, is he—"

"Not dead, from what I can see. The boys are bringin' him in now. I think it's goin' to be some time before he walks again, though. Well," he added, as he tipped his hat in her direction and holstered his guns, "I didn't know you had it in you. You're mighty quick with that there shotgun."

"You needn't worry about me, Mr. Terrell," Bethenia replied. "I can take care of myself . . . but thanks for your help," she added softly.

She watched the men who half-dragged, half-pulled the young Indian toward the campfire. Both of his legs were bleeding profusely. Bethenia moved toward him, but Haste got between her and the wounded man, stopping her.

"What do you think you're doing?"

"Going to help the poor man whose legs I nearly shot off! What do you think I planned to do?"

Haste stared at her, not believing what he'd heard.

"Oh, no! Don't touch him! We'll leave him here, and his tribe will come back and take care of him after we're gone."

"I'm *going* to help him," Bethenia insisted. "I shot him, and I have to *do* something."

She saw the flush of anger rise in Haste's face as he realized that this woman . . . this creature . . . was getting in the way of the management of his crew . . . of his job. He was so angry he could hardly speak.

He sputtered, trying hard to space his words and speak clearly as he started to explain. He was aware, too, that his men were eager to see how the trail boss would handle *this* situation.

"Miss, *I* am the boss of this cattle drive. Only one or two of us Negro men been given the chance to do this job . . . and I plan on doin' it right! Gettin' this herd to Wyoming and before too long. Mr. Connolly has entrusted me to do that, and no wounded Indian or runaway female is goin' to stop me."

"So, I suggest, sir, you do what *you* have to do and

I'll do what *I* have to do," Bethenia shot back at him. "That way we'll *both* be satisfied."

Haste had the last word, however. In his most powerful, strident voice he commanded, "Mount up men! Riding out now!"

He turned his back on the girl and the wounded Indian. His anger was clearly apparent in the way he sat in his saddle and urged his horse to the head of the herd.

Cook came forward with some rags and clean water. "Clean him up, quick as you can," he warned Bethenia. "He'll have to ride in the chuck wagon 'midst the flour and sugar bags ... best we can do."

He spoke to the Indian in a language so strange that Bethenia's ears hurt from the harsh, guttural sounds. He translated for Bethenia. "Says he's from the Ute tribe. Didn't mean to hurt you ... just wanted to steal a few horses."

The Indian spoke again to the cook as Bethenia cleaned and wrapped his legs. She noticed that he watched her every movement and showed no evidence of pain.

Al Page chuckled as he translated again. "Says he'll be your friend for life, but what are you ... a girl or a boy?"

"Tell him none of his business ... and he'd better not mess with me, whoever I am! Tell him he'd better keep his distance or I might shoot him again! This time, higher up. What's his name, anyway?"

"He is called Painted Owl, he says."

"Well, I'm sorry, Painted Owl, that you're in this fix," Bethenia said, as she helped settle the injured man in the wagon. "It might be rough, but you'll be traveling somehow."

* * *

Haste was worried. He had hoped to move the herd onto the more northwesterly trail through Denver into Cheyenne, where he would leave them; this was their destination before being shipped to the East. The Union Pacific Railroad had finally reached Cheyenne and would take the cattle to Chicago's stockyards.

From Texas to the dust of Oklahoma, they had progressed through a neutral strip of the country, the northeast corner of the New Mexico Territory, and now, with any luck, they soon would be in Colorado Springs near Pikes Peak where he hoped to get word of Bethenia's uncle. This morning's episode was only a forerunner of what could really happen. He chided himself. He should never have allowed Bethenia to stay with the cattle drive, despite Cook's manipulations. He didn't like the personal distraction she brought to his life. He found himself drawn to her, concerned for her welfare, and yes, even somehow content and happy when he was in her captivating presence. He'd never met a woman like her. He dared not voice his feelings, not even to himself. He had to control himself; he was the trail boss.

Haste would have been surprised if he had known how Bethenia reacted to his concern for her. She'd listened to his warnings about the Indians, but hadn't expected to be accosted so soon. Haste's masculinity intrigued her. It was evidenced not only by his physical presence, his long, muscular legs, trim hips, wide shoulders, and dark hair that curled beneath his large hat. It was more than that, she knew. It was in the way his men respected him, his judgment, his skill in managing the crew; he met everyday challenges with equanimity and composure. He was a man to be reckoned with, and she found herself attracted to him despite her earlier vow to have little to do with him. There seemed to be an invisible cord drawing them closer together. Could she maintain her passivity? She knew she'd have to try, especially if they were moving into wilder country. She did not want to cause him any more worry than she already had.

Painted Owl hobbled back from making his self-appointed rounds and settled down on his pallet at the foot of the chuck wagon. Since Bethenia's kindness to him, he had become an even fiercer protector of her than Al Page. He always slept on the ground, near her sleeping place in the cooney.

It was a dark night, the kind of night that seemed to call forth wolves who howled in the darkness, even an occasional cougar screamed, and the horses would whinny and snicker with inherent fear at what they could not see. Paint Owl whispered to them in the darkness, "Be still my brothers, all is well." Soon, he heard only movements of the night patrol and the soft crooning of Bart, the singing cowboy. Mother Night had tucked her creatures into their beds for a healing rest from the day's harsh labor.

Finally, Painted Owl, too, slept, but it was a light sleep, characteristic of his habits. He heard a twig snap, and his eyes flew open. He felt, rather than saw, two figures move toward the chuck wagon with great care.

He heard a mumble from one of them, something he couldn't quite make out, about Bethenia. He had some knowledge of English and recognized Bethenia's name. The sneaky movements of the two men meant trouble. He clearly could sense that, even in the dark.

Painted Owl's experience with white men had been limited to soldiers and government Indian agents whose mission was to keep the Indians in their territories. He had learned that the white men rarely gave any credence to the natives' pride or any justification for their own actions. "The only good Indian is a dead Indian," Painted Owl had heard more than once spat from their tobacco-stained mouths.

Tonight, his distrust of the men, who moved in furtive steps toward him in the dark, increased, and he felt his anger for them stream from his pores like perspiration. He could smell their rank bodies as they came closer.

He had only contempt for the two white men he had met in Haste's crew. Usually, he gave them a wide berth. He knew they recognized his feelings. "Just another redskin," Painted Owl had overheard them say.

Haste's other crew members—Mexicans, some of mixed blood, and Negroes—from Cook Al Page to Bart to the lowest young wranglers, called him "brother" and meant it. Painted Owl had long admired the buffalo soldiers. They showed the strength, courage, and stamina of the Indians' friend, the buffalo, the animal that both fed and clothed them. To Painted Owl, Bethenia, as well was to be cherished. She was like a western flower of the field to be protected and admired.

Even Haste recognized that truth, though he had little to do with her, or she with him. It was as if they were distrusting adversaries, yet bound together in the same circumstances by the cattle drive. Even Haste, by his deferential manner, protected Bethenia. It was almost as if . . . if they had done otherwise they would be denying the human, warm side of their individual selves.

Quietly, Painted Owl rolled from his pallet into the darkness. He could hear the two men whispering and jostling one another as they moved nearer the chuck wagon hammock where Bethenia slept.

Emboldened now, the two men started to giggle, each one trying to quiet the other with whispered shushes.

Painted Owl had learned long ago not to reveal all there was about oneself, and no one knew how gifted he was with a bullwhip.

When he was a small boy, Charley Garcia had taught him the intricacies of lassoing and using a lariat, as well as the long, plaited rawhide whip with the knot at the end of it. In the flick of an eye, Charley could clip a tick from a mule's back. Painted Owl was fascinated by the trick and pestered the man for days after his wounds healed until he agreed to teach him to use the long whip.

"Painted Owl," Charley had told him one day, "you're better than me! Can't teach you no more," he said, when he saw the young Indian whip off a button on a cowhand's leather vest.

Painted Owl now waited in the darkness and watched as the two men reached into the cooney to pull out the sleeping Bethenia. As they bent forward, their backsides were exposed, and Painted Owl released his whip. The air cracked with the snap of the rawhide whip as the missile reached its target. Both men yelped in pain as the whip, released again, threw them both to the ground. Quickly, Painted Owl unfurled his lariat, and the two were caught and bound together, as they struggled to free themselves.

Bethenia, her shotgun in hand, pointed it in the direction of the hubbub as lanterns appeared in the hands of the aroused crew.

"Didn't mean no harm," one of the interlopers Bulldog Steele said, trying to wriggle free of Painted Owl's ropes.

"Only playin'," the other Ray Young pleaded. "Tryin' to have some fun."

Bethenia's eyes widened as she observed the scene before her. Painted Owl held the two men hostage with his lasso, and the rest of the crew stood, making a ring with their lanterns, and watched as Haste, with raw anger apparent on his face, approached to rebuke the scoundrels.

"Get your gear and leave!" he told them.

To one of the young wranglers, he said, "Give them each a horse, one of the old mares." To Al Page, Haste instructed, "They can have a day's supply of grub, some dried beef and crackers."

"God's sake, man," one of the men declared, "you can't leave us out here on the trail like this! At least give us some coffee and decent horses. We need more food than a day's worth!"

The man's face paled a ghastly white. He glared, shaking his fist in defiance at Haste. A red, straggly fringe of facial hair stuck out untamed from his chin and broken, stained teeth gave him a wild look.

"We need food—"

"What you need is a swift kick in the ass, that's what you need," Haste raged. "I knew all along that you two didn't like taking orders from me. But, by damn, this is one order you're going to take! Up to you whether or not you ever get to take orders from anyone else again!"

"Why, you black bastard," the older man cursed, "wait till I tell the folk in Texas 'bout you!"

Painted Owl jerked the ropes even tighter when he saw the look of hatred the man sent in Haste's direction.

"Never git away with this. Leavin' two *white* men out here in the mountains." The other one forced between his tobacco-stained teeth.

"We'll see what kind of men you really are," Haste said, as two horses were brought to the men. "Here's your saddles and your gear. Your guns stay." Haste's voice was as cold as steel.

"No guns!" the older man spat out.

Suddenly sober now as their real plight dawned upon them, the younger of the two men pleaded, "At least give us our guns."

"Why, you suffering piece of dog meat, so's you can shoot me in the back?" Haste snarled. "You already got more than you would have given me or any of us. Now, git!" Haste slapped the mare's rump, and the startled horse took off.

"If the bears, wolves, or Indians don't git them, the weather may," Al Page told Haste. "It's goin' to snow, and we'll be lucky if the wind doesn't come with it."

Bethenia realized even more clearly now that it was her presence that had caused tonight's turmoil. Although, she crept back into the hammocklike cooney, there would be little sleep for her. Somehow, she'd brought only trouble to Haste and the cattle drive. She'd have to ask her uncle for some kind of compensation—somehow, some way. She hoped that she would reach her uncle Conroy's hotel soon.

Chapter Six

Haste managed little sleep the rest of the night. His mounting problems—the girl, the Indian, the would-be rapists—all caused him to shift uneasily in his bedroll. On top of that, now, he was short two men. His anger at himself for allowing the girl to remain with the cattle drive was mounting each day. He knew better than anyone that a cattle drive was no place for a woman, a young, single, inexperienced one at that.

Right after breakfast the next morning, Bethenia found Painted Owl. He was helping the wranglers to saddle the horses for the day's drive.

"Painted Owl," she said, "I must thank you for last night."

The Indian nodded quietly and shrugged his shoulders as if the matter was of little consequence.

"You cared for Painted Owl, not leave when Painted Owl hurt. Painted Owl care for missy. Same thing," he answered.

"But, now," she said, shaking her head, "Haste is short two men to ride 'drag.' And it's my fault."

"Aye, Painted Owl can ride 'drag,' " the Indian said.

"So can I!" Bethenia said, her face lighting up. "Let's tell him!" She was proud to be able to help. Once she and Painted Owl had searched and found Haste, Bethenia noticed the deep scowl of anger that crossed Haste's face as they approached him.

"Now, what?" Haste sighed to himself.

Bethenia was dressed in heavy woolen pants, a flannel shirt, and what looked like an old buckskin jacket that he recognized as once having belonged to Cook. She wore a wide-brimmed hat and a pair of leather gloves.

"Painted Owl and I are going to ride 'drag,' " she said. "We discussed the matter, and it's settled."

"That so?" Haste replied. "You know it's the worst job in the outfit ..."

"You need us, Mr. Terrell, and we both owe you. You know I can ride," she continued, as if daring him to stop her. "You know I can use a gun. I'm sure Painted Owl here can help, you saw him use that whip last night." She pointed to the coiled rope around the horn of Painted Owl's saddle.

"Listen, you're a girl—"

"No fault of mine," Bethenia shot back. "Right now, I'm another cowhand whom you need, and I might be the first woman to ride with a herd, but I won't be the last, I'm sure!"

Haste pushed his hat to the back of his head, a familiar gesture that she knew meant he was worried and concerned.

"What in God's name have I done to get a woman like you in my life?"

"You'll have to ask Him," she said with a casual smile. "Meanwhile, don't you have a cattle drive to run?"

The moment of ominous silence unnerved Bethenia. Perhaps she had gone too far this time. She did not mistake the steely anger when Haste finally responded.

"Don't need a woman to tell me my business, Miss

Cooper." His voice was low as if he was trying to control his anger. "All right. You've asked for the job. It's yours! You are going to see and hear some things, missy, you never thought existed on God's earth! Those few Indians the other day are nothin' compared to what we might run into durin' the next few weeks. You're going to hear wolves howl, coyotes bark, and cougars scream till you think you'll go crazy. You may have your horse shot out from under you, or he may step on a rattler that you don't even see. You're going to broil in the hot sun and freeze in your saddle if we come up on a sudden snowstorm. And God help you if any of our animals, steers *or* horses, get into a stampede! And try as we may, we might have to cross swollen rivers to get where we're going. So, Miss Bethenia, just so you'll know this ain't no picnic you've got yourself into, this is the roughest, hardest work known to man! Certainly, to a woman!" Haste thundered.

Bethenia tilted her chin proudly. "You'll get no complaint from me, Mr. Terrell. Right, Painted Owl?" Bethenia turned to look at the Indian who grunted a response. "Let's get to the back," she said, as she turned Jasper to the rear of the milling, bawling steers.

Damnation! Haste thought to himself, that is the most stubborn, bullheaded woman I have ever met!

He watched Bethenia ride off, her back straight with confidence as she sat in the saddle. Again, Haste begrudingly admitted he had to admire her spunk.

For Bethenia, she knew Haste spoke the truth. She realized that he was not trying to simply frighten her, only to prepare her for the hardships ahead.

Painted Owl grunted again as they rode to the rear of the herd.

"Boss speaks like strong wind," he told Bethenia.

"Strong wind push dust of lie from corners of mind. Only clean truth remains."

"I know, Painted Owl, I know." Bethenia's voice was quiet and reflective. She realized that she had cast her lot with a man of inner strength and certain ability. The way he had protected her with his twin guns when the Indians appeared, and his resolute decision to abandon the men who had nearly accosted her showed her that. She felt her edginess and hostility toward Haste lessen. She couldn't blame him for not wanting her along as extra baggage.

The days were long, hot, and dusty, but Bethenia and Painted Owl kept the rear stragglers in line. Bethenia was happy to have the Indian's company. As they passed through the foothills, he pointed out and named several flowers, cacti, purple fireweed, willowbrush, and talked in sparse terms of the animals and birds they glimpsed as they trailed the sprawling herd. She was intrigued by his knowledge.

"Aye, we come near water soon, I think," he told her. "The steers move faster, they smell water."

Bethenia's eyes widened, because, almost as soon as the words left Painted Owl's mouth, the animals started to run, even her horse Jasper. The bawling, shoving horde of steers swarmed, as if possessed, to the riverbank as the thirsty animals lined up a half-mile wide to drink. When satisfied, they moved across the river to the other side and started to graze on the fresh grasses there.

Bethenia had not seen Haste since early morning, and it was late afternoon when he sought her. As usual, his message was brief and to the point.

"We're campin' here tonight on this mesa. When we

leave here, we'll be headin' straight through some mountain passes before we git to your uncle's hotel."

"So, it's only a few more days?"

"If the weather holds, by the end of the week, maybe."

Bethenia tried again. "I know I've caused problems for you, Mr. Terrell, but my uncle will pay you," she offered, apologizing for her trouble to him and wanting to compensate him.

"Since I'm not in the business of escorting women, only cattle," Haste broke in, "I can't accept any pay."

Then, Bethenia's temper flared. "Mr. Terrell, I knew you had no intention of making this trip easy for me, and I didn't expect it to be easy . . ."

Haste noted that Bethenia's eyes sparkled with deep anger. She continued her tirade like a schoolmarm lecturing a student.

"You ought to know by now that I'm not the first Negro woman to try to make her life better, and I certainly won't be the last! And," she said, taking a deep breath, "as long as *my* God gives me strength, I intend to make my goal. So don't you worry, you *will* be paid for your trouble. You will be paid in full, even if I have to sell Jasper."

"Told you, that won't be necessary. I said we'll get you to your uncle, and that's what I intend to do," Haste responded, clapping his hat on his head.

He turned on his heel and walked away before Bethenia could reply. He felt some shame in his attitude, because, indeed, the girl had caused no real problems. She had even managed to become an asset with her culinary skills, giving Cook a hand. His biscuits were never as light as hers. And she was gifted around the horses. With carrots in her pockets, most of them followed her around like a puppy. Painted Owl had taught her to use the whip and the rope, and she did her part in keeping the steers in line. With her small but sturdy body, she was able to maneuver Jasper in and out of the animals with skill.

The next day they moved into a draw, a shallow valley. Painted Owl spoke to Bethenia. "Boss should stay here in draw."

"Why?"

"Keewadin comes. Big wind from northwest. Bring bad weather."

"Shouldn't you tell him?"

"Maybe you—"

"Me?" Bethenia laughed out loud. "What makes you think he will listen to me?"

"He likes you—admires you—wants to protect you. Painted Owl can tell."

"Now, Painted Owl, you *have* gone loco. Haste Terrell can hardly stand to look at me!" Bethenia laughed again.

"Do not laugh. Painted Owl sees inside boss's heart."

"The way he feels about me, I wouldn't dare tell him what to do. But I will tell Cook what you said."

It came as Painted Owl had said it would. The snow fell silently at first, large flakes that melted as soon as they hit the parched earth. Painted Owl's message had been passed along, and Haste had agreed when Al Page suggested they seek cover.

"You're right, Cook. We'd better hole up in this draw till this storm blows over. Already, it's startin' to bite and spit as the night comes on." Haste squinted at the darkening sky. He told the men to move as many steers as possible under a stand of trees. He hated to do it because it is always more difficult to remove a herd from shelter. Haste knew if the snow continued on into an all-day affair, some of the animals could freeze to death.

By the next morning, it still was snowing hard. The wind blew as the falling snow bit hard into Haste's face. His horse arched and bent his neck, his head turning sideways as Haste made his rounds of the camp. He had allowed a few fires to be made, and the men hunkered down beside them as they tried to keep warm. The men on guard patrol kept their large hats low on their brows to avoid the stinging pellets of icy snow and sleet.

Despite his precautions and worries, about a dozen of the young steers were lost to the storm. Even though the men tried to keep them together, they were separated from the herd.

"They keep goin' like they blind," Gus told Haste. "They look for forage in the snow, poor dumb animals. There's two of them over yonder," he pointed. "Frozen in their tracks, mounds of snow on their backs, eyes frozen open, and their legs frozen to the ground."

"I know, Gus. Makes me sick to see it," Haste replied. "But nature has her way . . . nothin' we can do."

Bethenia stayed near the chuck wagon and helped Cook with the food. All the men could do was eat, try to stay warm and dry, and wait for their assignments to go on guard duty. A card game or two broke up their boredom.

There was nothing fancy about the grub Cook and Bethenia prepared. Bacon, beans, hot coffee, and biscuits. But as Cook told her, "Give a man a full belly, and he can most always forgit 'bout his other troubles."

Later that day, Painted Owl spoke to Haste. "Chinook come soon. We can move by morning," he said.

"Think so, Painted Owl?" Haste poured a cup of coffee and handed it to the young Indian. "I'll be glad if the weather does change. A nice warm wind from the eastern side of the Rockies is just what we need."

Painted Owl agreed, nodding his head. He took another grateful swallow of the hot coffee before he spoke. "In two more suns, we reach missy's uncle's hotel," he offered.

"Not too soon for me," Haste said.

"She brave missy . . . good woman. She shoot Painted Owl, but she not leave him to die."

"I know. I told her your folk would come for you, but Bethenia Cooper would not listen to me. She's an obstinate woman."

"Strong woman is best kind you listen to," Painted Owl said.

At that comment, Haste grunted. The Indian was right.

Chapter Seven

Bethenia knew by Haste's purposeful stride that he was in a serious frame of mind. She watched him come close as she spread the wet flour sacks to dry on the low bushes near the chuck wagon.

"Evening, Miss Bethenia," he said. "How are you?"

He tipped his sombrero to her as he continued toward Al Page, who was storing pots and pans inside the chuck wagon. Cook's utensils always received special care and attention. He made sure his fry-pans, "spiders" he called them, were properly cleaned and seasoned. "Ain't nuthin' sorrier than a spider that won't fry right," he would say.

Bethenia responded to Haste in the same cool manner with which he had spoken to her. Civil, but with no hint of friendliness.

"Evening. Nicely, thank you," she said, as she snapped each cloth to straighten it and place it on the bushes. She watched as he moved toward Cook. The two conversed in low tones. She did not try to overhear their conversation. She knew that Cook would tell her about it later.

* * *

"Cook," Haste interrupted Al.

"Yep, Hat. What can I do for you?"

"Don't put the coffee pot where you can't get at it quick. Want to get an early start in the morning. Might as well leave it out."

"Earlier than usual? How so?"

"Seems like there's trouble ahead. Painted Owl went up furtha' on the trail. Found tracks, looks like some renegades, rustlers messing around. From what he saw, could be the Wards who Connolly warned me might be in these parts. Want to start early so we can get past their hangout before they know we're in the area. Painted Owl says they're about twenty-five miles northeast of here. Three o'clock too early for coffee and biscuits?"

"Three be just fine." Thinking back to their cavalry days, Cook asked Haste, "How many in this gang? Think we could take them?"

"Painted Owl says five men on horseback, plus a packhorse or two. Sure, we could take them, but I'd rather not have to, at this time anyway—"

"I know, got the steers to worry 'bout—"

"And . . . your *niece,*" Haste reminded him. "Wouldn't do for *those* men to spot her."

"I'll keep a close eye on her, Hat," Cook volunteered.

Haste grunted in agreement.

"Got to talk to the men, let them know what we're up against."

"We'll do all right, I guarantee." Cook tried to reassure his boss. How many times before had he seen the young man face other troubling odds with great success? He wanted Haste to know that he, Cook, knew he could succeed again.

Haste tipped his sombrero at Bethenia as he strode by her to join his men who were hunkered down by the evening fire. She couldn't help but notice the tight, grim lines around his mouth. He was concerned about something. She was certain of that. She was even more certain when she saw the serious attention the men showed as they listened to him speak.

Al Page came up to where she was standing and spoke to her as they both watched.

"Gittin' an early start in the mornin'. Haste wants coffee ready at three."

All at once, the hardships of the cattle drive—the tense anxiety that she had learned to tolerate, the long, dusty hours on the trail, her longing for a real bed, a decent bath, and a table to sit at and eat, the heavy animal smell of the steers and horses, a smell she believed she'd live with for the rest of her life—cracked her defensive armor, and she whirled to face Cook.

"And what Haste wants, Haste gets, is that it?" she said sarcastically. When she saw the pained look on Cook's face, she could have bitten her tongue.

He shook his head patiently before he answered. "So, *you* got twenty-five-hundred head of cattle, *you* got a remuda, a string of thirty-odd horses, plus eight, nine men, and a *woman* to worry 'bout, I suppose?" His face darkened with anger. "I don't *ever* want to hear you talk like that! Yes, Haste gits what he wants! He's the trail boss; his word is law. It's like the army . . . got one general and what he says goes. I'm goin' to put it to you straight, girl, you're in this outfit now, know you weren't wanted. *I* spoke up because I admired your spunk, wantin' to git to your uncle and all, but watch your tongue. I know you know why."

Bethenia realized that she deserved Cook's scolding. She accepted it and tried to apologize. "I'm sorry, Uncle Al, don't know whatever possessed me."

"You're a good woman, that's all," he said quietly. "Good women say what they think, let it out."

That was all he had to say on the subject; his mind was focused on the larger problem at hand.

"By the way," he said, "tomorrow stick close, either to me or Painted Owl. Don't stray, keep your head covered, wear a pair of pants. Better fork the saddle. No time for ladylike ridin'."

"Yes, Uncle Al," Bethenia answered.

"Now, get some sleep." She was relieved to hear the forgiving kindness in his voice.

When Bethenia finally settled herself in the hammock-like cooney under the chuck wagon, she thought about her impetuous remark.

I'm upset because Haste ignores me. To everyone else in this camp, I am either sister, daughter, or friend. But, to him, I'm a thing, like the handle on a coffee pot. Well, girl, she chided herself, *what do you want to be to him?*

She hugged her arms to her body as she felt a warm flush creep over her. She shook herself. *I want him to see me. You sure you don't want more than that?* her inner voice argued.

That night her dreams were very disturbing. It was the trail boss who moved close, his arms outstretched . . . and welcoming. Bethenia found herself accepting the refuge of his strong arms as she raised her face to meet his. She felt peaceful, serene, a feeling she knew meant she was where she belonged. She wanted to be in Haste's arms. She looked into Haste's deep brown eyes to validate her undeclared sentiments. She saw only love.

"Bethie," Haste whispered, and his mouth descended on hers.

Bethenia woke up, confused and shaken. Her lips still felt as if they had been caressed, but she knew she had been dreaming, she was still in the cooney under the chuck wagon.

She needed to walk in the brisk air. She sat up and reached for her heavy woolen jacket. Like the men, she slept fully clothed. She pulled on her boots and scrambled out into the cool early morning air.

A few lingering stars twinkled in the sky, and she sensed the peaceful harmony between the dark heavens and the deep brown earth. In an hour or so, the sun would rise over the eastern rim and bring radiant warmth to the huge boulders, sheer cliffs, and stone walls that surrounded the canyon. Somehow, she hated to leave this place. As much as she wanted to get to her uncle and safety, this spot would be special to her. She would probably never see it again, but it would always remain with her. Here she had made a self-discovery. She was attracted to a man who barely knew she existed.

She turned to her morning chores. Painted Owl greeted her, "Fire ready, missy. Water here for coffee."

Soon, the pungent odor of fresh coffee stirred the men. The wranglers had already brought up the remuda, the string of horses from which each man would select a fresh mount. The day's drive was about to start, and it was not yet daylight.

Bethenia knew she faced another day of hard work. She'd have to keep her feelings to herself. She hadn't bargained for this turn of events, but she'd live with it.

No one would see any change in her demeanor. As before, she would continue to keep her distance from Haste. It was just her misfortune to love a man who resented her very existence.

Her mind flew back to the bleak sadness she had experienced when she stood with her father beside her mother's rock-strewn grave. With a comforting arm around her shaking shoulders, her father, even in his grief, tried to reassure her.

"Honey," he had said softly, "life makes no promises to any o' us. What happens is just that, a happenin'. We can't change nuthin', hard as we try, and God knows, I tried. Did everythin' I knew, but your momma didn't have the strength."

"I know, Daddy, I know."

"Want you to promise me, Bethie—"

"Yes, Daddy."

"Promise me, whatever comes to you in life, meet it straight on. Hold your head high, don't try to shuck it, or run from it! Remember, you one of God's creatures, made from the love your momma and me had for each other. So be proud, independent, and take care of yourself. No tellin' how long I'll be round. You be strong!"

Bethenia recalled the sadness in her father's eyes. It was almost as if he was preparing her to be alone—as if he knew.

That day, when her father had bent to kiss her cheek, she had felt again the startling roughness of his unshaven face, and she remembered that first dark early morning long ago, it seemed, when she had seen him cry.

Resolutely, she threw her shoulders back. *Don't cry for me, Daddy. I'm going to be as strong as I can be. Neither Haste Allan Terrell nor anyone else is going to change that! I promise. Damn that man, anyway.*

When she closed her eyes at night, however, she still saw him, tall and straight in his saddle and his dark hair curled around his shoulders beneath his sombrero. He kept his eyes out for the well-being of all, men, horses, and steers, but she was invisible to him. So be it.

Chapter Eight

Haste never feared a fight. He was not easily angered, and he had deep compassion for his men, but his cavalry battles had taught him to fight Indians, Mexicans, or treacherous outlaws. And he reckoned there was a *time* to fight. He'd rather meet these unsavory renegades when his attention was not diverted by the cattle drive and the girl. But, realistically, he knew one faced a fight when one had to. Evidently, the renegades had been trailing them for days, obviously out to ambush them and rustle some of the herd. There could be killings, many of them, Haste knew. He would have to avoid their trap.

The gold rush and the opening of the West had attracted farmers, immigrants, army deserters, degenerates, and folk bent simply on trying to get rich in whichever way they could. The impulse to steal, rob, lie, cheat, and even to commit murder were vices which overcame what few virtues were around. The law, what there was of it, was administered mainly by the gun.

That morning, Haste directed his men to follow a trail that would lead them upcountry, several miles away from the established trail they had been using.

"See that mesa up there?" he asked his lead men, Gus

and Sandy. "Let the steers feed awhile, plenty good grass there, then make your way down on the other side and get back on the trail."

"Gotcha, Hat," Gus said.

Gus Bellamy was not a man to trifle with. Born in Kentucky of Irish immigrants, he was tall, rangy, and strong. His once black hair was now an iron-gray thatch. His beard was still black, and he wore it in the fashion of a Chinese warlord. Unexpectedly soft-blue eyes viewed the world from beneath shaggy eyebrows, but for all of his stern appearance, he was gentle and wise. It was only when he was crossed that his Irish temper would flare. Otherwise, as Cook had told Bethenia, "Old Gus don't git mad often, usually he's as cool as a skunk in the moonlight, but don't git on his 'off side,' not if you want to stay alive. Say this, though, he's one white man you can trust."

When Gus reached the mesa, a flat table mountain, the herd moved in bellowing swells around him and started to graze, grateful for the lush grasses they found there.

He focused his attention on the canyon valley below. Using his spyglass, he noticed a file of dark figures moving slowly behind and out of sight of the rest of the herd that brought up the rear.

"Darn," he said, "the renegades have doubled back and they're followin' the herd. Can only mean trouble for the gang in the back."

He rode back to give the unwelcome news to Haste. "What you want to do, Haste?" he questioned.

"Stampede the herd and get them out of here."

"Stampede? Sure you want to do that?"

"Think of any other way to get these Texas longhorns to safety in a hurry?"

"Guess not." But Gus knew that a stampede meant

danger, especially if the herd couldn't be turned. "But if you say so, that's what we'll do."

"Well, let the boys know, and do your best to hold them at the river," Haste told him.

He turned Red Chief back to retrace the trail over which he had just ridden. Bethenia, Painted Owl, and two of the young wranglers were bringing up the rear. "Renegades behind you!" was all Haste could shout to them before he heard the crack of a rifle shot. The earth shook as the horde of mammoth, unwieldy animals thundered across the mesa and disappeared in large dust clouds over the rim to the other side of an open valley. Fortuitously, the river compelled them to stop. It was like a flood, as wave after wave of cattle, their horns shining in the sunlight, moved as one being, an avalanche of a dark brown, undulating sea. Except for the throbbing, pounding hooves, they made no other sound. Nothing could survive in their path. It was over in a matter of seconds. The quiet that descended on the plain was eerie in its vast silence. It was as if the cattle had never existed. Only the rising cloud of dust gave testimony of their existence.

Haste gathered his remaining crew around him. He had Painted Owl and the two young wranglers, Max and Barney, and riding with them as part of the "drag" team was Bethenia.

Bethenia! The moment Haste had dreaded all during the long drive had finally arrived. He *had* to concern himself now with Bethenia's safety, as much as he had denied having done so before.

He looked at her, as if seeing her for the first time. He saw the warm flush on her soft brown skin, the result of her exertion from trying to manage the recalcitrant, straggling steers. He saw her deep, sparkling eyes that challenged him from beneath her smooth brows—as if daring him to deny her presence. And he couldn't help but notice her femininity that was almost enhanced by the heavy woolen trousers and jacket that she wore. All at once, the realization of what he had been trying to deny struck him. This young girl, independent and willful, but strong, determined, and beautiful, had become a most important person to him. When had it happened, he asked himself.

He spotted a hollowed out horse carcass lying on the ground near the fringe of the pine forest. He pointed it out to her.

"Better get your horse behind the trees and hide in that carcass. We've got company comin', and I don't believe they mean to make it a social call."

Bethenia made no comment. She hobbled Jasper in the grass beneath the trees and secreted herself into the stiff horsehide. When the animal had died some time ago, the coyotes had eaten away all of the soft inner parts; only the hide and bones remained. Surprisingly, it was so dry and stiff, and there was no smell or moisture. She crept inside the hollowed out hide and pulled her hat low over her eyes. She took out the derringer Haste had given her. She watched and waited.

Charley Garcia galloped back to tell Haste that the stampede was over and that the cattle were already some fifteen miles ahead, moving back onto the Goodnight-Loving.

"Boss," he told Haste, "renegades 'bout a mile back. Goin' wait for them?"

"Damn straight. Don't mean us any good."

"Well, I'll just stay round," Charley volunteered.

"Much obliged, Charley. Didn't want to do this ... they don't give me much of a choice. They're the ones following us, interfering with our drive."

He looked back over the trail, the woods were green,

the fields fertile and lush, such a peaceable land, he thought, but so rank with hostility. Would peace ever come, or would the land shudder with hate the same way it did when the hooves of the cattle crossed the land? Haste shook his head and turned again to speak to Charley, who seemed to understand his boss's hesitancy to fight.

"This is costing my boss time and money," Haste continued, "keeping me from getting this herd to market on time. Every day we're out here on the trail, they're bound to lose weight. And that's profit lost."

Charley Garcia grunted in agreement. "We goin' face them down, boss?" he asked.

"Never turned my backside to an enemy yet, Charley, you know that."

He turned to the two young wranglers. He gave them each a rifle and ammunition.

"Know how to use these?"

He was rewarded with enthusiastic grins. "Yes, sir," they both said.

"Boys," Haste said, with his tan face grim with worry, "we'll have a problem when those bastards get up here. They're going to be madder than a bunch of peeled rattlesnakes, especially when they realize we've moved the cattle. No-count murdering thieves who don't care about the lives of others. I know they want whatever they can lay their hands on."

Haste had a feeling that the experience he was about to face could very well end badly. If the men were the Ward brothers, he knew what to expect. It was said that they had been "spawned by a grizzly bear and suckled by a mountain lion." He remembered his last face-to-face meeting with them.

He had been stationed at Fort Gordon in Texas. He and his platoon were responsible for bringing these same outlaws to the county seat to stand trial. Murder, it was, but a "good" friend lied up and down that the Wards were, "Sure enough at his saloon playin' cards all night," when the murder took place. "Judge, I even lost a heap of money that night," the man had lied. Judge Parson had to let them go. Haste never had forgotten the victorious look on Franklin Ward's face.

"You might be wearin' a blue army uniform now, Nigra, but I'll git you! Someway, we goin' meet again!" He had spat a blob of viscous brown-stained tobacco juice on the floor, missing Haste's shiny boots by inches.

The wild cackle of glee and the dirty-toothed grin that Henry Ward had thrown at Haste when he had echoed his brother, saying, "We'll gitcha!" had remained in Haste's memory.

But now he looked down the trail as the men approached. Haste recognized Franklin Ward, his longtime enemy, the man Pinkerton wanted him to capture, atop a big chestnut horse. Behind him came his brother Henry who showed why he had a reputation of being somewhat wild. He rode his horse in a prancing manner as if he were out on a day's frolic or at a country fair.

They were about five-hundred yards away when Haste turned to Charley. "See who's with the Wards?"

"Damn, Hat, it's them hombres we ran off after tryin' to mess with Miss Bethenia."

"Yep. Steel and Young. Figured they'd tie up with someone like the Wards."

"What you aimin' to do, Hat?"

"Mosey over and see what they want, I guess. You keep close and don't do anything unless you see me push my sombrero back. Then, come in firing, hit anything that moves. Tell Painted Owl and the boys to lay low till then."

Then, the renegades came into full view, riding nonchalantly, seemingly unconcerned, even when they saw Haste.

"Well, well, if it ain't Sergeant Haste Allen Terrell of the U.S. Cavalry," Ward said, feigning surprise. He wore a wry grin as he reined his horse to a stop.

"What do you want?" Haste wasted no time. "I know you're not out on a picnic."

"Well, told you we'd meet again, Sarge. Wanted to *buy* some cattle from you, reckoned you might like to cut a few from Connolly's herd. Could make a profit, you and me. But seein' as how you done moved the cattle, that deal is off."

"I'll never deal with the likes of you, Ward, so why don't you move along?"

"Don't be so fast. If we can't git the cattle, we want the gal. My two friends here," he waved his arms toward his companions, "say that you were very inhospitable to them. Wouldn't let them enjoy her company at all. Now, is that any way for a Nigra to treat a white man?"

Haste was well aware of what would have happened to Bethenia. After the Wards had finished with her, she would have been turned over, for a fee, to a house of prostitution—if she lived.

He tried to control his anger. He stared at the outlaw and steadied Red Chief, his favorite mount. His horse understood by the slight pressure of Haste's knees that he was to remain stock-still, and he did so.

Haste was infuriated. His father, a hardworking farmer, had always warned him that he would be judged by what he did. He had tried to be the best trooper he knew how to be when he was in the cavalry. He was proud of the fact that he had been entrusted by Evan Connolly to be the trail boss, a rare responsibility for a black man. Here, he was, trying to do an honest job for honest pay, and scum like Franklin Ward and his brother were trying to stand in his way.

He thought to himself, always somebody out there tryin' to beat you. Well, look at it as another chance to prove yourself. Show no fear, because a white man ain't better than you, just looks different. Puts his pants on one leg at a time same as you, slid from his momma's belly like you did. So, don't let a mangy cur like Frank Ward take what you've worked for away from you. Don't let your self-confidence wither and die because of the threats of a man who only looks different.

Haste spoke quietly, pronouncing each word with distinction and clarity. He did not want Ward to doubt his intent. His dark eyes glowed fiercely with disdain as he challenged his enemy. "Get the hell out of here, Frank Ward. You're taking nothing with you, *nothing*, except your mangy crew."

He had noticed that Ward's brother and his men moved stealthily closer to the renegade leader as if to outflank Haste. There was one other man, a young cowboy, who hung back as if not quite sure of himself or the others, as if he'd rather not be with them.

Haste took stock of the situation. His father always warned him, "Check things out fore you make a move. Know your options." There were five in the outlaw party. He, too, had five. Besides himself, there was Painted Owl and Charley, both excellent marksmen. He was not certain of his young wranglers, but he knew Max and Barney could not have survived living in the West without some firsthand knowledge of guns. He knew for certain that Ward and his men would not have second thoughts if it came to killing any of them. He fixed his eyes on Franklin Ward and hoped that his own men had the others in their sights.

"The gal, Sarge, where is she?" Ward insisted.

"Where you'll never find her. So, be on your way."

Frank Ward's eyes narrowed with hate. "Now, I ask you again, since when does a Nigra tell a white man what to do?" Ward snarled.

"Anytime a Negro man is right. You know this one is," Haste shot back.

Angered by Haste's cool manner, Frank Ward impatiently shouted, "Let's take him, boys!" as he drew his gun.

In one motion, Haste pushed his sombrero back on his head, using the gun muzzle in his left hand, and he kneed Red Chief to move out of the line of fire. As he did so, he fired the gun in his right hand, knocking Ward's weapon from his hand.

Charley Garcia and Painted Owl sprang forward, with their guns blazing. With perfect timing, Max and Barney had slipped around and circled to the rear. They surprised the young cowboy, who dropped his weapon when he realized he was outnumbered. They shot his horse, and as it fell dead, the cowboy leaped from the stirrups and dropped to his knees with both hands up. His face was a contorted mixture of fear and relief.

"I give up! I give up! Don't shoot, please."

Haste, Charley, and Painted Owl had the drop on Henry Ward and the other two men, and they forced them from their horses. With a shout of the Rebel yell, Charley spooked the horses. They took off through the woods at the edge of the field.

"Just like a Nigra," Henry Ward complained in a whining, plaintive, weak voice, like that of a spoiled child. "You ambushed us, can't even fight fair, you black son of a bitch!"

Haste ignored the taunts. For the second time, Bulldog Steele and Ray Young were on foot, with Painted Owl's quick lariat secure around them.

The elusive leader, Franklin Ward, wounded and bleeding from his right hand, spurred his horse, and the big chestnut galloped out of range.

"I'll git you yet, Haste Terrell! Remember that!" His voice trailed back as he moved out of sight. Henry followed quickly after him.

"Leave the scum tied up right where they are," Haste told Painted Owl of the others.

"Damn it, Nigra, your not goin' to leave us out here again? Got no horses," Ray Young complained.

"Looks to me like you need another lesson. First time didn't teach you a damn thing," he told them.

Haste and his men rode away slowly, his heart closed to the pleas of the men who would have killed them without a second thought. At least, he was letting them live.

He turned his thoughts to Bethenia. Was she still safe?

Chapter Nine

Haste always remembered his mother's admonition: "Don't bother to worry none. Every problem you git is workin' clothes for a chance to learn and do better." Haste found himself thinking often about his mother, especially since Bethenia had come into his life. There were certain similarities between the two women: both were subborn, honest, and independent. Painted Owl was right. Bethenia Cooper was a woman to be reckoned with, and Haste felt his admiration for her increase with each passing day on the trail.

She did her share of the work; riding the range looking for stray steers, helping the wranglers hobble the horses for the night, and helping Cook with the meals. She did whatever she could, and she did not complain.

Haste became aware that her body toughened. They had been on the trail for more than six weeks. She could saddle and ride a horse with the best of them, and Painted Owl had been teaching her how to use the whip. Haste could see the increased strength in her hands and arms. Her skin had tanned to a berry-nut brown. She kept her hair hidden beneath her wide sombrero; only occasionally did wisps and tendrils escape as she concentrated on her tasks. She was as wiry and tough as any young boy. He knew he would miss her when they finally reached her uncle's hotel.

Bethenia looked lovely. She had told Cook, "I've got to clean up and make myself presentable before I turn up at my uncle's." Al Page had agreed, and he had helped her set up a small space near the chuck wagon. Shielded by hanging blankets and guarded by the ever vigilant cook, Bethenia had washed her hair, tucked her mother's tortoise combs into it, and after bathing as best she could, pulled on her one badly wrinkled calico dress. She had worn a pair of deerskin moccasins that Painted Owl had gratefully made for her, as well as one of Cook's old jackets. She had looked like the orphan she was, but she looked like a woman again. "You look plumb beautiful, Bethenia, girl," Al Page told her proudly.

Haste's eyes had widened with appreciation when he saw Bethenia. He had noticed the healthy shine in her luxuriant thick hair, worn unbraided now in an attractive bun. The tortoise comb added a simple elegance. Even though her cotton dress was wrinkled, nothing detracted from the lovely outline of the young graceful woman's body.

He touched her elbow as he accompanied her into her uncle's hotel.

"You look beautiful," he breathed. His voice almost choked because suddenly he realized he would not see Bethenia again. He realized, too, that she meant something to him. He would miss her.

"Thank you," Bethenia responded as she wondered what lay ahead for her.

"By God! It's Molly Mae!" Conroy Cooper exclaimed, as Bethenia and Haste walked into the lobby of the Marks-Ashton Arms Hotel.

"I'm Bethenia, Molly Mae's daughter," Bethenia told the man behind the hotel desk. "Your brother, my daddy, Lee, gave me this letter," she offered. "Said you expected him to come out to help work your mines and this hotel."

Her uncle silently accepted the letter from Bethenia. She stood uncomfortably at Haste's side as her uncle read the letter. the very same one he had sent to his brother earlier. She surely was his niece. She looked just like his brother's wife Molly Mae.

Conroy Cooper gave the beautiful young woman a hard stare.

Bethenia's disappointment was evident to Haste. She had expected a warmer greeting. Unexpected tears flooded her eyes. She swallowed quickly to stifle her sudden grief as the man's eyes, mouth, and coloring seemed almost identical to her father, but somehow was put together wrong. His air of controlled impatience was evident as he glanced briefly at the letter Bethenia had handed him.

"Who's he?" he asked her, pointing to Haste.

Haste, irritated by the cavalier attitude of the hotel-keeper (he'd seen better manners on a cowboy) spoke quickly and extended his hand for a brief handshake.

"Name is Haste Allen Terrell, sir. Your niece joined my cattle drive back in Oklahoma," he explained. "so's to get here. I'm trail boss of an outfit from Texas. Got to get to the rail junction in Wyoming next two, three days. Plan to leave Miss Cooper here and rejoin my outfit camped the north side of town."

"Why not stay overnight here? Rest up a bit." Conroy Cooper said, a wide smile appeared suddenly on his dark brown face. "Best accommodations right here, anything you want. We are the best in the West," he chortled. His pride was evident to Haste.

"I think, Uncle Conroy, Mr. Terrell is anxious to see the last of me," Bethenia said.

She noticed the brief scowl on the man's face when she addressed him as "uncle."

"I see. Well, Mr. Terrell, since you won't accept my offer of hospitality, what do I owe you for your trouble, for getting my niece here?"

Haste looked at the man, narrowed his eyes as he took his measure of the self-satisfied man who dared offer him payment for adhering to the code of an honest cowboy.

"When you've lived on the range as long as I have, Mr. Cooper, you know that out here in the West a man is judged by how he respects the land, himself, and others. I can't take all the credit for bringing your niece safely here, others helped, but every one of us has a great deal of respect for the courage and determination she showed trying to get to you. It was a pleasure to be of service *to her.*"

An awkward silence followed Haste's words. Conroy Cooper's face flushed with displeasure at Haste's caustic remark, and he simply said, "I see. Thank you."

Earlier, Bethenia had asked if her horse Jasper might remain with the remuda. She wouldn't accept money from Haste for the animal, said it was the least she could do.

She smiled at Haste to ease the tense moment and extended her hand. "Thank you for helping me, and thanks for taking Jasper," she said to him. "Good-by, Haste."

Bethenia had not anticipated what her feelings would be when she said good-by to Haste. Already she missed Cook, Painted Owl, and the other men. Somehow, the persistent feeling of deep loss unnerved her, and she wanted to leave the hotel with Haste and return to her friends.

Haste grasped Bethenia's hand. He did not trust himself to speak. He tipped his hat to her in a gesture of farewell, and his boot heels echoed as he strode across the polished wood floors to the hotel's glass front doors.

Bethenia watched Haste leave. Suddenly, she felt lost and alone. His long black hair curled at his shoulders beneath his deep brown, well-worn leather sombrero. His long muscular legs carried him purposefully from Bethenia's side. She knew she would never forget those wide shoulders and strong arms. More than once, she had seen Haste's strength as he roped a steer or threw a saddle across a wild mustang's back to tame the beast. She was not prepared for the feeling of unease she experienced when she realized she might never see this young stalwart cowboy again.

Stay well, Hat, she thought. Good-by . . . and thanks.

She turned back to her uncle. She could see he had been watching her, and as she looked at him, she caught a glimpse of something akin to impatience on his face. It was fleeting and so quickly removed by an artificial grin that Bethenia doubted for a moment that she really had seen it. She had the feeling that she was not welcome by her father's brother.

"Can you read and write?" He startled her with his question.

"Yes, sir, as sick as my momma was, she taught me."

"Good. Guess you can help out here at the desk. Never did have any women work out on the desk for me, but since you're kin. . . ."

Strange, Bethenia thought, he hasn't even asked 'bout Ma or Pa. How they died or nothing. It's like he doesn't care.

She searched the man's face for some of the loving

kindness and gentle warmth she had seen so often in her
father's face. It was not there. It was almost as if the familiar features had been rearranged in her uncle's face
into a farcical mask.

He led her to a small corner room tucked far back on
the second floor of the hotel. A small cot and a wash
basin and pitcher on a spindly table were its sparse fur-
nishings. Except for the single window, it could have
been a closet.

"It's yours long as you want it," her uncle said, "but
I'd just as soon no one knows you're my brother's
child. Try to keep my personal life separate from my
business one." He grinned facetiously as he patted
Bethenia on the shoulder.

She moved quickly from the unwanted touch.

"I'll call you Mr. Cooper, then."

A grim-faced, dissatisfied Haste untied his horse from
the hitching post in front of the Marks-Ashton Arms
Hotel. He guessed Conroy Cooper had a right to be
proud. Not many Negro men had been able to come out
west, discover a silver mine, and build a prosperous hotel. Bethenia had told him her uncle had come west to
seek his fortune after leaving the cavalry. She also had
told Haste that her father had said that after his brother
and his partner found the mine, whites jumped their
claim. Because of his color, he had been barred from
voting by Colorado law. No court would hear their case,
so he had given up the mine and opened the hotel with
his partner. He had been successful in that venture because miners, prospectors, trappers, and cattlemen were
crowding into the area and needed food and shelter.
Bethenia had said her father told her it was his brother's
intention to get the mine back. How he didn't know.

Years in the military, years on the range, and his undercover experiences as a Pinkerton man, gave Haste a sixth sense about criminal activity. There was something strange about Conroy Cooper. Haste could feel it.

He tried to dismiss the misgivings he felt about leaving Bethenia in a strange place with a strange man, but she had said the man was her uncle, and Haste had work to do. All the same, his anxiety and distrust of the man ran high.

He was surprised, too, when he realized that he was going to miss the bright, spunky, hardworking young woman who had been part of his crew. Somehow, she had made herself a key element of the crew. As focused as he always had been on the task at hand, Haste never would have thought that another person could change his life.

Painted Owl rode up quietly beside Haste as they left the hotel and asked, "Missy safe now?"

"Hope so, Painted Owl."

"Painted Owl stay in town. Keep watch on Missy. Painted Owl let boss know how she is. Two of my Ute brothers will ride 'drag' with boss."

"I'm much obliged, Painted Owl, much obliged. I'll need them. Okay if I give your pay to your brothers at the end of the drive?"

Painted Owl gave a short nod, turned, and disappeared down the town's dusty streets. Haste knew that the Indian would be true to his word. Bethenia had taken care of the wounded Painted Owl, and he owed his life to her. The Indian would never forget that.

Haste spurred his horse, anxious to get to the camp and resume the last leg of the cattle drive. Somehow, he had the feeling that the answers to some of his questions could be found only at the Mark-Ashton Arms Hotel.

As he rode toward the camp, his anxiety increased.

Another drive was almost over. His pride in his accomplishment was his alone. There was no one in his life to share it with. He wondered if it would be possible that, perhaps, someday, a person like Bethenia might be the one?

Chapter Ten

The long, weary cattle drive was finally over. Haste met Sam Donovan, Evan Connolly's paymaster, at the Black Dog Saloon near the railroad depot in Cheyenne. The twenty-four-hundred bawling, milling steers, some a little thinner from the long drive from Texas, had been herded into freight cars for their final destination, the stockyards in Chicago.

Later that day, the crew gathered around Haste at the Black Dog to receive their long-awaited pay. Each cowboy was eager to start spending their couple of hundred dollars, the average pay for each man.

Cook Al Page, Bart, Gus, Sandy, Charley, all the young wranglers, and the two Ute Indians, who had helped as "drag men," were paid. Haste decided he would keep Painted Owl's money because contrary to his earlier thoughts, he figured he'd see the man back in town.

"Now, boys," Haste said, warning them with a smile, "don't spend all your money at once." He knew his words fell on deaf ears.

"Hell," one of the point men said, "ain't nobody else to spend it on *but* myself."

Gus watched the saloon keeper set out glasses and line up bottles of liquor on the bar.

"Hey, barkeep," he demanded, "bring one of them there *full* bottles over here!" He slapped the table emphatically. "Keep them comin' till I pass out or run out o' money. Damn whichever comes first! That damn drive from the great state o' Texas was a damn hard one, I'm here to tell you! Don't want to see 'nother damn steer unless he's on my dinner plate!"

Some of the other men were crowding around the bartender, asking for directions to the nearest barber and hotel, to a store where they could buy new clothes, and to the nearest "fancy" house.

The bartender had ready answers. He knew if he played his hand right by the time the cowboys left the area most of their money would be left behind right where they had first received it.

"Well, boys, hotel's right down the block, and when you get slicked up, come on back to the Black Dog, and we'll treat you first-rate."

Haste went to the telegraph office and dispatched two wires. One to his boss in Texas, Evan Connolly, read, "Drive completed," and the other telegram went to the Pinkerton office in the Denver office. It, too, read, "Drive completed." This wire was signed with a different name, Gabe Skinner, the alias known only to Haste's Pinkerton supervisor.

Haste had served with the cavalry in Kansas and Texas and in the territories of New Mexico, Oklahoma, and Arizona. Their task had been to fight the Comanche, Apache, and Sioux. His commanding general, General Stiles, had been amazed at the ability Haste and his fellow soldiers exhibited. He had written to army headquarters in Washington: "These Negro men should be commended for their intelligence, their manner of discharging their duties, and their excellent care of the horses, arms, and equipment. I am proud to serve with them."

General Stiles had been impressed by the quiet, solemn young man, and when he pinned a commendation medal on Haste's tunic at the mustering out ceremony, had asked Haste what he planned to do after leaving the cavalry.

"Go back to Texas, sir."

"Look up my good friend Evan Connolly down there. Tell him Paul Stiles said to give you a job. He's outside Dallas. Fair Acres Ranch."

"Yes, sir. Thank you, sir," Haste said and saluted.

Evan Connolly liked what he saw in the young ex-soldier and farmer and hired Haste right away. It was not long before he put Haste in charge as trail boss.

Evan Connolly was a middle-aged rancher. Tall, with wide shoulders and slim hips. Little missed his piercing blue eyes as he looked at a man from beneath his twin white eyebrows. He took the measure of every man he met, assessing him for his worth and ability. Unable to ride, due to a fall, he liked what he saw in Haste. The relationship was more than one between a rancher and a cowboy. Each man respected the other.

When word came to Fair Acres that a renegade group, the Ward brothers and their gang, were rustling cattle, changing brands, and selling the cattle below price to the eastern markets, Connolly had hired a man from the Pinkerton National Detective Agency to look into the problem. There even had been talk they might be robbing banks.

"Now, Haste," Connolly had told him, "don't take any chances. I believe the Ward brothers are holed up in Colorado right now. George Benard, my Pinkerton man in the Northwest, will wait for your wire to let him know you'll be back, heading from Cheyenne. Use the name he gave you. We got to get these men and put them out of business, somehow."

"None of the crew know about this?"

"Better that only you and Benard know," Evan Connolly had said. "When you two start your hunt, whomever you put in on the deal is up to you. I know George Benard has a fine reputation as a secret service man, had experience with Allan Pinkerton himself guarding Abe Lincoln on his way from Springfield, Illinois, to Washington, D.C., for his inauguration. And Haste, I can't think of a better man than you to track these two outlaws. I'm counting on you, Haste, to bring the Ward brothers to justice."

Haste saddled Red Chief, and he put Bethenia's gelding, Jasper, who would remain with the remuda, on a lead and secured a packhorse. He figured it was about eighty miles to reach the Mile-High City and he would need several days' supplies.

A packet of food, dried potatoes, apples, beef jerky, cold biscuits, and coffee, were wrapped in a tight parcel. Several blankets, a rain slicker, another change of clothing, matches in a small tin, and a few cooking utensils that he would need were loaded onto the packhorse. Haste also carried two pistols, a rifle, and enough ammunition for his own protection. He wore his sombrero, a leather vest over a heavy woolen shirt, wool pants, and chaps to keep the sticky burrs from tearing at his clothing. A heavy woolen coat and an old fur hat were bundled into his bedroll. In his leather saddlebags were his identification papers and his authority to operate as a Pinkerton man.

It was a clear, cold, early winter day. The mountains

were crested with new snow, and the bright sun that sparkled against the whiteness made Haste blink his eyes. He pulled his hat down on his forehead to shade them from the glare. There was a fresh crispness in the air, and the sky was an innocent blue. Haste felt optimistic as he started on the trail. He had figured that perhaps Bethenia might want Jasper, and he was pleased that he had decided to take the gelding back to her. At first, they had decided that the animal might be better off with Haste, but now, after having met Conroy Cooper, Haste wasn't so sure. Bethenia might need to sell the horse, might need money of her own. And Jasper, a fine piece of horseflesh, would fetch a good price. Hell, he'd even buy Jasper himself if Bethenia wanted to sell. As soon as his assignment with the Ward brothers was over, he would be free to turn his attention to Bethenia and make certain that she was safe and secure in her new surroundings. She'd certainly been determined to get there.

He could not explain it, but whenever he thought of her, he felt a surprising quickening of his pulse. For some reason, her lovely face swam frequently in his mind. He couldn't wait to see her, and he realized that it was more than her physical welfare that concerned him.

"The Ward brothers?" Sam Donovan had answered Haste's inquiry with one of his own. "Rumor has it they held up the Union Pacific Railroad last month. Didn't have any trouble on this last trip. Course I *never* let on that I'm a payroll man. Never pick up my cash until I get to a bank here. Times are tough, you know, and to some folk life's not worth a plugged nickle."

Haste had nodded his head in agreement and had

said, "I heard that they rustled some cattle on the trail. Didn't have any trouble myself, but heard that they're stealing the cattle and selling at a cheap price."

"That so? Is there a price on their heads?"

"Don't know, Sam, but could be."

"Trouble with this part of the country is the need for law and order," Sam had said, shaking his head. "Can't have a decent civilization with thieves and cutthroats like the Ward brothers taking over."

The two men had shaken hands and parted, with Haste promising to extend Sam's best wishes to Evan Connolly.

Haste followed the trail below the timberline and made his way into the deep forest of the valley. His spirits were high. He had finished a successful cattle drive, and he was proud of that. And somehow he felt he would reach a satisfactory conclusion in this business with the Ward brothers. Could be he would be lucky in the venture as well.

Already, however, he missed the crew, the men he had worked and lived with during the long drive. Now, he had only himself and his present task to be concerned with, and his thoughts could be of matters that were important to him. It seemed to him that Bethenia Cooper, indeed, did top that list of items.

Chapter Eleven

Conroy Cooper was not happy to have his niece show up in his life. There were some tender feelings for his dead brother's daughter, but he would have been just as satisfied if she had not come.

Bethenia's resemblance to her dead mother upset Conroy Cooper. He had wanted Molly Mae for himself but Lee charmed her and she fell in love with the younger brother. After his time in the Union Army he found out the two had married. He never went back home, heading west instead.

Desperation alone made him write that letter to his brother. He never had expected Molly Mae to be dead. He never had expected a girl that would remind him of the woman he lost. But no woman would replace her.

At the outset, his hotel business had done very well. Visitors from the East were pleased to find an agreeable establishment so far from "civilization."

"I'd like to steal that cook away from the Marks-Ashton Arms Hotel," a prominent furrier once had told Conroy Cooper. "To find well-prepared and delightfully presented food out here in the Wild West is a sign of a discerning man, black or white. I'd like to hire her to cook for me back east."

"She won't go. Says no amount of money can make her go back. Have the feeling that Sophronia knows what she wants," Conroy Cooper had told the furrier. "She wants to be independent, be her own boss."

"Have to admire that," the furrier had concluded.

Years ago when Conroy Cooper and his mining partner Booker Marshall had been cheated out of filing their claim for their silver mine, it had been Booker's idea to ask John Owens, a white lawyer, to file their claim under his name. Owens was very agreeable to that, but when the two men brought in the silver ore, the scoundrel declared that the two men worked for him at *his* mine.

Booker had become ill with a wracking cough and decided to visit his elderly parents in upstate New York, where they had settled by way of the underground railroad. Although the trip was arduous, Booker had realized that he had little chance of survival from his illness, and he ought to visit his aged folk while he could.

"Sure, I'll buy you out, Booker," Conroy had said. "The way we always said, fifty-fifty." He had withdrawn the money from the bank, given Booker what they had agreed upon, and Booker left for New York.

After he had paid his partner, Conroy was short of cash. He would need money, and he would need it fast. He couldn't run a hotel without it. He had to keep his creditors satisfied. He decided to send for his brother Lee. After all, family would work for cheap. What he had gotten instead was Bethenia, an inexperienced young orphan.

Well, if the girl was anything like her father, she

would work out. She seemed like a quick learner. He showed her how to check in the hotel guests.

"Mostly they're menfolk, out here to make money—trappers, miners, some outlaws—once in a while a man will bring his wife along, but don't bother to question too closely on that, if you know what I mean."

Bethenia blushed at the implication, but understood very clearly what he meant.

Her uncle went on, "You can help serve the meals in the dining room, too, especially when its busy in there. Ask Sophronia for a white apron to put on over your skirt so when you finish in the dining room, you can come back here to the desk." He left her and entered his office, the door closing soundly behind him.

Bethenia sighed. She did not mind working. When she was busy, she had less time to think of Haste. It was when she returned to her tiny room and closed the door that her thoughts turned to the man whom she knew she loved. It wasn't until he left that she realized how much she missed him. She cried herself to sleep more than once. Would she ever see him again?

She had never felt more alone. Her uncle didn't like her. He used a matter-of-fact tone of voice when he spoke to her, and Bethenia accepted her relationship with him as that of an employee.

She straightened the hotel desk not noticing until too late the two men who had entered the room.

"Missy, get me Conroy Cooper."

Her heart dropped from fear. She was almost sure she had recognized the Ward brothers. She nodded yes and went quickly to her uncle's office. She opened the door.

"Mr. Cooper." Bethenia's voice broke into her uncle's reverie as he sat in his office pondering his future and that of his hotel.

"Mr. Cooper, there are two men here to see you."

"Yes, gentlemen, what may I do for you?"

Conroy Cooper had grown a thick, dark beard in the years since he'd seen the two men. Due to worry about the hotel, he'd lost considerable weight despite Sophronia's excellent cooking. As he moved toward the two burly white men, he tried to suppress a rattling cough that bubbled up from his chest. He held a white handkerchief to his mouth, wiped his lips, and hid his anxiety as best he could.

"You own this place?" Frank Ward asked, looking about surreptitiously.

"Surely do. Have rooms to rent, a fine dining room, and a decent barbershop, all right here." There was unmistakable pride in Conroy Cooper's voice.

"Got a stable out back?"

Cooper stood and went to the desk. His blood nearly froze when he recognized the two men. Conroy forced himself to remain calm. He was aware of Bethenia's close scrutiny of what was taking place. Had the past finally caught up with him?

"Yes, sir. Your horses can be well-fed and cared for. A dollar a day for each horse, and five dollars for each night's stay here in the hotel."

"Fine. Name is Franklin Ward, and this is my brother, Henry," he said with a crooked smile. He reached for the pen to sign the register.

Bastards, I know who you are, Conroy thought. But he turned to Bethenia with forced enthusiasm.

"Yes, sir! Bethenia, go and get Will to take care of these gentlemen's horses, and tell Sophronia that there will be two more for dinner."

Conroy turned to the rough shaven men. "You will be here for dinner, gentlemen?"

"Expect so, long 'sthings here *suit* us. There are some other things to discuss, Mr. Cooper."

A distinct chill rode down Conroy's spine as the meaning of Ward's words penetrated his brain. He had hoped never to see these two men again. Would his luck ever change, or would bad luck always follow him? He had a feeling that he wouldn't die in peace.

Through a scrim of dust, Haste rode through the valley. He kept aware of his surroundings. There could be unfriendly Indians or rough mountain men who wouldn't mind relieving a solitary traveler of whatever he had and they wanted. He hoped to reach town before nightfall the next day.

Having ridden about thirty miles this day, he decided to make camp and to rest the horses and himself. He found a spot shaded by some trees, fir, aspen, and cottonwood, with a nearby meadow of long grass for the horses. A swiftly running brook about fifty yards from the meadow gave him fresh water. He unsaddled Red Chief, unloaded the packhorse, and led Jasper and the other two animals to the stream. He filled his own canteen and his coffee pot with fresh, cool water.

After he had staked the horses, he set about getting his own camp ready. He had picked a spot with several large boulders arranged in a rough semicircle. The sun's heat had warmed them, and Haste constructed a rough lean-to of branches and logs to give him protection, both from the elements and animals. He stretched out his ground sheet, placed his blankets over it, and put his saddle down sideways as a pillow for his head. He started a small fire within a pile of stones and had a serviceable flame going in minutes. He put his coffee on, and in his small fry-pan, he cooked some bacon and opened a tin of beans, adding them to the bacon.

Never had such simple food tasted so good. After he

finished eating, Haste cleaned up his utensils and settled back to rest against the saddle. The horses grazed contentedly, and Haste's thoughts turned once more to Bethenia. He closed his eyes and saw her young face: her large, dark, luminous eyes, her determined chin that she would thrust forward whenever she was challenged. Her thick black hair that she most often wore in long twin braids had become intriguing to Haste. Now, as he lay silent, thinking about the girl, he felt an instant arousal. Who would have thought six months ago that he, Haste Allen Terrell, would be stumbling, mumbling, and bewitched by a female? And why this one, when she had been such a problem to him?

Haste shook himself, placed his pistols within easy reach and drifted into a light sleep. In his mind, he could see Bethenia, a nebulous cloud of dark hair floating free from her face and her mouth opening as if she was trying to speak, but Haste heard nothing.

He awoke with a start and looked around. Nothing seemed to be amiss, yet a feeling of urgency came upon him. Darkness had fallen but a full winter moon hung on the horizon, ready to move across the black night sky. Haste decided to move, too.

Chapter Twelve

Bethenia stopped in the basement kitchen long enough to tell Sophronia that there would be two more men to feed that night. Sophronia, a small brown woman of unbelievable strength, was a woman of few words. Bethenia received the response she had expected.

"Two more, ten more," the wiry, birdlike woman snapped, "makes no never mind, child." Sophronia prided herself on her ability to meet any challenge, either in the kitchen or out of it. Her master, a Cajun connoisseur, had come into the kitchen of the big house to inform her of her freedom, and said, "Slavery is over, and the government says you're free." Sophronia had placed her mixing spoon on the table, walked out of the house, and never looked back. She had continued to walk, behind a wagon train, from Louisiana to the West. When she had reached Denver and the Marks-Ashton Arms Hotel, she had stopped and told Conroy Cooper, "I'll cook for you, but you pays me. No more work for nuthin'." Conroy Cooper had agreed and paid her well. It was her culinary skill that made his hotel's dining room famous, and he knew it. What no one knew was that Sophronia was saving her money to be able to send for her children whom she had been forced to leave be-hind with relatives when she walked to freedom.

"These two men are bad folk . . ." Bethenia started to describe them to the cook, then stopped herself. *It is better to keep my ears and eyes open and study them a little more.* She had sensed, that her uncle had been un-comfortable with the two outlaws. She wondered what their connection was. The more she could find out, the better, she figured.

She wished that Haste were around. *He* could handle those two. She would never forget how he had handled the men who tried to rape her. That incident would be always in her memory. She was lucky to know such a good man.

She smiled as she remembered one night, shortly af-ter she had tricked her way into the cattle drive with Uncle Al Page's help, he had tried to tell Bethenia just what kind of man Haste Allen Terrell really was.

"I'm goin' tell you 'bout Hat," he had said. They had just cleaned up after serving the crew their evening meal.

"I know you think he's strict and stubborn, but he's a fine man. He believes in the Good Book, 'Do unto others,' you know. Always willin' to help them in need . . . man, woman, or child. But it's a rough, tough life, and more than one man couldn't take it and went back east. I remember when Haste first came to Fair Acres Ranch. Mr. Connolly knew he'd been in the Tenth cav-alry, but them's tame horses and men. Cowboy life is different. He was a tall, skinny kid, but he had strong muscles. Hat had that same look in his eyes you see now. Determination, I calls it. Knows what to do and don't quit till he does it."

"How long have you known Haste?" Bethenia had asked.

Cook had pushed his weather-beaten sombrero back on his head, used a straw to pick his teeth, and sat back against the wagon wheel of the chuck wagon before he had answered. "Let's see now. Years gone by so fast, hard to recollect. He was a boy of seventeen when I first met 'im. 'Bout thirty years old now, I'd guess. Out here folk don't talk much 'bout their years."

"Know how old you are, Uncle Al?" Bethenia asked with a teasing twinkle in her eyes.

"Who wants to know?" Cook had grinned, throwing a dishtowel made from a flour sack at Bethenia.

"You're still a young man, aren't you?"

"Old enough to be your daddy, and don't you forget it." Cook had smiled. He had enjoyed the company of this young woman, and he would have killed anyone who harmed her. Al Page had lived with Indians, was skilled with a bow and arrow, and his experience as a buffalo soldier had made him well-equipped in the use of firearms. He always had carried his two Colt revolvers, even under his voluminous white cook's apron.

"So, how long have you and Haste known each other?"

"He was my sergeant in the cavalry, and believe it or not, we mustered out 'bout the same time. Course he got honors when he got out, recommended by the general and all, but I got drunk when I got out. Went our own ways for a while, and boy, was I surprised when we met up on the Connolly ranch."

"Glad to see each other?"

"Glad? You betcha! But let me tell you what happened to Haste. He'd only been on the Connolly ranch for a few days, and as usual, everybody gits after the new man, so's to speak. Wasn't no different with Hat. I remember some white cowboy, didn't know nuthin' 'bout Hat, dared him to ride an 'outlaw' horse."

"And 'outlaw' horse. What on earth is that?"

"An 'outlaw' is an animal that's been so mistreated, so abused all his life, he don't know how to act. He'll bite, kick, buck, do anything he can to keep from bein' rode."

"Sounds terrible."

"It is. Them horses been treated so bad—hollered at, beat to tame them—acts just the opposite. They get meaner than a hound dog with a toothache."

"What happened?"

"Well, the way I remember it, Hat wasn't 'bout to let that dude git the better of him. So, he knew he had to ride that there old Red Chief. He was one bad animal—big, with haunches that looked like coiled springs and muscles that rippled under his reddish-brown skin. Had the wildest white eyes you ever saw, and he had one mean spirit . . . like the devil he was. That brute hated hisself, the world, and everybody in it! I whispered to Hat that old Red Chief might be the last horse he rode, but if he planned to stay on this ranch, he'd been called out, so what else could he do?"

"So he rode him?"

"Did he! Hat went into that corral that mornin' . . . never forget it . . . everyone standing round, watching. Had him a pocketful of carrots, apples, and sugar lumps. See, bein' in the cavalry, he knew horses. He went up and pitched a rope over Red Chief's head. That horse started to buck and snort, but all the time Hat talked quietlike. Hat just kept talkin', all the time workin' hand over hand up that rope, watchin' out that he didn't get kicked, till he was able to slip a half-hitch over the Chief's ears. Pressed the bit in his mouth with another piece o' carrot, plus a bit of apple, and that horse was just a chewin' and relaxin'. Then, Hat threw the saddle over Chief's back. Well, that did it! That son of a bitch pitched

and kicked and jumped and twirled around, hoofs sound-
ing like thunder! But Hat held him steady, talkin' and
pattin' when he could. Took 'bout twenty, twenty-five
minutes 'fore he could finish with the saddlin', tryin' to
keep away from them flyin' kicks. That animal was one
mean brute."

"Was Haste able to ride him?"

"You betcha. Hat has got plenty o' patience, and little
by little he got hold o' the reins, bent the horse's head
down, grabbed the saddle horn, got his foot in the stirrup, and there he was, sittin' on Red Chief!"

Bethenia laughed lightly, "What did the horse do
then?"

Cook had grinned at the memory of that day.

"I never seen such buckin' and jumpin'. That mean
bastard even tried to run up against the fence to git Hat
off his back. He put Hat through *everything;* buckin',
whirlin', all four feet in the air, dust flyin'. Naturally,
the cowboys was watchin' and yellin'. It was somethin'
to see! Hat held on. Told me later that he thought any
minute he'd be throwed to kingdom come, but he knew
he'd die tryin'. That Red Chief, evil though he was, was
smart, too. See, Hat hadn't hollered, hit him . . . none o'
those things the other riders had did to him, so after
what seem to be a lifetime, he gave up. Just stopped,
sides heavin', froth at the mouth, and turned his head
and looked back at Hat with them big white eyes as if
to say, 'All right, boss, you win.' Know somethin',
Bethenia? Hat was the onliest one ever could ride that
animal. Still is to this day. Ridin' him right now on this
cattle drive. I believe that horse would do anythin' that
Hat ask him to do."

"What about the man who dared Hat to ride Red
Chief?"

"Well, I'd have to say he knew he'd met a Negro

man who was every bit and more the man he thought *he* was. Came right over, put his hand out to Hat, and said he'd be pleased to shake his hand, and the rest o' the crew agreed. Hat never had no more trouble, and that's when Mr. Connolly started givin' Hat more responsibility. Till he decided this year to make him trail boss."

She nodded, pride growing in her heart. "Thanks for letting me know, Cook. I don't want to be a problem to Haste. I'll carry my own weight."

"Appears to me you are two of a kind. Independent *and* stubborn," Cook Al Page had concluded.

"Could be," Bethenia had agreed, with a sigh. "Could be," she repeated wistfully before helping Sophronia with the dinner.

Chapter Thirteen

It was noon the following day when Haste spotted a faint plume of white smoke that rose into the bright blue sky. Someone has a camp nearby, he thought. Better move cautiously ... could be hostile Indians or renegades. Former cavalry men were always suspicious.

He rode a few miles closer, then decided to approach the camp on foot. One of his horses could snicker, step on a twig or rock and thereby give away his presence. He dismounted and picketed the horses in a leafy glade where they would be hidden but where they could crop safely.

He told Red chief, "Rest, old man. You may have to move quickly if I come back on the run. Don't know what's out there. Be back soon."

He patted the horse's nose, and Red Chief's ears twitched as if he understood exactly what Haste had said.

With his two pistols holstered, Haste took his rifle, plus adequate ammunition, slung his canteen and knapsack over his shoulder, and crept quietly toward the camp he had seen from the distance. When he got closer, he relaxed because there was Painted Owl, seated Indian-fashion beside the campfire, his right hand raised in greeting. He sighed with relief. Painted Owl greeted him.

"I figure, boss, you come this way soon. You see message Painted Owl send?"

"Sure did, old friend. Is that coffee hot?"

Haste knew that he was welcome to help himself to a cup of coffee, but it would not be polite to do so without first asking permission.

"May I have a cup?" Haste would always honor the Indian tradition of respecting another's possessions.

"Coffee hot and corn pone, too," Painted Owl said, indicating that Haste was welcome to help himself.

Both men ate and drank in a friendly silence. Haste ate eagerly showing appreciation for the Indian's food, then he reached into his buckskin jacket and handed Painted Owl a small roll of bills.

"I owe you this, your pay, Painted Owl. Your brothers' help was much appreciated, too. They did fine."

Painted Owl took the money without counting it and grunted his thanks.

"Missy is well, but the Ward brothers are at hotel," he said abruptly. "Others sleep in stable, not pay uncle for sleep, sneak up in hayloft, and leave before stableboy come in mornin'. But Painted Owl wonder about missy—"

"Why, Painted Owl? Is she all right?" Haste asked, aware that the Indian sensed his concern.

"Aye. Works for uncle in hotel. But missy does not smile much these days. Not happy like when on cattle drive."

Haste swallowed his last few drops of coffee. He had a job to do tracking the Ward brothers but Bethenia . . . she haunted him. What difference could a short trip make? "What if I bring her gelding, Jasper, back to her. Think that he will make her smile again?"

"She be glad to see him, boss. And you, too, Painted Owl believes."

By dusk, Haste and Painted Owl had reached the outer edge of the dusty town. On the main road, there was busy traffic of a sort: mules, wagons, horses, and all types of people, Indians, mule skinners, many prospectors, and cowboys. Haste even glimpsed a black-robed priest who seemed out of place amid the mercenary, money-grubbing crowd. A dust storm of greed and avarice hung in the air as all the activity seemed to focus on a single destiny—money, land, gold, and a selfish, if fleeting, prosperity.

Haste looked to his companion's face and recognized the shadow of sadness. By believing in Manifest Destiny, the government had decreed that to explore and conquer the West was its preordained right and duty. But Haste understood the pain the Indians felt as they viewed this offensive scene. Mother Earth was being scourged and raped, and they could not help her.

Each man shook his head as they rode wordlessly into the crowd. Little notice was taken of the two strangers on horseback who made their way with their packhorses and the gelding to a stable located near the Lee-Ashton Arms Hotel at the far end of the half-mile long street.

"I need to know more about these men, Painted Owl. The ones you saw at the hotel."

"Aye, I take horses to stable."

"Good. Tell the stableboy to give them a good rub and plenty of food. I know Red Chief is tired. Deserves a rest."

"Haste happy to see missy?" Painted Owl said teasingly, with a sly grin.

"The question is, will she want to see me? I'm just a cowboy, and here she is livin' in a grand hotel."

"Painted Owl be plenty surprised if missy not glad, boss."

"Come to the dinin' room, and we will eat and find out what we can 'bout the strangers."

Bethenia tried to remain calm, but there was no mistaking the galloping leap her heart took when she saw Haste Terrell push open the hotel's glass doors. She wondered if the wild flush that she felt show on her face?

The late afternoon sun flicked through the western windows of the large hotel lobby. Firelike rays of light played on the shiny pine wood floors. Haste felt welcome, but nonetheless, he remained cautious. There were several tables in the lobby where men in groups of three or four were smoking, planning, and waiting for the dining room doors to open for the evening meal.

Haste removed his sombrero, placed it on the counter, and gave a quiet whistle as he looked at Bethenia. Gone was the tomboy in the wool trousers, flannel shirt, and old, rough jacket. Haste reached his hands across the registration desk, reaching for Bethenia's hands.

"By God, Bethenia, nothing I like better than seeing you in a dress. Why, you're a young woman, by damn!"

"No need to swear, Haste," Bethenia spoke calmly, hoping her voice didn't betray the joy she felt at seeing Haste.

"Bethenia Cooper, by God, you're plumb beautiful!"

Bethenia's thick, lustrous black hair was piled high on the crown of her head, and her slender neck was exposed by the upswept fashion with only a few soft cascading tendrils escaping. Her deep brown eyes focused on Haste as she watched him sign his name. Though she tried not to show her anxious pleasure as she handed him the room key, somehow communication passed between them. Bethenia realized it was the first time they ever had touched each other. Her face flushed even more deeply against the demure white collar of her cotton blouse. Haste could only guess that her uncle wanted her to be noticed as little as possible, because she wore a plain long brown corduroy skirt. The schoolmarm look did not deter Haste. To him, she was radiant with her soft glowing skin and warm smile.

The sincerity in Haste's voice pleased Bethenia. She was happy to see her friend. She felt safer already, but she realized that any moment her uncle might appear from his office to check on her. He was apt to do so, especially if he heard a man's voice.

"Will you be staying at the hotel, Haste?"

"If I may. You know Painted Owl is with me. We'll be sharing a room for a few days. We're on our way back to Fair Acres. Can't get over you," he repeated. "All grown up and pretty as a Christmas doll. Can you take a walk with me later?" Haste asked. "There is someone here I'd like you to meet."

"Me? But who, Haste? Who is it?"

"You'll see. I'll stop here for you after dinner is over."

Haste could hardly wait to see Bethenia's face when she saw her beloved gelding, Jasper.

Chapter Fourteen

Most of the men eating in the dining room paid appreciative attention to Bethenia as she moved from table to table, replenishing coffee cups and refilling glasses of water. The diners concentrated on the extraordinarily good food, rarely found on the frontier, and on their own intimate conversations of deals and plans, legal and otherwise. Like all servants, Bethenia listened for any bits and pieces of talk that she could remember and perhaps later put to her advantage. Her small brown face concentrated on her task. It proved not to be a bad job; she was busy and was learning something about the hotel business.

As she refilled the coffee cups of the Ward brothers, who sat at the corner table where they could view the whole room and its occupants, she heard one of them speak to the other in a coarse whisper. Bethenia shuddered as their rank body odor engulfed her.

"Said the train pulls in 'bout midnight."

"Quiet, Henry!" Franklin hissed at his younger brother, whose slow wit often caused problems. "I heard what he said. Now, shut up!" he admonished.

Bethenia moved in an unhurried pace to the next table. She was certain that the men were the Ward brothers. She heard the older man scold the younger one again, "Be quiet, I said. She could hear you."

"Oh, Franklin, she's only a dumb colored serving girl. Don't know nuthin'."

"Ain't so sure. I seen her watchin' us when we talked with Conroy. He *sure* don't want nobody to know that we know him! So, keep your trap shut! His information better be right."

"Franklin, you worry too much!"

"Henry, you dumb ox! If *I* didn't worry we'd be six feet under by now. Shut your mouth. Tell you, let's get outto' here so I can check things. The boys still sleepin' in the hotel stable?"

"Yep, ready to move anytime you say."

As the two rustlers strode unhurriedly and confidently toward the dining room entrance, they were unaware that they were being watched by Haste and Painted Owl. Haste noted his old enemy, Frank Ward and his lame right hand.

"There, boss," he whispered. "The Ward brothers."

"You're right, friend." But Haste wondered, what if there *is* a connection between Bethenia's uncle and these criminals? What would it mean to *their* budding relationship?

With the meal finally over, the room thinned out as the dinner guests made their way to the bar, the lobby, or out onto the street in search of other diversions— mainly female companionship.

Haste had promised Bethenia that he would wait for her on the verandah. It was nearly nine o'clock when her chores were completed and she was relieved at the desk by her uncle's night receptionist. She wore a heavy wool jacket, and her dark brown shawl protected her head and face from the sharp night air. To Haste, she was suddenly the most beautiful of creatures. Her eyes, like pools of deep water, reflected her excitement at the thought of the surprise Haste had promised her. His heart pounded with unexpected joy as he sensed her eagerness to discover his secret.

A full moon rose over the roofs of the town's two-story buildings on its single main street. It's glow offered a shiny silver patina to the mercantile building and the saloon with its bright lights. Raucous laughter from the saloon patrons filtered out onto the street, spiced with the brassy chords of a piano. The one substantial brick building housed the bank and stood alone, with forbidding bars at the windows and doors that defied entrance. Across the street were the wood-framed post office, assay office, and the sheriff's office, with two cells for prisoners.

Haste knew that soon he would have to speak to George Benard, his Pinkerton contact, but for tonight, he wanted to try to begin a new relationship with this lovely, headstrong woman who had compelled him to do so, unwilling though he had been to help her. He was glad that she had.

The bare ground was frozen beneath their heavy boots. They crunched around the corner of the hotel, and down a dark alley. Bethenia's breath quickened in anticipation as they neared the stables.

Her hand trembled on Haste's arm when she saw the open door of the lighted, warm stable. She started to run.

"It's Jasper! Haste, you brought him back!"

When she ran into the stable, the big gelding recognized her voice and scent and whinnied with excitement, snorted, and pawed the earth with his front feet as Bethenia threw her arms around his neck. Painted Owl let go of the reins as Bethenia hugged the animal.

The visible love between the young woman and her

horse was so palpable, Haste and Painted Owl could only grin at each other. Words were not necessary; indeed, they would have been inadequate.

Bethenia turned to thank Haste; her tears of gratitude sparkled in her eyes and moved his heart.

"Never thought I'd ever see my friend again. I'm not sure my uncle will let me keep him, but thank you, Haste, for bringin' him to me. He and a few other things are all I have from home. My Jasper."

She patted the horse's neck and spoke softly to him. His ears pricked, recognizing her voice, and he whinnied again softly as he welcomed her.

Painted Owl spoke, "Here, missy." He handed her some carrots and apples, which the horse eagerly accepted from her familiar hand.

"Thank you, Painted Owl, you are a good friend, too. Isn't that so, Jasper?"

From the shadows of the stable stepped two more buckskin-clad Indians. Silently, they had watched the young brown woman greet her horse with honest love and affection, and they felt a kinship to such a person who could understand the heart of a four-legged brother.

"My brothers, Running Fox and Deer Cloud," Painted Owl explained. "Good brothers to missy, too, now."

Bethenia nodded solemnly to each man who raised his right hand, palm outward in greeting.

"How did you know?" she asked Haste.

"That you needed friends?" he answered. "It was a feeling that I had when I left you here, Bethenia. Was I right?"

"I think so. I'm worried. There are two men in this town, came in a few days ago, and I've got the feeling that my uncle fears them. Hasn't said anything, but he seems uneasy."

"Let's get back to the hotel. You can point them out to me. Might be of interest to me." But Haste already knew.

He walked Bethenia back to the hotel. It was such a cold night; the air was bitterly freezing as it streamed from the mountains, that it seemed only natural for Haste to tuck Bethenia's hand into the crook of his arm. She welcomed the warmth of his body and accepted the gesture without question.

"Haste," she said, "it was real nice of you to bring Jasper back to me. I've really missed him."

"I thought you might. Know I'd miss Red Chief. Be good to have Jasper close by. Think your uncle will mind having him in the stable?"

"I don't know, but he's paying me a small salary, so I can pay for Jasper's room and board. He's the only link with my family," she said quietly, as she reflected on her losses.

"Bethenia," Haste asked, "you plan on staying here in Denver?" He surprised himself with the question.

Bethenia was startled by Haste's question and realized she should have asked him why he wanted to know about her future plans. She wondered what he would have said if, by chance, she *had* decided to leave? Would it have made a difference to him? He had been away from her long enough for her to have some warm feelings for him. She had missed him.

"Don't really know yet." she said instead. "My mother's sister lives in Boston . . ."

After a few moments, Haste spoke again. "I'll bet you never let on to your uncle how hard a time you had, how rough it was for you to get here. You haven't told him, have you?"

"No, Haste, I haven't. You do what you have to do, that's all."

Her shorter legs scrambled to keep up with him. Automatically, he altered his stride to accommodate her. Somehow, he did not want to get back to the hotel ... too soon, anyway. He wanted more time with her.

The sharp night air frosted their breath, and Haste was delighted to be sharing this precious time with the young girl he had traveled with the past weeks, but of whom he really knew so little. Except ... he knew that he cared, cared a great deal. Never before had he believed such a powerful feeling as love would come into his plain cowboy life. As he had once told Al Page, "I'm just a mustered out trooper ... now a cowboy. Never did have dealin's with the finer things, like women and girls." But this evening he knew with certainty that he wanted to protect, to share, yes, to love, this woman, this Bethenia, who had been daring and bold enough to claim to be his "wife" to get what she wanted. Recalling the words, "your wife," jarred him as much as they had that day when he first heard them.

"Bethenia?" He spoke gently as they finally reached the hotel verandah.

"Yes, Haste?" She looked up at him and saw concern in his face.

"Are you ... are you satisfied? I mean ... being here with your uncle? Is everything all right? You feel safe here?"

Her answer was slow in coming, as if she were reluctant to speak. "Well, Haste, guess I'm satisfied. My uncle's not what I expected. I don't know him well. Course he looks a lot like my daddy, even sounds like him, but," she scowled, "a lot of him is not like Daddy at all." She thought about her uncle's questionable relationship with the rough-looking men she had seen approach him in the hotel.

She continued thoughtfully, "In a way, yes, I'm disappointed. I'd have to say. I believed they'd be more alike."

"He's not mean to you, is he?" Haste wanted to know. "Work you too hard?"

"No, not that. And I really like the work. Some of the men are rough and tough, but I can manage—"

"I *know* you can manage, Bethenia," Haste broke in. "Seen you do that with my own eyes," he commented laconically, remembering her relationship with the men on the drive.

Bethenia smiled. Al Page had once told her she could wrap *any* man around her little finger. She wondered if she could do that to Haste.

"And," she continued, "Miss Sophronia has been like a mother to me. She misses her own children, so she's kind of adopted me. No, Haste, it's just that somehow my uncle doesn't treat me like kin. I feel like a stranger around him."

"Oh, Bethenia." Haste stood ramrod straight, and the intensity in his voice alarmed Bethenia as he took both of her hands in his.

"All these weeks, I've been telling myself that you had no place in my life. I was damn mad when you thought you could join my cattle drive! Not a woman, and a young woman at that! I couldn't let such a thing happen . . . and when Cook convinced me by allowing that you were his 'niece,' I was madder than hell. I tried, by damn, not to acknowledge that you were around—"

"Haste," Bethenia interrupted him, "I knew from the first that you thought I'd be a problem, but I declared I wouldn't."

"But ... let me finish, Bethenia. Somehow *you* showed me. You *wouldn't* be ignored. And I saw how quick you learned. You have a natural way with horses, and you weren't skittish round the steers. And my eyes were really opened when I saw how you could handle the men. There's not a man in my outfit who wouldn't give his right arm for you. Every last one of them cares about you."

Suddenly, Haste knew that everything in his life had brought him to this time, this place, this woman.

He almost shook his head with the startling clarity of it. He loved her! Was such a thing possible? How could he manage to fall in love now with all the responsibilities he had facing him? One thing he knew for sure, he'd have to speak tonight. He'd have to let her know what was in his heart.

Haste's pressure on Bethenia's hands tightened as he continued his apology.

"How can I make up for the times I've ignored you, been cold and unpleasant to you?" he continued. "I'm sorry. I've been a stubborn cowboy with only one thing on my mind—to prove that I could handle a herd of cattle and run a cattle drive, same as any other man."

"I would never fault you for that, Haste. You had a job to do, and you did it."

"Yes, I'm heading back to Fair Acres Ranch as soon as I can. And Bethenia ..."

Bethenia sensed that Haste's next words might be ones that could change her life. As much as she longed to hear them, she wanted to resist. What did she really know about this man? Only what she had seen during the cattle drive. Did he plan a life on the trail? How could she—did she—want to live a life like that? Did *he* know what he wanted from life beyond running a cattle drive?

She wondered. Would he truly be committed to her? He was a man used to being alone. Yet she knew she had been attracted to him from the beginning. And the day he had left her in the lobby of her uncle's hotel she knew she loved him. Her known world had vanished like smoke. Barren isolation surrounded her as if she was somehow on a raft on a gray-green sea, unanchored, adrift, and purposeless. She'd had all she could do to prevent herself from crying.

Haste, don't leave me here with strangers! I want to be with you. Always it seemed to her, she'd had to steel herself—to make hard choices. It seemed to be the pattern of her life.

Her mind reeled with conflicting thoughts about a future with Haste. She shook her head as if to clear her mind, and listened.

"I've dreamed about you, Bethenia. And it wasn't only to bring Jasper back to you that I have returned. I had to see you. Had to tell you that I realize the truth . . . about how much I care for you . . . ."

He gently raised her chin toward his face, and Bethenia could see strong, powerful emotions reflected in his eyes.

As she stood beside him, his handsome brown face close to hers, she experienced a deep longing. She wanted a safe haven, a secure future, a real, honest love. But should she trust Haste's arms, depend upon his judgment, lean on his shoulders? Or would he, too, bring a greater, more disastrous disappointment to her, and . . . leave her, all the worse for having tasted his affection?

She gasped involuntarily as she realized that at last she was about to feel Haste's strong mouth upon hers.

Eager as she was to savor his masculine lips, to feel his strong arms around her, to align the length of her body with his, something held her back.

What was it her father had said, "Depend on yourself. Follow your own conscience." But what in God's name was she to do about the forces that were propelling her into Haste's arms, toward that beautiful mouth that she so wanted to feel upon her own?

Did she dare trust the physical signals her body was sending to her? The unexpected moisture in her most secretive place, the erratic thumping of her heart, the heated flush that she knew enveloped her face despite the cold night air? Did Haste know, could he tell, how much she *wanted* to respond to him?

In her mind, fears and uncertainties swirled—her uncle, Haste, and her own future. Confusion rose above everything, and she knew if this moment ever came again she would have to be ready to receive it, to grasp and hang on to it. Tonight, however, she was not ready.

With strength she didn't know she had, she pulled both of her hands away from Haste and thrust them against his chest.

"Got to go," she murmured. "My uncle," she started to say, then abruptly she changed to another subject as if to return to the original focus of their outing.

"Thanks for bringing Jasper back," she said, as she pushed open the glass doors and disappeared into the warmth of the hotel.

Haste stood where she had left him, unaware that on the other side of the closed doors Bethenia stumbled to her room, her eyes filling with tears as she forced the newly aroused feelings of love back into the secret places of her heart. All she really had wanted from life was someone to love her.

* * *

It was a sober, reflective Haste who sat in George Benard's office the next morning. After the unhappy results of his thwarted meeting with Bethenia, he knew more than ever he'd have to conclude this Pinkerton business quickly, return to Texas, and ask Evan Connolly to release him from another cattle drive so he could get back to Denver and Bethenia. He couldn't lose her.

"Gabe Skinner, is it?" George Benard inquired of Haste.

"For this job, yes. What information do you have on the Ward brothers?"

"I know they are here in town, in Conroy Cooper's hotel. Also know they have been blackmailing him for sometime."

"Blackmailing him?"

"Yep, the information I have is that Cooper received a less than honorable discharge from the cavalry. He was an amateur boxer with a reputation for gambling. One night he lost some money *and* his temper. Rumor was that he had 'fists of stone,' and he put his enemy in the hospital. Subsequently, he was drummed out of the military. Well, anyway, he found his way out west and took up with a miner to help him work his claim. He and Booker Marshall were so angry that they had been cheated out of their own valid claim that they bushwhacked the unsuspecting man and tried again to claim the mine as their own. Again, they failed because of their race. The miner had died of his injuries but not before naming Cooper and Marshall. He told the Ward brothers, who vowed vengeance against the pair. 'Can't stand a smart Nigra,' they said. Begging your pardon, Gabe."

Haste nodded. "Go on."

"The Ward brothers play their own games. They've toyed with Conroy Cooper. The ante went up when they realized Conroy owned the hotel."

"So, now," Haste concluded, "the Wards are black-mailing Cooper."

"Right. Information I have is that he has to give them a base of operation and alibis as they follow their other pursuits of rustling cattle and robbing banks and trains. They could implicate him as a partner if necessary. The word I have now is that the train robbery is going to be pulled off tonight."

"You think they mean to try?"

"I do. Say, how many men do you have?"

Haste said, "I have three Ute Indians, good men, all. How about you?"

"Just myself," Benard answered, "but we can count on the railroad security man who will be riding in the express money car. I sent a wire out this morning to put them on alert."

"Train pulls in at midnight?"

"Right. I suggest that you station your men in the gully on the opposite side o' the platform. I'll signal to you when I see the Wards show up. You boys got enough ammunition?"

"Plenty. But the sheriff, he in on this?" Haste wanted to know.

"Ah, yes, the sheriff. Well, you know, as Pinkerton men, we have been hired to stop this gang. Some Texas ranchers have laid out money for us to apprehend this bunch of rustlers, and I guess we can bill the railroad if we save *their* money, don't you think?" Benard said with a grin. "So, yes, I've spoken to the sheriff. He's glad of the help. He'll be there."

"Should be! We're helping him do his job," Haste insisted.

Later that night, the town was quiet, with most of its citizens asleep. However, the saloon remained active with a few die-hard revelers making merry as long as the barkeep was able to keep the liquor flowing.

Haste and his three companions walked their horses carefully and quietly to the train depot behind the row of buildings on Main Street. They positioned themselves in the thick brush and trees that bordered the ditch beyond the train bed. It was eleven-thirty.

Painted Owl put his ear to the ground and announced solemnly, "Train come soon. Mother Earth shakes and trembles."

His brother Running Fox agreed, saying, "Enemy come near, too. Rider come this way."

"Keep your horses quiet," Haste told them. "We'll wait for Benard's signal to attack." He had explained before that it would be the owl's hoot.

In the distance, a train could be heard thundering toward the depot. As it came closer, the ray of its steady headlight pierced the dark night.

Haste and his men waited. A shrill steam whistle announced the train's arrival, and like a weary, mechanical beast, it sighed as the great wheels ground to a stop. Haste could see the blazing hot flames from the furnace reflected on the faces of the firemen and stoker as they worked, faces blackened with soot. He and his men kept quiet positions in the dark.

As the men stepped from the train, gasping for a breath of the cold night air, they were accosted by two men whose faces were covered below their eyes with bandannas.

Haste watched the four figures. Two had guns which they pointed at the other two men, who now stood silent, with their hands in the air.

Haste knew they were the Ward brothers. How many more times, he wondered, are these two men going to cross my path? They have been dogging my footsteps since the days in the cavalry. Plague take that Frank Ward! This time, I hope he gets what's coming to him. All I want is to marry the woman I love and find a peaceful life somewhere. If only he could know Bethenia's feelings for him.

As Haste waited for George Benard and the sheriff, he felt rivulets of perspiration, chilled by the night air, crawl slowly into his eyes and down his cheeks. He blinked to clear away the smarting sweat.

Then, he heard the distinct nasal drawl of Frank Ward. "Keep both hands up! Make a move, you're dead!"

Stopped in their tracks, both men were quickly gagged and bound. Hissing could be heard as the engine cooled down, and an occasional puff of steam exhaust flared like a baby cloud into the night sky. The old train gave one last snort, then was quiet.

Haste and his men kept their horses still in the darkness with a hand over the animals' mouths to prevent an untoward whinny or snicker. They waited for the signal.

Soon, three of the Wards' men rode single file right in front of Haste and his men, unaware of their presence. They faced the armored car of the train.

Franklin Ward moved to the engineer who still sat in his cab, open-mouthed with fear as he saw the robbers with their guns drawn for an imminent attack.

"Open that there express car door!" Frank Ward demanded.

The engineer complied, and the pressure lock was released. The wide door slid noiselessly on its runners. Bright interior lanterns flooded the scene. A single train employee was at his desk in the money car, his face shielded by a green eyeshade. When he realized the car was being robbed, he reached for his gun, a grave error. Franklin Ward's gun spat a lethal flame, and the train employee fell to the floor.

Ignoring the wounded man, Henry Ward sat on his horse and cackled in glee, saying, "Boys, we never have to work 'nother day in our lives! Help yourself!"

On the floor were several bags of gold coins with *U.S. Mint* marked on the outside of the bags. There were flat packages that contained paper currency, all destined for the Bank of Denver.

"Shut up, Henry," his brother warned him, as he threw several bags to his waiting gunmen, who seized them with open arms.

Haste and the Utes watched. Then came the lonely hoot of an owl. Haste motioned to them. He and the Utes sprang forward from their hidden places among the trees and brush of the gully. The element of surprise for the Ward gang was doubled when the door on the opposite side of the money car slid open. George Benard and the sheriff leaped into the car with their guns blazing.

Franklin Ward and his brother had each grabbed a bag of coins from the floor, and as they tried to turn to fire at Haste, it was their undoing because Haste's twin pistols found their marks. Henry fell from his saddle, seriously wounded, and now, Franklin's left hand dangled from the wrist where the lead ball had struck. He was virtually defenseless. Haste saw the hate in Frank Ward's eyes.

The three other bandits went down the gully as fast as

their horses could take them, but the Utes were behind them. Painted Owl used his whip to snare one of them, and each of his brothers roped the other two.

Chapter Fifteen

Bethenia found her uncle's body the next morning. As usual, her day began by opening the dining room drapes and windows to let in the daylight and to allow fresh air to cleanse the room of the prior evening's smoke-filled air. At first, she thought the body slouched over the table was just another drunk sleeping off a stuporous binge. Then, she recognized her uncle, saw the small hole in his temple, blood in his hair and the gun on the carpeted floor. Her screams brought people from all parts of the hotel. The quick-stepping, flour-dusted Sophronia, up from the basement kitchen, reached her first and assessing the situation, folded the horrified girl in her arms.

"Child, child," she spoke softly, "you done see death fore, and you goin' see it again."

Not since her parents' deaths had Bethenia felt so pained. It came as a shock to her, because she had not really known her uncle, and now, she realized she was truly alone again.

"Alone once more," Bethenia sobbed.

"No child, don't think like that. You got friends, good friends, too. Don't think you are by yourself. You got me . . . may not be kin, but—"

"Oh, Sophronia! What'll I do?"

* * *

Sophronia was relieved when Haste arrived, sending the curious onlookers out of the room and dispatching Painted Owl to find the sheriff. While they waited for the lawman, capable Sophronia ordered that tables be removed into the hotel lobby, and she provided hot coffee, biscuits, jam, corn bread, and grits for those travelers who wanted to eat quickly and get on about their business.

The sheriff accepted a fragrant cup of hot coffee from Haste as he explained, "Seems like a suicide to me, with the gun being near his hand, and there's a note. Actually, two. One to his niece, Bethenia Cooper, and the other one to me, believe it or not! Says he took his own life cause the hotel was losing money and that he was afraid and tired o' the Wards and their blackmailin' him. It can be quite a burden, between those two evils, don't you know."

He pulled a large watch from his vest pocket, checked the time, then asked Haste, "Think Miss Cooper could see me now? Could get this matter settled right quick."

"She's in the kitchen with Sophronia. Said she wanted to be busy. Her way of dealing with this, I guess."

"Yes, well, it's too bad," the sheriff commiserated.

Conroy Cooper was laid to rest on a quiet hillside grave outside of town. When the last words had been spoken to the few mourners by the old Negro preacher, and when he had dropped the last clods of earth onto the desolate grave, Bethenia turned to Haste who stood, hatless, beside her and asked, "Why? Why, Haste, did he do this?"

"I believe he had a lot of sadness, Bethenia. Can never rightly say."

Haste never told Bethenia what he knew of her uncle's past and his involvement with the Ward brothers.

As they walked down the hillside to the waiting carriage for the ride back to the hotel, Bethenia said sadly, "He was the last of my father's family." Reaching the carriage, she turned and raised her black-gloved hand in a last wave to the just buried man she had scarcely known.

Haste and Bethenia rode back to the hotel in the undertaker's carriage that was hired for the deceased's family. Each was burdened with overwhelming thoughts. Haste was worried about Bethenia. What was going to happen to her? Would she stay in Denver? Would she inherit the hotel? What would all of this mean to him? To the woman he loved? He hadn't been able to tell her how much he loved her. Would she go to Texas with him? He was so close to revealing his love the night he'd brought Jasper back, but she'd bolted like a scared rabbit. Could he dare tell her now? She looked so small, so vulnerable, dressed in black with her hands resting quietly in her lap.

Bethenia sat in the corner of the carriage, her own thoughts jumbled and confused. She felt disembodied, as if the cloth of her life had been shredded and scattered. Could she get her life in order? What would she do now? What was left for her? She knew she loved Haste, but he had not spoken . . . perhaps, he wouldn't. Should she have encouraged him that night? How could she? She wasn't ready, didn't know really what it would all mean. Was she ready now? She dared not look at him for fear her aching heart would show on her face. Instead, she breathed a long, audible sigh.

Instantly, Haste asked, "Bethenia, are you all right?"

Bethenia turned to him quickly as if released by a wound up spring. The silent tears that Haste saw in her eyes broke his tentativeness. He gathered the weeping woman in his arms.

"Oh, Haste, I don't know what I'm going to do! How will I manage to keep going . . . if, if, one after another, everybody dies?"

"Don't cry, Bethenia. I'll always be here, always, if you want me."

"Oh, Haste," Bethenia sobbed as if the floodgates of all her recent sorrows had been released.

"Bethenia, I know it's not the time or the place, but you know I love you, have loved you since the day you rode into camp, claiming to be my 'wife.' Bethenia," Haste raised her chin to face her tear-stained gaze, "can you forgive me for being so stupid, so hardheaded? Say you can and that you love me. Please, Bethenia."

She smiled through her tears. "Dearest Haste, I love you, too," Bethenia told him. "I thought I'd die when you left me at my uncle's hotel," she sobbed. "Wanted to call you back. And when you came back with Jasper, I was so happy to see you, but I was confused and I didn't know—"

"Sh, sh, my love, now you know," Haste assured her quickly. "I want you to marry me, be my 'real' wife . . . no more pretend, not ever again."

He pulled her close to him, and when their lips met, Bethenia felt, at last, her world was turning right again. She prayed it would stay that way.

They walked into the hotel dining room, each aware that although death had been with them that morning, this time they faced a brighter, hopeful life together.

Sophronia noticed it in their faces, and she grinned to herself. Now, maybe, things would be better.

Sophronia had prepared a lunch for them of fried chicken, sweet potato casserole, and potato salad. There was a big bowl of salad greens, plenty of hot coffee, and an apple cobbler.

Haste thought, What is it about funerals that makes people need to eat? Guess it's cause they feel such a deep loss they need to fill it ... or perhaps, cause it's somethin' to do when you don't know what else to do. He concerned himself, too, with his new-found relationship with Bethenia. Damn, he still had to get back to Texas and Evan Connolly. Perhaps, she would go with him. Dare he hope? He'd let her know as soon as the legal business was finished.

The local law required that both Pinkerton men appear at the county courthouse to testify in the matter of the train robbery and the bloody aftermath.

George Benard and Haste met in the office to prepare their testimony for the trial. Both were anxious to conclude the unsavory business.

"I know you're as eager as I am to get this business done with," George Benard told Haste.

"I sure am," Haste answered. "Have you heard when the circuit judge is due?"

"Tomorrow, if we're lucky."

"Suits me just fine," Haste said. "I got to get back to Texas." He did not let on that it was Bethenia whom he wanted to get to as well.

"Shouldn't take more than a day or two. I have the reports ready for the railroad's insurance company. You need to sign them, and I believe they will be satisfied."

The next morning, they arrived at the courthouse together, and the sheriff met them at the door.

"I'm much obliged to you Pinkerton men for helping

me out," he told them. "Those Ward brothers have been gettin' a mighty tough reputation in these parts."

"Will the trial be starting soon?" Haste asked him.

"You betcha. Just as soon as my deputies haul them outlaws over from the jail. The judge is ready and waitin'. Gentlemen," he gestured to George Benard and Haste, "come on in." He ushered them into the county courthouse.

It took only a few hours. The testimony was brief. The railroad engineer and other railroad personnel identified the Wards and their men as the train robbers. The sheriff related the fortunate roles of the two Pinkerton men and the Ute Indians in helping him do his job.

Even though the lawyer for the Wards tried desperately to place his clients in a brothel, the evidence against them held, and the judge gave them each a sentence in the prison. "It's time we got rid of all of you bandits who think you can ignore the law," he told them. For the attempted robbery and the attack on the train employee, the judge gave ten years to each man.

As he was being led from the courtroom, Franklin Ward singled out Haste with a glowering look of pure hate. His bandaged right hand was handcuffed to his left hand which had been crippled from their previous encounter. With venomous eyes, he glared at his enemy and spat at Haste's feet.

"I'll be thinkin' 'bout you, Nigra, every day I'm in prison. And when I git out, I'm comin' after you! I *know* who you are. Don't need no *uniform* to tell me, either."

Will their paths cross again, he wondered. Once an enemy, always an enemy . . . till one is victorious, Haste figured. He'd have to handle that situation whenever and however it came. He shrugged his shoulders, turned to bid George Benard good-by and begin focusing his thoughts on Bethenia. Now, with his responsibilities finished, he was free to go to her.

When Haste finally returned to the hotel, he couldn't believe Sophronia's words. His disappointment was obvious to Sophronia, and she felt sorry for him.

"She's gone? Where? When did she leave?"

"Left yesterday on the early train out o' here. Got a letter from her mother's sister. Goin' to Boston. Left a note for you, son. Here it is," she said gently.

> *Dearest Haste,*
> *I know you said you love me, and I love you, too, but I know I can't take the life of a cattleman's wife. I would be a worry to you on the trail, and I wouldn't like waiting at home alone while you were driving cattle. I wouldn't dare to ask you to change. I don't think either of us thought this through. I love you too much to make you miserable. Sold the hotel to Sophronia. Couldn't think of a better person.*
>
> *Bethenia*
> *P.S. Please take Jasper back to Texas with you and turn him loose in green pastures. He deserves the best.*

Red-faced, Haste threw the note on the table and turned to the new owner. "Sophronia, tell me where she went. I've got to find her."

"Said somethin' 'bout her aunt Lacey, who runs some kind o' music school in Boston."

"But where in Boston? She leave an address? That's a big city."

"No, she didn't. But ... wait a minute, son." Sophronia's face broke into a wide smile which reassured the anxious young man. "Haste, I've got it! Her address is here on the deed I signed for this property."

Haste wrote the address on a slip of paper, kissed Sophronia good-by. Her jovial voice rang in his ears, "Don't give up, Haste! You'll find her!"

"Got to," Haste replied, "She's my life!"

"Hat, you old son o' a gun! Took you long enough to git back home!"

Cook Al Page tossed his cigarette butt to the ground and stamped it out before he grasped Haste in a bear hug. The two men exchanged hearty slaps on each other's backs as they celebrated their reunion.

"Almost time to start another drive, Haste. You just 'bout in time."

"Not this time, Cook. Got somethin' else I've got to do."

"Let that little gal slip away, huh?"

"Long story, Cook. Talk with you soon 's I report to the boss."

He made a full report of his activities to a grateful Evan Connolly, and then, he explained why he could not make the next proposed cattle drive. The wise rancher understood. He knew Haste was a valuable employee, but he would be an ineffective worker if he was an unhappy one.

He spoke quickly, without hesitation, raising Haste's hopes. "O' course, I'll let you go, Haste. No question. Take whatever time you need. You're a good man. I don't want to lose you."

"Thanks, Mr. Connolly."

"With what you've accomplished," the rancher went

on, "I *owe* you. Couldn't have been successful without you. Haste, find her and bring her back to Texas. We'll make her welcome."

"Thanks again, Mr. Connolly."

"Evan, Haste, call me Evan," the rancher prompted. He saw Haste as an equal.

Haste thought back to his early days in the Tenth Cavalry when the white officers resented having to lead the buffalo soldiers. Thought they weren't worthy of the name "soldier." Well, perhaps, he had proven his worth. For once in his life, he was being accepted for who he was, Haste Allen Terrell, trail boss.

Evan Connolly was still talking. Haste could hardly believe the man's next words.

"You know, Haste, I guess I told you ... meant to, anyway, that the cattlemen here put up reward money for the capture of the Ward brothers. Five thousand dollars o' that reward is yours."

"Mine? I was only doing my job, Evan. Didn't call for no reward."

"Whether it did or didn't, it's there and it's yours."

"I don't know what to say, Evan," Haste remarked.

"But I'm sure you know what to do, don't you?"

Evan Connolly grinned and thrust his hand out to shake Haste's hand.

"Get to Boston as fast as I can, I reckon."

"Now, Haste ... Josh Carpenter, who used to be my foreman, told me just last week that since his wife Mattie died he wants to sell his little spread and move to Dallas to be near his daughter. You be interested in buying his place 'bout ten miles south of here? It would get you off the cattle drive."

"Most surely would, Evan."

"Well, all right then. I'll see about letting Josh know, and you get up north and bring back your bride."

Still, Haste worried. Would life on a Texas ranch be enough for a subborn, independent girl like the Bethenia he knew and loved? Did she love him enough to move to Texas? Most of all, did she love him enough to marry him. He knew now his life had no meaning without her. Funny how his life had turned around. He was so angry when he first saw her; she was like a millstone around his neck—a burden he didn't want or need. Now, that same girl had become the most important part of his life. Life had strange turns and twists to it, he mused.

"Aunt Lacey, you know I want to work. What I do to help earn my board and keep?"

Her aunt chuckled. "Child, I'm so glad to have some family here in Boston at last. I came up here to git this music school started. And now to have some of my kin, well, that's even better."

Bethenia had little memory of her mother's sister, only fleeting recollections of someone in the family who had kissed her good-by with promises to send gifts from "up north." Bethenia did have one strong memory of a white crepe dress sent from one of Boston's largest stores. Her mother had promised that if she was a good girl she could wear it on Sundays, but only to church. She always had felt so special in her Boston dress.

Aunt Lacey did favor her mother, except that her creamy colored face was open and cheerful, with a bright smile that welcomed Bethenia. She remembered, sadly, that her mother's face was frequently furrowed and pale, and framed by lank, unkempt hair. Everyone always said it was a shame what had happened to Molly Mae because she was the prettiest of the sisters.

But Aunt Lacey was different. Her hair, black, thick,

and abundant, dignified her and only enhanced her stately appearance. A tall woman, she wasn't strict or unyielding, but you knew nonsense wouldn't please her at all. She just made you want to please her, Bethenia had decided.

Bethenia had arrived two days before, unannounced, but in the tradition of her family, her mother's sister had received her warmly. They had talked for hours about the family, its hopes and eventual tragedies, and Aunt Lacey, only a few years older than Bethenia, had listened with dismay to her niece's litany. But her comment had been comforting.

"Don't worry, Bethenia, you got family long 's you got me. We'll do all right. But what about that cowboy? Seems to me you kindo' stuck on him. You know, I can hear somethin' in your voice," she had teased.

"Oh, Aunt Lacey. I never expect to see *him* again. Texas is a long way from Boston. He's probably back on the trail, glad I'm not round anymore."

Bethenia's aunt Lacey had shaken her head as she patted her niece on her knee and had said, "Sometimes, honey, the longest way can be made short when the heart decides. From what you say 'bout the young man, wouldn't surprise me at all if Haste Allen Terrell showed up right here in Boston."

Bethenia had shaken her head. That life was in her past. Now, she was in Boston, and although she had no knowledge of music, the one thing she was no stranger to was hard work.

"You do your schoolteaching, Aunt Lacey, and I'll do the rest."

Bethenia cooked, cleaned, kept the classroom neat, its floor was polished to a glorious shine. She tended the small iron-fenced front yard of the brownstone and even

learned how to take the streetcar to Haymarket Square
to haggle and cajole the vendors she met there. She tried
hard not to think of Haste and what her life might have
been like with him.

"Aunt Lacey," she told her aunt, "you should use
some of the money that I got from the hotel sale
for your school. I don't need it long 's I can live
with you."

"Oh, no, Bethenia," her aunt protested, "you keep
your own money. You know they always say, 'God bless
the child that's got his own.' Not that I don't appreciate
your offer ... and you needn't worry that you can't
stay, not the way you work round here! Already, I'm
able to take in more students—"

"But, the money—"

"To the bank, child, that's what you do. Put it in the
bank where it can draw interest. You never know what's
ahead of you. May need that little nest egg some day."

Haste had finally left the Chicago Station for the final
leg of his journey to Boston. He was weary and travel-
worn from the train, the hotels, and the unsatisfying
meals. He longed to return to Texas: to its wide-open
spaces, its natural beauty, its fertile acres, and the
rolling fields of grass, undulating for endless miles as
far as a man could see. He hoped Bethenia would want,
as he did, to ride under the benevolent Texas sky, to be
content watching horses and cattle graze on open plains,
and, yes, to watch their children grow and flourish. He
knew he loved her from the moment he had seen her
standing defiantly beside her horse, declaring that she
was his "wife." He reached into his pocket for the hun-
dredth time to check the address.

Mrs. Lacey Reed
c/o Harmony School of Music, South End
181 Pontilla Street
Boston, Massachusetts

Haste leaned his head on the back of the seat and closed his eyes. Bethenia's lovely, warm brown face floated into his mind. She was so alive, so quick, so strong, willful, and determined. By now, he thought, she has probably become accustomed to the excitement of the city, the fast pace, the sparkling effervescence of life in a major city. What can a cowboy from Texas offer? His mother had once told him, "Nobody but you know what you really want, son, so it's up to you to git whatever it is. Nobody's bound to *give* you what you want—you just go and git it."

No one but himself ever could know how much he loved Bethenia. He'd not be satisfied until she knew it, too. Haste stared out at the landscape that moved through his vision like a panoramic exhibition. Small cities, towns, farms, rivers, and lakes passed by outside the murky, smudged train window.

The rocking motion of the train's wheels kissing the steel tracks that lay like twin silver paths beneath it comforted Haste. He was getting closer to his love. Many times in his life, his nerves had tantalized him as he faced his destiny—on the trail looking for wayward, marauding Indians, searching the western hills for renegades and robbers, bringing bootleggers and swindlers to the local lawmen, helping to chart and map the unknown West, and finding water and forage for men and animals—but nothing, none of these experiences, compared to the inner anxiety he felt as he neared the northern city where he hoped to find Bethenia. He had to convince her to become his wife and return with him to Texas.

Now, with the promise of a farm, there would be no reason for her not to be willing to marry him. He would never let Bethenia Cooper get away from him again.

Chapter Sixteen

Bethenia crossed the cobblestoned street, intent on getting her bundles into the brownstone. She was very pleased with herself. She had secured some fresh codfish from the fishmonger, some beautiful greens and okra from the greengrocer, and rosy, luscious fresh peaches. She would have an exciting meal for Aunt Lacey that night. After a hard day's work of trying to instill classical music into the hearts and minds of Boston's colored children, her aunt deserved a satisfying meal, and Bethenia was glad she was able to cook well.

"You know, Bethenia," her aunt had told her once after a busy day of teaching, "it's music in the soul that helps make life bearable sometimes. I intend to see that these children have the chance." Although mostly self-taught until she had come to Boston to study, Lacey Reed had what she said was a "calling." She was devoted to her students. "They are goin' to need all the help they can git to make it in this tough old world."

The evening meal that they shared allowed the two women to be together like family. After only a few weeks, Bethenia realized how much she had missed. Aunt Lacey had even given her a place of her own.

"Every woman on this earth needs her own space," her

aunt Lacey had said. So, she had given her niece the third
floor apartment as her own. "No two women, don't care
how close, can live together without buttin' heads. We'll
take meals together, but it's nice to have your own. I want
you to be happy, child, cause I know you've had a rough
row to hoe all your life, what with your mother Molly
Mae sick so much."

"Aunt Lacey, it's perfect!" Bethenia had clapped her
hands delightedly. "Never had a place of my own."

She loved the two cozy rooms tucked up under the
eaves of the brownstone. For the first since her parents'
deaths, she felt secure. She had decorated with warm,
earthy colors: bits of tan, orange, yellow, and deep
brown. The draperies at the cheerful windows and the
bedspread were complemented by a woven bluegrass
rug that welcomed her feet when she stepped out of bed
each morning.

The modest living room had the same draperies at the
windows, an ancient wicker chair that she had found in
a secondhand store down on Boston's lower Washington
Street, and a sofa her aunt had given her. Bethenia had
added a small table and a kerosene lamp with an ornate
globe. She was happy there.

"Aunt Lacey, you work so hard with your students. I
wish I had someone to look after me when I was growing up."

Her aunt answered wisely, the understanding of gen-
erations in her voice, "Never *wish* for anything. My
sister was the sweetest, happiest girl on this earth, and
how she loved your daddy! But she had a weakness in
her, don't know where it came from, and she let it take
over. In this life, you got to fight! My poor sister didn't
fight for what she had."

Aunt Lacey picked up her fork and took another bite of the peach cobbler that Bethenia had made. "Best I've ever tasted," she said, and she sipped a little of her tea before she went on. She peered seriously into her young niece's face, as if to emphasize her words.

"What *you* have been through, my child, is goin' to fix you for whatever else life has in store. I know it's been hard, but . . . look at every stone in your path as a firm foothold . . . won't be sinkin' in no sand when you step in life over the rocks o' hardships. And don't waste your time wishin'. Wish in one hand and spit in the other. See which one fills up the quickest. 'Bout all wishin' 'mounts to."

"Guess you're right, Aunt Lacey. I thought I was all set when I went to my uncle, like my daddy told me to do, but well—"

"Honey, you keep on bein' as strong as you can. And be patient. Good thin's will come to you, I know." She smiled, caught up in her feelings for her orphaned niece. "Believe me, I know," she repeated.

After the evening meal was completed and the dishes were washed, Bethenia said good-night to her aunt, who was busy with her school work. "Good-night, Aunt Lacey. See you in the morning."

"Good-night, my dear. Will you be goin' to church with me? I want you to git to know some of the young people—start to have some friends your own age."

"Yes, ma'am, I'll be ready."

Bethenia made her way up to her small apartment on the top floor of the brownstone. She wondered if her aunt was right. Would good things come to her? Would she ever see Haste again, the man she loved, or was he out of her life forever? The young men and women she'd already met at the church seemed just that, *young*. Although her same age, they seemed so inexperienced, so hollow. Well, perhaps, her aunt was right. She should make a start toward a new life. There were too many miles now between her and the man she would always love, Hat Terrell.

"Raymond, this is my niece, Miss Bethenia Cooper. She's stayin' with me."

Bethenia saw a neat-looking young man dressed in a blue suit. His serious brown face and slicked back hair warned her that this was a solemn, sober individual. His offered hand was so soft it almost shocked her. Never worked hard a day in his life, she thought. A pianist's hands, she guessed.

"Raymond is a student at the conservatory now," her aunt remarked proudly.

"Miss Cooper, I'd like to take you to our next concert. I'm sure you'd enjoy it."

A week later, in the early evening, Raymond Peterson had escorted Bethenia home from the conservatory's music concert.

And she had tried to enjoy it, although she really had not understood the program or the performers. It was all so new to her.

I'd rather be riding my Jasper out on the plains, she had thought, not sitting in this stuffy hall. But she had smiled through it all, and she had thanked Raymond for a lovely evening when he had taken her home.

One day after having shopped, Bethenia made her way up to the front door. She had not seen the figure at the parted curtain of the living room's bay window. Before she could place her key in the lock, her aunt opened it, with a soft, knowing smile on her face.

"Honey, you got company," her aunt said. Her face looked as if she had a secret she was trying hard not to reveal.

"I have? Who?"

"Come on in, you'll see. Here, hand me the bundles."

Aunt Lacey took the heavy shopping bags that were awkward and cumbersome, having been filled almost to overflowing with fruits, vegetables, meat, and fish. She pushed Bethenia toward the closed double doors of the living room. "In there," she directed.

Bethenia grasped a door handle in each hand and thrust open the carved mahogany doors.

"Haste!" She stood stock-still at the sight of the cowboy who she thought was out of her life forever.

His height, his wide shoulders, narrow hips, and muscular legs seemed to overcome and fill the space of the proper Boston living room. Haste had removed his sombrero, and as Bethenia remembered, his long dark hair curled around his shoulders. His ruddy brown skin was burnished to a glowing patina from his days in the western sun.

Bethenia clung to the door handles as Haste reached for her in two powerful strides. She had no way of knowing, but Haste was not as certain of himself as he wished. He had no idea what he intended to do once he saw her. Would he take her in his arms . . . would he try to hold her to make her realize how much he loved her, wanted her?

He was not prepared for his own reaction when he saw her. As usual, her lively eyes challenged him. A half-smile of welcome formed on her lips, and she stood calm and unperturbed. She was as lovely as Haste had remembered, and his heart almost stopped at the sight of her. A glowing warmth extended from his groin, to his face, to his fingertips. His face flushed with emotion as he blurted out, "Why did you leave, Bethenia? Why did you run away? Sophronia said . . ."

"Run away?" Bethenia interrupted quickly. "Haste Allen Terrell, *I* never ran away from anything in my life! I might run *to* something, but 'run away,' never!"

"Well," Haste insisted, "you knew I had to testify about the robbery and all that—"

"Mr. Terrell," Bethenia said, with her voice taking on a formal tone, "you never told me that, and there was *no* reason for me to stay. My uncle was dead, so I sold the hotel and I left."

"But you knew—"

"Knew what, Haste?"

"Bethenia, you knew I'd be back."

"No, I didn't know that." Bethenia walked to the bay windows and turned to face Haste. "How could I know? Did you tell me?" Her chin rose defiantly as Haste crossed the room to stand in front of her. Bethenia saw determination and purpose in his eyes as her reached for her hands.

"Damn, I'm going to tell you something right now, Miss Bethenia Cooper! I've come all the way from Texas to ask you to be my wife and to return to Texas with me. Now, I'm not going to beat around the bush, you know me better than that! I just want an answer, one way or the other!"

"And you expect me to fall into your arms simply because you came all the way from Texas?" She thrust her chin forward again as she waited for his answer.

"No, not just that. I didn't know how much you meant to me till Sophronia told me you'd gone. Bethenia, it was as if the world had come to a stop. I knew I would not be able to go on if I didn't find you . . . to tell you—"

"Tell me what, Haste?" Bethenia prompted, looking deeply into his eyes.

"That I love you . . . want you . . . need you."

Bethenia heard the soft passion in Haste's voice as he took her into his embrace.

There was a light tap on the door, and Aunt Lacey brought in a tray with tall glasses of lemonade and a plate of cookies.

"Thought you two might enjoy a cool drink," she said. The scene was not lost on her.

"Aunt Lacey," Bethenia said, "this, is Haste Allen Terrell."

"Yes, he introduced himself to me, or else I would never have let him in *my* house."

"He has asked me to marry him."

"And . . . ?"

Bethenia turned to Haste.

"I'm going to," she said simply.

Shortly after his arrival in Boston, Haste had sought out a barber, saying, "No proper Bostonian walks around with long hair." Bethenia missed the shoulder-length dark hair that she was accustomed to seeing under his wide sombrero, but her breath had all but been taken away when she saw how the young western cowboy had turned into an elegant city gentleman. With his shorter hair, his dark eyes seemed even more piercing. And he seemed even taller, with a broader, firmer chest and shoulders than she remembered from his cowboy days. But he was still the man she loved. She even loved the strong masculine smell of him, and she pressed herself closer to him, hoping that the urgent need that she had denied for so long would at last be satisfied.

* * *

The wedding took place a week later in the second floor music room where Aunt Lacey usually held her annual recitals. Aunt Lacey, with the help of her students, had transformed it into a lovely wedding chapel.

There was a raised platform on which a white wooden trellis, decorated with red and white roses, had been placed. Pink and white ribbons had been formed into rosettes and tied to the end chairs to form a colorful aisle down which the bride would walk. Planters of pink geraniums were on the floor in front of each of the three long bay windows.

One of the most gifted piano students had been selected by Aunt Lacey to play the wedding music. Two other students acted as ushers and seated the wedding guests, mainly friends of Aunt Lacey. There were two vacant seats in the front row on the bride's side of the aisle. A red rose had been placed on one chair in memory of Bethenia's father, and a white rose on the other, in memory of her mother.

Aunt Lacey had planned to not only "give the bride away" but also to serve as maid of honor.

"I declare," Aunt Lacey said as she helped Bethenia with her wedding dress, "it's a lucky thing we found this dress ready-made. It would have taken me more than a month to make a dress like this, and we both know that Haste wasn't about to wait that long to take you back to Texas."

"Aunt Lacey, it's so beautiful," Bethenia said, as she admired the minute tucks alternating with lace on the full sleeves. "I do love the heart-shaped neckline. Think Haste will like the way I look? Don't answer that, Aunt Lacey, he'd better, that's all I have to say."

"Honey, every bride is beautiful. To me, you're the most beautiful one I've ever seen, and I know Haste is goin' to think the same. Let's do your hair now,

Bethenia," her aunt suggested. She placed a clean towel over Bethenia's shoulders to protect her wedding dress.

"Child, your hair is just like your momma's: thick, smooth, and heavy. We'll braid it, and you can wear it like a crown on the top o' your head. Otherwise, the pins will slip out and be all over the place. There," she stepped back, satisfied with her work.

Aunt Lacey's eyes clouded over when she placed the gossamer veil over Bethenia's head. "Just wish Molly Mae and Lee were here to see their child all grown up and gettin' married."

The signal was given to the pianist, and Aunt Lacey and Bethenia started down the aisle toward Haste who waited beside the preacher. Haste could hardly believe the vision of loveliness he saw floating toward him. Bethenia had been transformed from a spunky tomboy-ish horsewoman into a graceful, sparkling beauty. Her dark hair had been piled high into a high coronet braid with a few soft tendrils curling down beneath the veil. Haste held his breath. His dream was walking to him. He smiled and extended his hand to grasp Bethenia's. They both turned to face the minister. Their new life was about to begin, at last.

The reception was a sit-down meal in Aunt Lacey's dining room. She had insisted on using her best china and glassware. The table, covered with a white lace cloth over a sparkling white tablecloth, looked regal and inviting. Aunt Lacey's church group prepared and served the meal. There were a dozen people present, including the minster, Reverend Royal Holt, and his wife Minerva, the students who had assisted at the ceremony, a few of Aunt Lacey's closest friends, and the bride and groom.

The meal was sumptuous. Roast turkey with giblet gravy, corn pudding, rice and peas, succulent, meaty pink slices of ham, candied sweet potatoes, greens, and the lightest biscuits Haste had ever eaten.

Minerva Holt prided herself on her baking ability. She had insisted on making and decorating not only the bride's cake, but she had made a rich, dark fruit cake saturated with rum and brandy. "The groom's cake," she announced, as she placed it in front of Haste.

Haste, somewhat flustered, exclaimed, "A cake for me?"

"Why, o' course, son," Mrs. Holt answered. "In my country, the Islands, we always have cake for the groom!"

With banter, small talk, and much food to be eaten and punch to be consumed, it was late before the last guests left.

Aunt Lacey closed the front door firmly and locked it, turning to Haste and Bethenia with her arms wide to embrace the pair.

"Don't want to see your two faces till late tomorrow. Off with you! I thought Reverend Holt would never stop askin' you 'bout Texas," she said to Haste.

Bethenia kissed her aunt.

"Thank you, Aunt Lacey, for everything."

"Go on, girl, it was little enough. Go, you two." She smiled as she waved them toward the stairway and watched the young couple head toward Bethenia's third floor rooms. "God be with them," she sighed, as she wearily padded off to her own room. It had been a long, exciting day.

Bethenia's happiness was complete when she saw the agreeable smile on her new husband's face as she led him to her third floor haven after their wedding. His six feet two inch frame dwarfed the tiny rooms, but as he told Bethenia, "I am happy just to be anywhere with you. Anywhere!" He closed the door, held out his arms to her. She went to him without a moment's hesitation.

"Haste," she moaned as her husband's mouth closed over hers. She had not guessed how sweet, how loving the gesture was going to be as his lips teased hers with a sweetness, a honeyed elixir of love that moved her to impulsively clasp both arms around his neck. Her right hand released the small bridal bouquet of pink and white roses, and it fell, unheeded, to the floor. Bethenia reached for the back of her husband's head to press his mouth closer to her hungry one.

Haste whispered her name, "Bethie, Bethie." Then, she felt his searching tongue seek a response from hers. He traced his tongue along the inside of her mouth. She thought her breath would stop. The soft young curves of his bride's delicate young frame seemed perfect in his arms.

She responded with gestures of her own as she grasped Haste's face between her hands and rained kisses all over his eyes, his nose, chin, cheeks, and back to his mouth again. She continued ravenously and gasped when she felt her husband's fingers inside the bodice of her wedding dress. Those same fingers that he had roped steers with, managed wild mavericks with, and wrestled men and horses with, were as gentle as a hummingbird's wings on her skin.

Their mouths still fused, Haste carried her into the bedroom. Gently, he placed her on the bed and lay beside her. Slowly, savoring the moment for which they both had waited, Haste patiently and lovingly removed each article of clothing from Bethenia. Her lace dress, shoes, and stockings, then the silk slip her aunt had given her as "something borrowed," then the wispy corset bra from which Bethenia's young breasts sprang like golden-brown orbs into Haste's hands. When she lay naked before him, almost quivering in anticipation, Haste quickly removed his own clothing. Silently, he reached down to pull a soft coverlet over their bodies. Slowly, he removed the pins from Bethenia's hair, releasing it from her bridal coiffure and allowed her lustrous black hair to fan out over the pillow and her shoulders.

"I've wanted to do this for such a long time," he whispered. "Bethie, I love you with all my heart. I'll never be able to say that often enough. Tell me you love me."

"I have always loved you, Haste, from the moment I saw you come to the Yorkes' farm. I knew that night when I saw your face glow over the blacksmith's flame that I loved you and wanted you in my life. To me, it was the most natural thin' in the world to follow you, to go wherever you went. I couldn't help myself."

"Thank God you did, my love, otherwise this poor old ex-trooper-cowboy would still be out there, alone, unloved, and wonderin' why."

Bethenia laughed and buried her face into the curly hair of Haste's chest. Again, she felt the flaming heat from her own body envelop her as Haste pulled her face up toward his to kiss her parted lips. She felt his fingers tenderly caress her breasts, and her nipples rose to respond. She realized she had not control over her body's reactions to the sweet ministrations her husband gave to it, nor could she explain her own body's behavior. Her physical needs were being satisfied, her mind having long ago assured her of the rightness of it all.

Haste looked at his bride. The soft lights from the kerosene lamp in the living room cast ethereal shadows into their bedroom. Bethenia's dark luminous eyes were wide, reacting with excited expectation as Haste's fingers moved gently over her smooth skin. Her lips were parted as her breath moved huskily from her throat. Haste closed his own eyes as he bent forward to place his mouth on the delicate buds of her breasts. Bethenia drew in her breath in quick gasps as her husband plucked from her body sensations and longings she never had dreamed existed.

Later that night, they slept. Bethenia's body tucked close to her husband's. Her back was to his chest, her small bottom rested on his strong loins, and his arms held her close, each hand caressing her smooth, loving breasts. It was the early morning sunlight that rose over the rooftops and through the rounded windows under the eaves that woke Bethenia first. She turned in her husband's arms and watched him sleep; her heart full of love for the man she had loved even as he tried to deny her existence. She laid her head on his chest and listened to the soft beating of his heart. She prayed silently, "God, please don't take this love from me."

A few moments later, Haste woke up to find Bethenia observing him.

"Good morning, Mrs. Haste Allen Terrell," he said. He kissed Bethenia's nose, her mouth, and her eyes. He saw the diamond drops of tears that sprang from her tightly closed eyelids, and his own heart nearly exploded with the love that he had denied for so long. He would never, ever deny her again, he vowed.

He kissed the wetness from her eyes, and soon, they reentered the world of lovemaking again. This time their journey was sweeter than the first, and both were stunned by the intensity and fervor of it. The power stunned them.

"Bethie?" Haste spoke quietly as they lay, sated in each other's arms.

"Yes, husband mine?" She answered with a wide smile.

"We have to make our plans to leave Boston, get back to Texas."

"You still work for Mr. Connolly?" she wanted to know. "Driving cattle to Denver?"

"Well, now," he teased, "I don't know . . . what would you think of having a small ranch of our own?"

"Of our own? How can we do that? It would take money, wouldn't it? I do have some from my uncle's hotel—"

"Don't need *your* money, my love. I got paid for the cattle drive and got reward money from the railroad and the Texas ranchers for that Pinkerton business. Got 'nough to get us a little spread. Got a line on one, too."

"Oh, Haste, you mean a place where we can have Red Chief and Jasper, raise horses, maybe . . . I've dreamed so many times of having a real home."

"No more than you should have, Bethie, my sweet. I was so hopin' you'd be happy 'bout goin' to Texas with me. Wait till you see it! Wide-open spaces, the biggest, bluest sky, the brightest colors of wildflowers scattered over the blue-green plains. I want you to love it as much as I do."

"Why not, Haste. If you love it, I will, too. I want what you want, always." She snuggled closer to him, content at last with her life.

Haste intruded into her reverie with his next words.

"You know, Bethenia, what made me fall in love with you?" he asked.

"What?"

Haste reached for her face and kissed her softly on her lips.

"You, going after what you wanted. I never met a woman like ... so ... so determined, so sure of what she could do."

"You have the same mind yourself, Haste."

"Yes, but little did I know there was something about the way you stood beside your horse, Jasper. By the way, he's doing fine. But there you were, a mere girl, determined to do what it was you wanted to do."

"You always knew what you wanted, didn't you, Haste? Couldn't have been easy being a buffalo soldier, going through all of that, and leading a cattle drive when folk didn't believe a Negro man could do that. So, what's the difference?"

"Guess that's what makes us love each other, Bethenia. Can't wait to see Cook's face when we get to Texas."

"He won't be surprised, Haste. He was the first person whom I told that I was the trail boss's wife. He won't be surprised."

"Good thing he didn't let me run you off back to the Yorkes'."

"It would have taken more than two buffalo soldiers to do that." Bethenia laughed as she snuggled again into her husband's arms. "More than two. Not even a whole regiment of buffalo soldiers. You must know that by now, Hat Terrell!" she said, teasing him as she tried to scramble from his grasp. He reached for her quickly, and they tumbled back onto the rumpled bed.

"Oh, no, you vixen!" Haste countered. "You followed me till I *caught* you! You're mine now, and that's the way it will always be!"

"I wouldn't change that for the world, my lord," Bethenia mocked. She raised her face to Haste's to receive the kiss that she knew meant, at last, that she had all she'd ever wanted ... someone to love her. A little orphan from Tennessee had won the heart and soul of a stalwart cowboy, her happiness knew no bounds. She was safe at last.

Chapter Seventeen

For the young couple, their six-week honeymoon train trip from Boston to Texas turned out to be a memorable adventure. Haste delighted in Bethenia's reactions as they savored new experiences. They decided to spend a few days in New York City. Might not have the chance again, Haste had decided. He teased Bethenia about her dislike of the crowded city.

"Don't tell me a strong, outdoors girl like you is afraid of people," he said, shaking his head at her.

"I'm not *afraid* o' them, Haste, there's just too *many* o' them. So many different faces, voices, clothes . . . I thought Haymarket Square in Boston was unbelievable."

"This is just another seaport town, like Boston," he reminded her. "And people come from all over the world."

"Well," she said sharply, "I'd rather be out west where there are fewer people. I'll take horses and steers any day."

"I *knew* it," Haste said, grinning at her, "knew you'd be a real ranch woman. You're a woman after my own heart."

They spent that day sightseeing, and they took a horse drawn carriage back to their hotel.

Exhilarated and thrilled by the city's tall buildings, narrow streets, and downtown bustle, they needed the quiet ride to allow them what they wanted most—time to focus their attention on each other.

They had dinner in a secluded corner of the hotel's gaudy, gaslit dining room. As she looked around, Bethenia realized that her uncle's "grand" dining room paled in comparison. She shook her head to erase the sad memory and turned her attention to her new husband. He had been watching her.

"Bethenia," Haste said, picking up both of her hands, "have I told you how beautiful you are? There's not a woman in this room who can hold a candle to you, and I'm not saying this just because you're my wife. Honey, you're a stunner!"

"Because of the new clothes you made me buy today, Haste." Bethenia pressed down the lapels of her new jacket. Her small frame was perfect for the pale gray woolen skirt she wore. Twelve-inch pleats graced the bottom of the garment, and her kid and cloth high-buttoned, shiny black shoes peeked demurely from beneath the skirt as she walked. She wore a white muslin shirtwaist that fitted over the top of the skirt. Rows of pearl buttons from the top to the bottom of the blouse accented Bethenia's slender neck. Her gray woolen jacket was trimmed with black and gold braid on the lapels and cuffs. Her hat was a tiny, black velvet pillbox that framed the soft tendrils that escaped from her hair that had been braided into a matronlike bun. "Although, where I'm going to wear such fancy clothes in Texas is beyond me."

Haste rubbed her hands gently. He could feel her warm pulse beat against his fingers. His love for her almost choked him. How had it happened that this lovely woman was his wife? His mind reeled with the thoughts of how meaningless life would have been without her.

"I want you to have the best there is, my love," Haste assured her. "Only the very best." He had already felt a few pangs of jealousy when he noticed other men fix their gazes upon her.

"Let's go to our room." he decided quickly. "We will be leaving early in the morning for our trip to Chicago."

They moved slowly and silently to the stairway that led to their room. Neither spoke.

The room was lit only by the soft, wavering gaslights from the street, but there was just light enough for Haste to view the exquisite form of his wife as she undressed wordlessly, tantalizing him as she shed the cloth constraints that had covered her. Haste, hungrily gazing at her, wondered if Bethenia really knew the power she held over him. Hurriedly, he dropped his own clothing to the floor. From the bed, he welcomed her with open arms, and she came to him, her hands outstretched as he moved to make room for her beside him.

They still had not spoken. Their actions gave voice to their feelings. The great need to be together as one was finally met, and at last, they lay comforted in each other's arms. Bethenia was awe-struck by her own astonishing capacity to love her husband. As she snuggled closer to him, their bodies cooling from the flame of their intense love, she idly traced her fingers along her husband's face and neckline and along his broad shoulders and chest. She murmured into his ear, "No one told me that it would be like this," she whispered, her voice hoarse with emotion.

"My mother died when I was young, but my aunt told me how much Momma loved my daddy. I wonder . . . if she had happiness like this, how come she couldn't fight to keep it, to live, to hold on to it?"

"We'll never know, Bethie. I'm sure she tried to."

"I'll always love you, Haste, and I'll fight for this love as long 's there is breath in my body," she whispered, as she moved her foot along his leg. She moved it slowly up and down the length of his muscular leg from his foot to his thigh. Her knee rested lightly on his crotch. Her husband's arousal was instant, and bent over her, reaching for her mouth to kiss her.

"My sweet love," he groaned, as he tasted the glorious essence that flowed from her lips to his. Their bodies flamed anew with vigorous passion, and this time, Bethenia saw tears of deep emotion seep from Haste's closed eyelids as he held her to him.

They lay quietly. Haste rubbed his hand over Bethenia's shoulder as she nestled closer.

"You know, Bethie," he confessed, "life was never easy for me. Everything came the hard way. Never had much schoolin' at all. I remember trying to learn to read from the time I was a little boy. I never will forget that Union soldier whom I hid in Pa's barn, teaching me to read in the dirt on the barn floor . . . the stories he told me, things I'd never heard fore about the world—different people and their different ways. Made me want to see more, know more. But, after the war, there was nothing, nothing. There I was, seventeen years old with no future. That's when I joined the cavalry." He continued to tell her about his life in the cavalry and as a cowhand and cattledriver. "Everyone thought I couldn't do it."

"You proved them all wrong. I'm proud of you, Haste, because you got that something in you that won't let you give up."

"I guess . . . but I'll be damned if that isn't the same

thing I admire in you! You're the most stubborn, intractable woman I've ever met. You *never* give up!"

"Don't that make us two of a kind?" she teased.

"Damn straight, it does! Look out, Texas, here come the Terrells!"

Haste's earlier reflective mood had turned lighter, and Bethenia delighted in the pleasure she saw in her husband's eyes. Silently, she prayed that all would be well for them when they reached their new home and started their married life.

Al Page met them at the depot. Bethenia could not hide her happiness when she saw her old friend grinning at her from his high seat on the platform spring wagon.

"Uncle Al!" she cried aloud, as she turned to greet him. She did not try to disguise the welcome eagerness in her voice.

"Whoa, girl, hang on there!" Al greeted her with outstretched arms, his face framed with his familiar grin. He looked over her head across to Haste, who was wrestling with Bethenia's trunk, trying to hoist it into the back of the wagon.

"Got some sense at last, didn't you, son! Brought your wife *home!*"

He helped Haste with the trunk after giving him a hearty hug, plus a few vigorous slaps on the back. They heaved the trunk, along with a few valises, into a corner of the wagon, leaving room for Cook to slide in beside it.

"Evan Connolly said to get you folk over to the Carpenter place," Al told Haste. "Had it cleaned up nice for you."

In his eagerness to find Bethenia, Haste had not questioned Evan Connolly's offer of the former ranch foreman's property. He had assumed that from what the rancher had said he would find himself the owner of a decent, livable house.

Disappointment flooded his face when he finally saw the sod houses with a connecting roof between them, forming an attachment the Texans called a "dogtrot."

Sod had been cut into blocks to form the walls. A rough wooden door, one window front and back of each structure, a roof made of boards, tar paper, a thin layer of sod, and finished with a rough coat of ashes and clay formed the simple dwelling. It was a house, but not what Haste had expected.

As he helped Bethenia from the wagon, he searched her face for a reaction. His relief was a joyous one when she looked at him and squeezed his hand.

"Haste, we can make this place a home."

Chapter Eighteen

It did not take Bethenia long to make the old rancher's place livable. Josh Carpenter, the previous owner, had left a plain rope bed, a stove, and a few cooking pots blackened from years of use. But, when she saw them, Bethenia said to her husband, "These won't be hard to clean. All I need is some wood ashes, some lye, and plenty of fat. And, yes, a good stiff brush."

First, though, she opened the windows and doors, "To let the Carpenter smell out and to bring our own smell in," she said. The dark, earthen colored sod walls she decided to plaster with newspapers and to hang on the wall the bright patchwork quilt that Aunt Lacey had given her.

"Don't know, could git cold down there in Texas," Aunt Lacey had said, as she pressed still one more gift on her niece. Well, it could stay on the wall for now, Bethenia thought. The vibrant orange patches and blocks of crisp yellow, mixing with shades of blue and green, did create a cheerful focal area in the otherwise drab room that served as their living room. Cotton curtains fashioned from the always available discarded flour sacks framed the windows.

"We're beginning to look like quality folk," Haste said when he saw what Bethenia had accomplished.

"We *are* quality folk, Haste," she insisted.

Al Page brought a belated wedding gift, one of his favorite "spiders." "Didn't have much," he explained, "but had to give you something."

"Oh, Cook, not one of your good fry-pans!" Bethenia hugged the pan to her chest. "How will you get on without it? I know it's so special."

"Same's I did 'fore I had it."

"Don't know how to thank you."

"An invite would be nice, I guess." He smiled.

"Of course! How stupid of me! You know you're welcome. Potluck tonight, though. Beef stew and biscuits."

"Well, now," he drawled, "this here cowboy will be damn happy to put his feet under your table."

"Our first guest, that's what you are, Uncle Al, our first guest," Bethenia said.

"Good. Well, I'll just mosey out to the lean-to and see how old Hat's doin'. By the way," he stopped in his tracks, turning in the doorway to look at her, "he treatin' you right?"

Bethenia grinned at him and raised her eyebrows in an expressive manner.

"Enough said" was his reply, as he closed the wooden door behind him.

Bethenia watched the two old friends greet each other. Those two have shared a lot of their lives with each other. I can't take that comradeship away from them, or interfere. But a deep part of her wanted to share everything with Haste, she reasoned.

However, Al Page's news was not what Haste wanted to share with his wife.

"Heard you were in a bit o' a ruckus up there in Denver." Cook started right in when he found Haste replacing one of Red Chief's shoes.

"What did you hear?" Haste asked, intent on his task. He was not at all happy that his cover had been blown. What problems would that mean for him—and Bethenia?

"Boys at the ranch sayin' that some Pinkerton men teamed up with the sheriff, got hold of the Ward brothers tryin' to rob a train."

"That so?"

"Yes, and somebody said one o' them Pinkertons was you."

"What you think, Cook?"

"Dad-gun it, Hat, don't know what to think. Wouldn't put it past you."

"Evan Connolly asked me. Course he had no way of knowing that Ward and I had crossed paths fore when I was in the cavalry. All he knew was that he and the other ranchers were losing steers to a gang of thievin', murderous rustlers. He had asked the Pinkerton agency for help, and they figured it would be a good idea to have an 'inside' man on the job, so I was recruited. I couldn't say no to Evan. After all, he had given me a job. So, I was sworn in for the Pinkerton job as Gabe Skinner."

"Great day in the mornin', Hat!" Al exclaimed, thrusting his sombrero to the back of his head. "You never let on? No wonder you was upset when Bethenia showed up in camp!"

"Know you thought I was crazy, but I couldn't see how I could let her stay. Then, when you 'convinced' me to let her stay, well I knew I couldn't afford to lose you. It would all have been over, shot to hell."

"But, now, that she's your wife, it was worth it, eh?" Cook threw a side glance at Haste.

"Damn straight, but not a word of this to her, you hear?"

Al shook his head. "Don't know, son, talk in camp is that there's a chance that Frank Ward has threatened to come back and git the Nigra who sent him up to the penitentiary. Know he's got some o' his gang left in this part o' Texas. Might try to git together with them."

"I don't know 'bout that, but all the same, don't want to worry Bethenia."

"Might be makin' a mistake, son, not to put her on notice. It's a good distance from the next house out here."

" 'Bout five miles to the Harrison ranch, I'd guess."

"Well, the way I see it, Hat, that Ward is one mad hombre. You know, every time you done met up with him, you bested him. That white man never goin' forget that, you hear me?"

Hat's face froze into a cold mask. There was no doubt of his intent with his next words.

"Cook, when the time comes, *if* it comes, I'll handle it." His voice was calm. "In the meantime, if you so much as let on to my wife that there's a problem, you'll have to answer to me! Got that?"

"Got it. And, son, if I hear anythin', I'll let you know."

"Good. Now, let's go eat."

Haste slapped Red Chief on the rump and watched with pleasure as the horse trotted out to the pasture.

"See you in the morning, old pal."

"Sure do love that horse, don't you, Hat?"

"One of the best friends I've ever had. Four-legged ones, that is." He threw his arm around Al's shoulder as they walked to the sod house. "You know you're my best two-legged friend."

He was rewarded by a broad, open smile on Al's face. They understood each other.

They washed up outside. A basin, a pail of water, and

some soap had been placed on a small table. A towel
hung on a nail beside the door. Sheltered by the connecting roof of the dogtrot, both men washed their
hands and face. Haste discarded the soiled water and
hung the basin beside the towel.

Tantalizing aromas whirled in the warm air of the
kitchen, and both men drew in deep, satisfying breaths
as they entered the room. A red-and-white checked tablecloth was on the table, along with tin plates, cutlery,
and cups. Bethenia was in front of the oven door. Her
face, flushed from the heat, wore a happy smile as she
placed the biggest, fattest brown biscuits on the table
that Cook had ever seen.

"My God, girl, where did you learn to make food like
that?"

"From a very good teacher," Bethenia said, smirking
"and you know it."

In their bed later that night, she wanted to question her
husband about his conversation earlier with Al Page. At
the evening meal, all had been sweetness and light, the
conversation warm and friendly. But the occasional dis-
tant look that she saw in Haste's eyes troubled her.
She'd be patient, she had decided and somehow discover what was worrying him. She sighed softly. She
prayed for guidance as she listened to her husband's
quiet breathing. *God, please help me be a good wife to
this man of my heart.*

But Haste did not tell her what he and Al had discussed. Each day, he went about his tasks, caring for
their two horses, Red Chief and Jasper, and he worked
steadily on the stable he was building for them. It would
be much better than the lean-to that poorly housed them
now. Texas winters could be harsh at times, and pro-

tected animals had a better chance of staying healthy and surviving.

He had ordered barbed wire from a company in Illinois, and preparing for it's arrival, he had paced off his land, staked poles along the perimeter, and persuaded some of the cowboys to help him fence the land.

Their cattle herd was increasing as well. Cattle drives passed by the old Carpenter homestead, now named the T-C Ranch after Terrell and Cooper, its new owners' names, and they would drop off newborn calves that were not allowed to accompany their mothers on the drive. Already, there were six young calves of various ages from several days to a few months. Haste called it, "Bethenia's nursery."

Her favorite was a bull calf, only a few days old, whom she had named Thunderhead because the cattle driver said the calf's mother had "dropped" him during the worst thunderstorm he had ever seen. Bethenia had fashioned a nipple from the finger of an old kid glove, and she had been able to keep him healthy and alive until he could be weaned to hay. Everyone who visited the T-C Ranch—and the young Terrells had many cowboy visitors who admired Haste and his bride—laughed at Bethenia. It was obvious that the calf thought she was his mother, because he bawled every time she left him. He was quiet only when she fed or talked to him. Whenever he was allowed out of the makeshift pen, he would bump his way along and trail behind her like a lost puppy

Haste teased her, "What am I going to do with all these animals falling in love with you? Even got Red Chief spoiled, feeding him apples, carrots, and lumps of sugar—"

"Never hurts to have a friend, Haste, I always say. I know Red would never let me ride him, only you can do that, but I want him to know I'm his friend. Anything wrong with that?" she asked.

"Not that I know of. But, when time comes to sell the cattle, you won't want to part with them . . . they'll be your friends."

"You're teasing me now, Haste. Just don't part with Thunderhead," she pleaded.

"What can we do with him? He has to be castrated and dehorned if we keep him."

When the day came for the procedure to be done, Bethenia stayed indoors, covering her ears so she would not hear the pitiful bawling of her pet.

"Poor Thunderhead," she sighed when she saw him, his underside covered with tar to coagulate any blood. He had been dehorned as well. She tenderly rubbed the soft spots where the horn buds had been removed.

"It's safer this way," Haste assured her, noting her distress. "Safer for us and for him."

"He's only a baby," Bethenia crooned. She put her arms around the calf's neck.

"Won't be able to say that in another six months. I'm going to turn him out to feed in the pasture. Make him feel better, forget what's been done to him." He slapped the calf on the rump and headed him toward the field. "Let's go, old man. The worst is over for you."

His words to the calf brought a worry to Bethenia's mind. Was the "worst over" for them, or was there some unknown danger in the future? She continued to be concerned because she had not discovered what Cook had discussed with Haste. Something bothered Haste, she knew. Ever since Al Page's visit, Haste thrashed restlessly in his sleep, and his frequent nighttime mutterings disturbed her. She was worried.

Chapter Nineteen

"Aunt Lacey is coming to visit us!" Bethenia announced excitedly to Haste as she waved the letter she had received from Boston. One of the cowboys from Fair Acres Ranch had delivered it.

"Oh, Bethie, that's great news! Great news! I hope your aunt Lacey won't be too upset by our simple home," Haste said, grimacing.

"Pshaw! Not Aunt Lacey! From what she has told me, she had a hard time when she first started out in Boston, living in one room, boarding with a family with a passel of children. She knows what it means when you're just starting out."

"All the same," Haste persisted, "I wish we were living in a real wooden house, not in this muddy sod house. But," he looked at his wife, his eyes intent on her face, "listen to me, Bethie, I promise that as soon as possible, I'm going to build one of the finest houses in Texas, for you, my love."

Bethenia smiled at his serious intensity.

"I know you will, husband mine. And I'll be satisfied, surely will, with whatever you build."

"When your aunt gets here, talk over with her what you'd like to have in your new house."

"Haste, that's what I'll do. I'm glad we ordered that davenport from the mail-order catalogue. Be perfect for Aunt Lacey."

"Sure, she won't mind sleeping on a couch that opens into a sofa bed?"

"She has one herself, so she knows what sleeping on one is like. I slept on hers when I first got to Boston. I didn't mind, don't believe she will."

"I hope she'll be comfortable, and never mind what anyone says, you've done a good job with the house. When I first saw this pitiful place, my heart dropped . . . looked so hopeless."

"Never say that, Haste, my love. Nothing is hopeless long as we have each other."

She reached for him and reassuringly patted his cheek. Impulsively, as her nearness excited him, he grasped her hand, turned it to kiss her palm, and gathered her closer.

"Tell me again, Bethie," he whispered into her hair, his voice solemn with passion, "tell me that you love me, that you'll fight to keep our love alive, that you believe in our right to be together."

Bethenia rested her head on her husband's strong, broad chest and listened to the reassuring beat of his heart, and she felt his arms tighten around her fiercely, as if defying heaven itself from separating them. She murmured quietly, "Told you fore, husband mine, it would take more than a regiment to drive me away from you, more than a bunch of wild horses!"

She clung to him and looked into his face, seeing that his copper-colored skin had reddened from his deep emotion, and she saw, too, the intensity of his feelings for her reflected in his eyes. He bent his head forward to kiss her.

Each would have been distressed if the thoughts of

the other's mind at that moment had been voiced. Bethenia realized that this man truly loved her, but could she convince him to share *all* of his life with her? It was what she wanted, to share wholly with the man she loved. For Haste, unknowingly, Bethenia's words, "wild horses" had made him draw her small body even closer.

He had not told her that Evan Connolly whom he still worked for, had asked him to help round up a herd of wild horses needed for a remuda. A rancher always required a fresh string of horses, especially for the long cattle drives.

Haste had informed Evan Connolly earlier that he would no longer be willing to leave his young wife on a six-months cattle drive, but, "You know, of course, Evan, I'd be willing to help round up a herd of mustangs," he had told him.

"You'd be willing to leave her for a week to ten days?" Evan had asked.

"Her aunt will be here, and I'd be happy if you could spare some of the men like Cook, Gus Bellamy, maybe Charley Garcia, to stay a few days and watch over her."

"No question about that, Haste. Charlie says he's too old to go after wild mustangs like he did years ago, when he was a young vaquero, but I know he wouldn't mind helping the others to keep an eye on things."

Evan had walked with Haste to the corral and both men had looked over the horses there. Evan had continued to speak, observing the animals, "My string of ponies is 'bout wore out from that last drive we made. Don't take long to break them down. Moving at top speed and handling and turning cattle, they need rest after four hours of steady work like that."

"I know, Evan, and it wouldn't be so bad if they had fodder and oats to feed on, but, as you know, all they can get on the trail is grass, and that stuff is really not nourishment enough for a hard workin' animal."

"Then, it's settled. As soon as your wife's aunt arrives, we'll go after the wild mustangs. Got some good men to help. Scouts have found a sizable herd just fore the crossing over the Rio Grande. Wouldn't want you to have to deal with the Mexicans."

"We'll do our best to avoid that," Haste had assured him.

Now, as Haste held Bethenia in his arms, his worry was compounded by the distressful news that Al had brought to him. Frank Ward. How could Haste leave his wife with the spectre of his declared enemy around?

The tension that Haste tried to hide from Bethenia was not successfully concealed from her discerning eyes. There was something bothering him, something was wrong. She simply had to find out what it was, or she would have no peace of mind. She'd go crazy with worry.

After their evening meal that night, she broached the subject. Haste was busily mending a hackamore, a rawhide halter with a wide band to go over a horse's eyes. It would be used for breaking a horse. She was working on a quilt that she was trying to complete before her aunt's arrival.

"Haste?" she said bluntly, "what is bothering you?" She had been patient long enough.

"Bothering me? What do you mean, Bethie?"

She put aside the quilt pieces and directed her gaze at her husband. "Ever since Cook's been here," she took a deep breath and plunged forward, "and you two talked, you have been upset. You know I've been with you, on the trail, after my uncle's death, the bad situation with the Wards, I *know* when you're upset. You've got to tell me. Sometimes it seems to me that you're someplace else, not here with me at all."

"Course I'm here."

"You know what I mean. You've got something on your mind, and I know it. You might as well tell me, cause I won't let up till you do."

"Bethenia . . ." Haste started.

"Don't Bethenia me! Didn't you tell me once that I am the most stubborn, intractable woman you've ever known?"

"But you would be worried if you knew."

"If I *don't* know, I'll be worried," she broke in. "Don't think I haven't heard you playin' your mouth organ out there in the dogtrot. Know whenever you do that, you've got a problem. And don't think I haven't heard your sighs and noticed your restless sleep."

By this time, her eyes flashed angrily toward her husband, and she strode purposefully to stand in front of his chair.

"Haste Allen Terrell, listen to me! We are in this life together to share whatever comes, and I aim to do my part. I'm not *afraid* of anything, Haste, and I know I can handle anything long 's you love me. That is the only thing that I couldn't manage! I do love you, Haste," she said simply.

Haste saw the tears of frustration in her eyes. He placed the hackamore on the floor and pulled his young wife onto his lap.

"Bethie." He kissed the tears from her eyes and held her tense body close. "I'll always love you. There's nothing that can stop me from loving you. You know you are my heart, my soul, my life. And I swear to you that if Frank Ward or anyone ever harms you, I will hunt him to the very depths of hell."

Then, Haste told her of how Franklin Ward and his

gang had crossed paths with him when he was a soldier, how he had blackmailed her uncle, although for Bethenia's sake, he told her he wasn't sure of the reason. And, as if she really didn't want to know, she did not question him. He told her of his Pinkerton activities and the fact that the Wards had been sent to the penitentiary for the attempted train robbery, due to his capture of him and his testimony as a Pinkerton agent. He did not tell her of Ward's threat to him.

"But is he's in jail, why are you worried?"

"He's got friends in these parts, gang members, and he may come back. No telling what he might try to do. I believe he is a jealous, crazy hombre whose life has not turned out like he wanted. I don't know."

"Don't worry, Haste, I'll be safe."

"That's just it. I'm not sure," he worried. "When your aunt Lacey gets here next week, I've promised Evan to help out with a round-up of wild mustangs. Be gone about a week to ten days. I figure with your aunt here . . . and Evan has promised to send over some o' the men who are not going on the hunt to keep an eye on things."

"I know you have to help Evan, Haste. He's been a good friend to us. Do what you have to do and don't worry about us."

"While I'm gone, promise me, Bethie, you'll stick close to the house and keep that derringer I gave you close by at all times."

"I promise, Haste."

Aunt Lacey arrived a few days later, laden with gifts. Her valises, hand luggage, and suitcases were bulging with all sorts of surprises. A new vest and tie for Haste, a dimity blouse and heavy woolen skirt for her niece, plush Turkish towels, sheets, and kitchen curtains. In addition, a new lamp and globe that she had carefully hand-carried. Ribbons, bows, colorful yards of cotton and silk material spilled from her bags as she opened them. She even brought new cutlery for Bethenia, who exulted when she saw the shiny pieces: spoons, knives, and forks.

"Now," Bethenia exclaimed, "I can set a proper table. No more tin pieces."

That evening, when Haste explained to Bethenia's aunt that he would be away for a while, she assured him that she would be able to stay as long as she wanted. "This is my first vacation in years, and I intend to make the most of it," she told him. Later, she took Haste aside and said, "I'm so glad to see that Bethenia is happy. You don't know what peace o' mind that gives me, son."

Haste thanked her for her compliment, saying, "I hope, Aunt Lacey, that it will always be this way. And if I have any say in the matter, it will be. Count on it."

"Have a successful hunt, Haste, dear. Be careful and come back soon."

"Thanks, Aunt Lacey, will do my best."

Cook looked in on the women early in the morning the day of Haste's departure.

"So, this is Aunt Lacey," he said, when Bethenia introduced him. "Pleased to make your acquaintance, ma'am." He bowed low in a courtly fashion to shake Aunt Lacey's hand.

Over his head, Aunt Lacey beamed at Bethenia. Her glance said, "What a pleasant surprise."

Chapter Twenty

That morning, Haste had ridden out early to join the Connolly crew of cowboys to start the wild mustang roundup. Never, he thought, had he seen the sky so light, so luminous, so bright with expectation. The sun's rays filled the sky, and even though it was early summer, the morning air swirled cool and crisp. New young prairie grasses bent like waves of blue-green water. This great land should be peaceful and serene, like the powerful forces of nature that shape it, he mused. Instead, there are evil aggressions brought by men to ruin it.

He had said his good-by to Bethenia in the early morning hours. It had been a restless night for each of them, and neither would admit to the other the apprehension each felt.

He had held her close. Bethenia had tried not to let the tears that stung her eyelids fall. She was afraid of being alone without her husband, but at least, she had Aunt Lacey, and there was enough work around the sod house to keep them busy. She could not let Haste know. She snuggled closer to him.

"Oh, Bethie," Haste had murmured, "I hate to leave you, God knows, I hate it."

Haste had been shocked by his own feeling of vulnerability, almost a weakness, when it came to his over-whelming love for the woman in his arms. He had stared at her face as if memorizing it. He could hardly believe this lovely, spunky young woman had come into his life. He had wanted to speak, to tell Bethenia how much he loved her, but the words wouldn't come.

Bethenia had seen the tension in his face, and she had moved her fingers lightly along his jaw, impulsively pulling his mouth toward her own.

"Haste, I love you," she had whispered quietly. "Come back soon. I need you."

It had been then that Haste had seen the diamondlike tears, that his young wife had tried so hard to control, slip silently down her cheeks.

He had gathered her even closer as their mouths joined in a kiss so desperate, Haste had shuddered as he tried to control his emotions.

"This is the first and the last time I'll ever leave you," he had murmured. "Never again, Bethie, I promise, never again."

He had sighed deeply as he had kissed her again. "Never again, no matter what."

Bethenia had spoken then, her voice caught in her throat. "You will be careful out there, won't you, Haste? Wild horses can be so dangerous."

He had answered her quickly, "Don't worry, little one, by the time we run them down, they will be so tired they'll be glad to settle down in the corral. It's you I'm worried about. I know how fearless you are, but I don't want *you* to be careless."

He had turned in the bed, rested on one elbow to look down at her. His heart had thumped in fierce stabs as her young loveliness took his breath away.

"Promise me," he had moaned into her hair, "take no

chances. I know how strong you are, but I also know
that men like the Ward brothers don't care."

She had looked up at him. His bronze coppery skin
had shone with the love he felt for her. His hair, grown
long again, had framed his face as he had bent forward
to kiss her repeatedly. She had welcomed the fullness of
his firm mouth and had opened her own to receive his
probing tongue. She had felt her insides quiver with excitement as she had acknowledged the sensuous caresses
of his hands on her body. She had been on fire, aflame
with mounting desire.

"Haste," she had whimpered, "love me, love me,
now!"

Then, his mouth descended to her breasts as her arms
tightened fiercely around his neck. The world had been
forgotten, the muddy sod walls disappearing as they
rode the crest of almost unbearable fulfillment. Their intimate world had been one of passionate beauty as it
took them into unforgettable realms of blinding joy.

"Bethie, oh, God, I love you so."

Bethenia's response to her husband had been a cry of
pure rapture as her excitement spiraled to meet his, to
soar into limitless space. Their welded hearts had beat
on in unison, and together, they had defied the world to
try to thwart their future.

Later, as he had sat astride his horse, Haste had taken
one last look at the sod house where his life, the only
life he wanted, existed. Would all be well while he was
gone? Had he done all he could to protect the woman he
loved? Why was there a nagging doubt in his mind?
Why was he upset about trusting his responsibility to
someone else, as much as he did rely on Cook, Gus,
Charlie, and the others? Was he being spooked, appre-
hensive for no real reason? Reluctantly, he had turned
his mount away from the house and had ridden hard to

catch up to the thirty men who had been decent enough not to intrude on his farewell to his wife.

It was a sixty-mile ride to the wooded, hilly area where the wild herd of horses had been located. A good-sized area had been cleared where the fringes of the forest thinned out. There a trap had been formed. At the very end of the trap, a fenced and stoutly wired wooden corral that was large enough for fifty horses had been built with a wide opening that could be secured once the horses had been chased into it. In front of the corral was a wider heart-shaped funnel of space about fifty-yards wide, like a huge mouth to envelop the wild animals. Wings on each side for a mile or so leading to the heart-shaped funnel were formed by stringing wire along pickets and trees. Rags of various colors and shapes were tied onto the wire about every four feet or so. The fluttering rags would spook the horses, and they would run into the trap, chased by the yelling, noisy cowboys.

But, first, the herd had to be found. The cowboys stationed themselves around the gaunt rocks, tall pines, and birch trees about a half-mile apart. They watched diligently for the stallion. Once he appeared, the herd of mares and young colts would be close by.

On the third day, Angus Fenton, a young Scotch immigrant, spotted him: a magnificent creature, black as coal, with a luxurious black silky mane and tail. Angus told Haste excitedly, "Aye spotted the beast comin' out o' the forest! Like a devil's ghost he were! God, black as the witches o' hell, exceptin' a blaze o' white slashed down his face!"

"Good job, Angus," Haste said, praising him. "Now, we'll have to start runnin' him and his ladies, day after day, till they're so weary they can be driven to the trap."

The men knew they would be in the saddle for the

next eighteen hours or so, running and forcing the herd, so most of them pulled their bedrolls from their saddles, hobbled their horses for the night, and hoped to get what little rest the hard ground would give them.

For Haste, the news was welcome. They had been out for four days, and if they could succeed in capturing the herd in another two or three days, he could be on his way back to his wife and home. That night, he prayed hard for success.

Bethenia and Aunt Lacey spent their mornings working in the small garden that Bethenia had asked Haste to spade up for her. Her vegetables had been planted, and she delighted each day as she saw the new sprouts push through the dark earth. In the afternoons, they rested in the quiet, away from the hot sun, and their evenings were spent in talk about the future.

"You do expect to have a family, don't you, dear?" Aunt Lacey inquired gently one evening.

Bethenia blushed lightly, her hands busy with her sewing. "I certainly hope so. Don't know why I'm not in the family way already," she conceded.

"I believe it takes time. Really, you and Haste both have been workin' hard, and you've both been under a strain. It will happen. I can see how much you love each other."

"I'd *die* if anything ever happened to him, Aunt Lacey. Wouldn't want to live."

"Nothing is goin' to happen to either of you. Bet my life on that," her aunt answered. "Not you two! By the way, that cowboy, Al Page, Cook, you call him sometimes, he's the one who helped you join the cattle drive?"

"Sure did, Aunt Lacey. And he's been a good friend to me ever since. Sometimes, I call him Uncle Al."

"So, I've noticed," her aunt said dryly. "Seems to be quite a character."

The "character" turned up an hour later as the women were preparing to retire for the night.

"Thought I'd mosey over to see how *my* womenfolk were doin'," he said, when Bethenia let him in the front door.

"Already checked round, and all is quiet. Thought I'd sleep in the bunkhouse, the other side of the dogtrot. If you need me, bang on a pot. The rattle of pots and pans always wakes up a cook," he said grinning.

"By the way, did you check on Red Chief?" Bethenia asked. "Haste was real upset that he couldn't take him on the mustang roundup. He loves that horse."

"Yep, he's doin' a little better. Got him to drink some water, but he still won't eat. 'Notha' day, two, he'll be hungry, and we'll see."

"What's wrong with Haste's horse?"

"Don't know how it happened, Aunt Lacey, but somehow he got hold of some locoweed."

"Locoweed? What's that?"

Bethenia looked at Cook, who explained, "It's a weed that most of the time animals won't eat, but if they do, it is like whiskey is to a man. They want more and more of it. They'll go off their feed, won't eat or drink, their eyes get all wild, and they stagger, bump into things, just like a drunk."

"That's awful, never heard of such a thin'. Can you cure them?"

"Oh, yeah, but you got to pen them up till the mess gits out of their systems. That's why they call it 'loco-weed.' Drives them plumb crazy. Must say, Red Chief looks bad, coat all dull and shaggy, but," he reflected cheerfully, "he'll come round. Like I say, tonight got him to drink. That'll help git him well. Got to! Haste loves that horse, you know. And that animal loves him. Ain't nobody else can ride him except Haste. Don't know, Bethenia, do think that animal's gittin' sweet on you, always givin' him sugar, carrots and such."

"But, since he's been sick, he won't take anything from me, Cook."

"He'll come round. Give him time."

"Hope so, for Haste's sake."

Chapter Twenty-one

As soon as he saw the man weaving his way through the wooded, rocky path toward their one-room shack, he knew that his father had been drinking over at old Mr. Fowler's homemade whiskey still. The young boy watched as the man he called Pa stumbled and reeled. The boy could see by the wavering lantern that his father carried that his eyes were wild and bloodshot. The saliva from his gaping mouth dribbled down the front of his already deeply stained overalls.

He was doing it again, reciting that obscene poem at the top of his lungs, as if the silent dark trees were a captive audience. His hair, steel gray and lank, hung limp from his large head like some old weather-beaten scarecrow's wig. His voice, hoarse and craggy, reverberated among the rocks and trees.

The boy trembled in anger and fear as he watched and listened from behind a tree. His stomach alternatively churned and tightened as his father lurched closer and the wild verses were flung into the night.

Oh, my sweet lady, mistress mine,
Let me kiss your breasts devine,
Fold me to your loving bliss,

I yearn only for your kiss,
But for your love, oh, mistress mine,
I fain would leave this world behind.

Terrified, the lad sprang from his hiding place to run into the back of the house and warn his mother. "Ma! Ma! He's back, and he's blind drunk, he is!" He sucked in his breath as he tried to help his sick mother get to her feet so she could hide in the cave behind the house until his sodden father slept off his drunk.

But, his mother, weak from the birth of her last child whose month-old body lay buried in the small cemetery along with four other siblings, could not move fast, despite her eldest son's assistance.

"Take your brother Henry and go!" she hissed, as they both heard the thudding footsteps of her husband on the front stoop.

"Hide, son, hide," she pleaded. "And no matter what you hear, don't come back till I calls you."

"Oh, Ma! Don't stay, he's goin' to beat you again, I know!"

"Hush, now. Go! Come only when I call. Stay hid with your brother. Be satisfied if I know you're safe."

The hoarse, cracked, demanding voice of his father sounded through the thin walls of the shack once again, "Would fain leave this world behind . . . ." Then, came the thunderous voice that the boy dreaded.

"Maggie, Maggie, where are you? You worthless, sufferin' bitch! Come tend to your husband, your lord and master, and be quick about it!"

"Comin', Malcolm, on me way, love," she said, as she pushed her two surviving sons out the back door. "Run, run," she insisted, as her pale fingers clutched her flannel nightgown close to her frail body. "Till I call," she whispered, and she closed the door on their bleak faces.

They did as she told them, running breathlessly into the night, guided only by the stars and a full moon, not stopping until they reached a small cave that they had stumbled upon one day when they were out exploring.

Huddled together in the darkness, they listened as their mother's screams swelled out into the night air. They had witnessed many times the hard slaps and shuddering blows their mother suffered from the drunken hands of their father. They heard one last scream, "M-a-a-l-col-m, do-o-n't!" It hung in the air for what seemed to them to be an eternity. They listened. There was quiet, broken only by the occasional hoot of an owl.

Their mother's call to come home never came.

Early the next morning, as soon as it was daylight, the boys crept silently toward the gloomy hovel. Neither spoke. The quiet was deathlike; only the noisy chatter of a busy squirrel broke the awful stillness of a new day.

With gestures, the older boy cautioned his brother to be quiet as he tiptoed to the back door. He insisted that Henry remain outside until he investigated. Slowly, he opened the door. His unspoken fear of what he might find made it almost impossible for him to move.

He was fourteen years old. The sight he viewed that day never left him. From that event grew a hate so large, so strong, it flowered from inside him like a huge bulb of animosity and loathing. It changed him. His innocence was gone forever.

He saw walls painted with blood, bits of hair smeared on the bedclothing held there by bloody clots, broken furniture, splintered wood on the floor, and then, his gaze was drawn to his mother's sightless open eyes staring at the ceiling where flies buzzed aimlessly. His father's body, half-undressed, lay across his mother. His pitiful nakedness had reduced him to a wretched, impotent shell. He had died, choking on his own vomit. The man had soiled himself as well, as his death purged him of his anger and his bodily wastes. The room reeked of sour, foul odors.

The boy pulled a blanket over the bodies and walked out the door without a backward glance.

"Come on," he said to his waiting brother, "we can leave now."

Together, they walked down the stone-filled path five miles out of Stewart Hollow to their nearest neighbors, a Swedish family named Feldson.

Mrs. Feldson, a large, friendly woman, greeted them at her front door. She had been baking, and her ample boson was dusted with flour.

"Look, Oscar," she called to her husband, "it is the Ward brothers! Come in, boys," Her welcome was warm and sincere. "And how are your ma and pa?"

"Dead," Franklin Ward blurted out with no emotion on his stony face. "Both dead, they are."

Mr. Feldson mobilized the scant community of Stewart Hollow, and a brief burial was held for the couple. He stood at the graveside in the small cemetery where both parents were laid to rest with their dead babies. As the last pieces of earth were dropped, he felt the trembling anger of Franklin Ward as he rested his arm across the boy's shoulder.

Poor laddies, Mr. Feldson thought, what a terrible way to start life. He looked across the quiet grave to his own sons standing beside their mother. Thank you, God in heaven, for my wife and children. Make me a decent man, please.

Everyone went back to the Feldson house after the burial. Other neighbors had brought food, pies, cakes, loaves of bread, meat pies, and plenty of vegetables. The Ward boys sat by themselves in the Feldsons' yard as neighbors offered condolences. Women gave pitiful glances and sucked their teeth at the horror of the boys' dilemma, but no one offered any solutions.

That night, the Ward brothers slept on pallets on the floor of the Feldsons' living room.

"We *can't* keep them," Frank Ward overheard Mr. Feldson whisper to his wife. "We've enough problems as it is."

The Feldsons needn't have worried. As soon as breakfast was over the next morning, Frank stood up, pushing his chair back to the table, and announced, "My brother and me, leavin' now. Thanks for your help with Ma and Pa. Now, we're goin'. Come on, Henry," he said reaching for his brother's hand.

"Oh, God," Mrs. Feldson exclaimed as she rose hurriedly from her chair, "Where are you going?"

"Out west," Frank said grimly. "Goin' out west."

Mrs. Feldson had tears in her eyes as she watched the Ward brothers leave. Each carried a knapsack with a few of her older son's outgrown pants and shirts. She also thrust upon them a bag of meat sandwiches, some dried apples, and a few hard-boiled eggs.

"Oscar, we should have made them stay here," she insisted to her husband.

"They didn't want to, Elsa. Can't say I blame them. This old hollow here in Tennessee don't have nuthin' for them but bad memories, I'd say. And, well—"

"Well? So, what is well? Two young ones on their own," she said defiantly.

"The older one is determined, Elsa. Could see it in his eyes, no doubt of that."

The man was correct in his assessment of Franklin Ward. He never looked back, and he never spoke of their parents again, not even to his brother. He became mother and father to Henry, who was four years younger. Henry was dependent on his older brother and looked up to him. Although not stupid, his thought process was not as quick as Frank's, nor was his imagination as flexible.

The rest of that summer found them working on various farms as they traveled. A few days here or there picking fruit—peaches, apples, oranges—or perhaps, another week helping a farmer raise his barn. Another month spent hanging tobacco to cure for a tobacco planter. They moved as transients. Jobs and boardinghouses were offered, but Franklin rejected them.

"Goin' west," he said. "We're headin' west."

By the time he was eighteen, they had reached Oklahoma. There, both boys fell in love with horses. The freedom of movement, viewing the world from the saddle, the exhilarating thrill of seeing the earth move beneath the flying hooves of their steeds—it released the binding tensions they had endured, and they were like newborns, testing and searching, and finding energy and purpose.

And they discovered firearms. Henry proved to be the more gifted of the two when it came to guns, although both handled their new acquisitions easily. He was single-minded enough to spend hour after hour drawing twin guns from his holster and working at shooting targets.

His skill did not go unnoticed by the Oklahoma gangs of rustlers and renegades who frequented the taverns of the frontier towns. It happened in the town of Gunsell, named, no doubt, because guns could be purchased there.

It was there that the Doherty gang took special notice of the two brothers. Rafe Doherty, the leader, sat with his cronies, drinking and reliving the exciting events of the day when the Wards showed up. Not one to let an opportunity pass by, he hailed Henry, who stood beside his brother at the bar.

"Hey, you," Rafe shouted, pointing his half-smoked cigar toward Henry.

"Who, me?" Henry turned, surprised at being singled out instead of his brother. He was aware that Frank had stiffened, unperceived by the others, to full attention at the sound of the leader's challenge.

"Yep, talkin' to you. Hear you're some kindo' exceptional with your firearms."

Frank made a quick survey of the room, sensed no hostility, so he relaxed slightly, but remained alert. He and Henry were new to the town and not yet privy to the politics of the place. He always wanted to be on the "right" side, not necessarily of the law, but of the strong and powerful.

"What you want to see?" Henry asked.

Aware of what could happen, the saloon owner spoke quickly, "Outside, please, gentlemen. Outside! Please!"

Rafe Doherty laughed at the man's anxious concern.

"Ah, Zeke, you know I'd pay for any damages, but . . . this once we'll take our business outdoors."

"Jesus, Rafe, you know I can't help it. All my savin's in this place," the saloon owner whined.

"Yeah, yeah, come on, son, let's see what you got." He led the way onto the dirt street. As soon as most of the patrons and onlookers had filed outside, ready for some exciting entertainment, Rafe Doherty took a twenty-dollar gold piece from his vest pocket, tossed it into the air, and shouted, "Hit it!"

The white curl of smoke from Henry's revolver hung in the air as the coin tinkled to the ground, a round hole in its center.

Rafe chewed on his cigar for a moment as whistles, yells, and murmurs of approval came from the crowd. He looked steadily at Frank as if he had recognized him as the spokesman for the brothers.

"If you can shoot half as good as that, I'll take you both into my gang. Can always use good sharpshooters."

"Yes, sir," Frank agreed. At last, this was what he'd hoped for all along, to someday be a part of something that was strong and certain. Now, he could start to learn all he could—keep his eyes and ears open. Soon, he'd be the leader of his own gang and would take orders from no one. He'd be *giving* the orders.

As the homesteaders came west, the criminals, con artists, ne'er-do-wells, thieves, cutthroats, and murders came, too. Along with other gangs roaming the West, Rafe Doherty and his gang planned their schemes to meet, rob, plunder, and even murder the ill-prepared newcomers.

"Your money or your life" was the demand heard again and again by the families that streamed over the plains and mountains to struggle for a new life.

Frank Ward never saw the faces of his victims. After his gun had spoken and his victims lay where they had fallen, Frank and his brother became bold in the pursuit of the wealth and power they sought. The law of the West was the law of the gun.

The inevitable day came when Frank challenged Rafe's leadership. It was Rafe's custom to bury the dead. He always insisted on it. "Poor bastards, it's the least we can do," he'd say. "Can't leave these people out here for the animals and buzzards to pick at them."

"Why not?" Frank replied, with the familiar stony look from his cold, slate-blue eyes fixed on Rafe.

"Cause it's not decent. I may be a rogue and a rustler, but I ain't uncivilized," he argued.

"Boys," Frank turned in his saddle to face the men who were aware of the crisis, "the longer we stay here, the more likely we'll be caught by the troopers in these parts. I say let's ride and let the dead bury the dead. Let's move!"

"Why, you sufferin', stinkin' polecat!" Rafe muttered. "You forgit, Ward . . . I make the rules, and you follow them."

"Not anymore, Rafe."

Frank's gun was out of its holster, and the shot he fired found its mark. Rafe Doherty was dead before his body hit the ground.

"Anybody want to stay here on a buryin' detail is welcome to it." Frank Ward's voice was pure steel. He kneed his horse, and rode away from the area. Not once did he look back. His brother caught up with him.

"God, Frank, you killed Rafe!"

"Had to. It was him or us."

They heard the thundering of horses' hooves behind them.

"The men are joinin' up, Frank, they're not stayin' back," Henry said, looking over his shoulder at the approaching men.

"We got *us* a gang now, Hank. Nobody is ever goin' forgit us. We're the Ward brothers gang," he vowed.

One eleven-year-old boy survived the massacre, and when found by the cavalrymen of Haste's troops, he was able to describe in detail the men who had slaughtered his parents and the other members of the wagon train.

"What kind of men could do this?" one soldier asked. "These people are not the enemy, these are only people tryin' to find a new life."

"Men who killed unarmed people have no conscience, no feelin'," his sergeant, Haste Terrell, said. "The death of a human being means little to them. I guess somebody or somethin' that happened in their lives has made them cold and hard like this."

Chapter Twenty-two

Bitter hatred nagged constantly at Frank Ward. Ever since he had crossed paths back at Fort Gordon with that colored trooper, Haste Terrell, he had been almost eaten by his hatred for him. *Didn't that bastard know that this country was for white people and that he should stay in his place?*

To anyone who might presume otherwise, he would have denied being envious of the cavalryman, but he could not deny to himself the deep set feelings he felt. He envied the man. He had heard that Haste, like himself, had come from a bleak childhood, but, so far, Haste seemed to have succeeded in his life. Frank Ward, a white man who should have had the advantage, was in prison. Not for the murders he had committed, nor for the cattle he'd rustled and resold. Not even for the blackmail scheme he'd perpetrated on Conroy Cooper. But because of the failed attempt at the train robbery, caught red-handed by that Pinkerton man Haste Terrell. It was that damn Nigra that caused the sore horn of rage that twisted and burned in his gut whenever he thought about his plight. If it was the last thing he ever did in this life, he'd repay that black bastard for every anguished moment he'd spent in jail.

Even his brother Hank had suffered. Crazy kid, unable to tolerate the confines of the prison walls, had tried to escape them by hanging himself. He had been found by one of the guards one morning hanging from the cell's bars, naked, his cotton trouser leg tied around his throat. He even had failed at that. He was still alive when cut down, and an attempt was made to revive him, but the prolonged absence of oxygen to his brain left him with no future.

"Poor bastard," the prison doctor had said, "now, he will be in prison for life. He'll live, but only as a vegetable . . . won't even know he is alive."

When Frank was given the news, he had smashed his already maimed hand into the wall. When asked if he would like to see his brother, he had responded with snarled obscenities and had spat at the guard who'd brought him the message.

"*You* go see him, you goddamn son of a bitch! You made him like that! *You* look at him!" He had glared at the guard, who understood his anger and hatred. Even so, he had maintained his authority over the prisoner.

"That spit will cost you your supper," he had said, walking away from the hostile, cursing prisoner who hurled one more invective at the guard's retreating back.

"Damn you and your god damned supper!"

But after that day, he changed. For six months he became a model prisoner and eventually became a "trusty." He worked in the stables, keeping them mucked out and clean, and he worked in the storeroom where he saw that the harnesses were clean and repaired. He was at ease with the animals, loved being near them and caring for them. But, most of all, he was happy to be in the sun and fresh air, even though the prison walls surrounded him and he could not see past them.

Deep, corrosive hate still lived within his mind and soul, but those in charge, his jailers, saw the change he wanted them to see. Working in the storeroom, he realized that his jailers trusted him.

Always quick to take advantage of any situation that would benefit himself, he waited for his opportunity. One evening when the guard was at supper, Frank simply walked away. Thin, wiry, and strong, the eighteen-foot wooden wall was no problem for him. He took his few belongings and the few dollars he had earned in prison and headed for Texas. He had unfinished business there.

"Your uncle Al, as you call him, is a very interesting man," Aunt Lacey said to Bethenia. Her face was serious as she voiced her observation.

They were putting the quilt together, "Like a sandwich," Bethenia said. She looked up from her kneeling position on the floor where she had spread papers to protect the quilt, and she was about to tack the pieces together with bits of thread.

"Uncle Al has been real good to me, Aunt Lacey," she said, as she spread the muslin on the floor. "Sure glad you brought these yards of cotton muslin. How'd you know I'd need it?"

"Just knew it might come in handy. Can always use good cotton muslin."

"Right. But, well, yes, Al Page is mighty like my pa. Course no one could ever take Pa's place, and I felt so alone when he died, left me with those awful people that didn't care a thin' 'bout me! But I remembered Pa had kept tellin' me to get to his brother, Uncle Conroy. *He* didn't turn out to be much of an uncle to me. Guess he didn't know how, but Cook did. I could always de-

pend on him . . . to be in my corner. You know," she
laughed at the memory, "he even went against Haste in
my favor."

"I must say, Bethenia, I never expected to meet anybody like him here in Texas. The stories he tells—his
cavalry experiences, fightin' Indians, Mexicans, renegades. Even speaks two, three languages."

"Learned that living with Mexicans and Indians for a
time. Can talk with some Indians. And a lot of his roping and riding he learned from the Mexicans."

Aunt Lacey's eyes softened with a faraway look. She
handed Bethenia more pins to secure the quilt.

"He really is an interestin' man. There's no one quite
like him in Boston, I don't think."

Her niece looked up at her aunt and observed the
thoughtful expression on her face.

"Aunt Lacey, I do believe you're getting sweet on
Uncle Al" she teased brightly.

"Not really, but as I said, he's had lots of experiences
to talk about, and I do love the way he tells his stories."

When Frank Ward left the prison, physically he had
been a changed man. His once russet-colored hair was
now granite white, and the prison food had left him
tough and wiry. Prison life had also etched deep furrows
across his forehead, but it had not dulled his mind. He
was forever thinking ahead and planning his future.

As he walked out the prison door with eyes forward,
he had known he needed two things . . . a gun and a
horse, and he had set about acquiring them.

Walking briskly, his first stop had been at a remote
farmhouse about fifteen miles south of the prison.

"Sure, I could use some help," the farmer had said.
"Can't pay you nuthin', but can feed you. Wife's ailin',

and my son ain't but six years old. Need all the help I can git."

Frank had worked beside the grateful farmer all day, repairing fences, chopping wood for the man's wife . . . and planning his next move. He had been gratified to see that the man's one horse was strong and well-cared for, and he had learned that the horse's name was Ned. He was the farmer's pride and joy.

That evening, he had shared a meager meal of beans and fatback, some well-cooked greens and rather hard biscuits with the family.

"Can stay the night, if you want," Clem Durant, the farmer, had said.

"Don't mind if I do," Frank had answered.

He had been given a blanket and quilt, and he had rolled up in a corner of the room which he had shared with the six year old who was on a cot. He had waited until he heard deep, rhythmic snores from the bedroom. He had moved stealthily so as not to wake the boy. He had made his way out to the stable and with one hand clamped over the horse's nose to prevent him from snickering, had led him away. He had walked the horse until they were safely out of earshot.

He had been on his way, headed for Texas. He still had needed a gun. He had ridden hard all that morning, driven, propelled by the need to seek revenge and regain his rights as a man to be reckoned with. He owed his brother, as well as himself. That ex-trooper, buffalo soldier, wagon boss, whatever he called himself, was his enemy. Frank Ward knew he'd have no peace on this earth as long as Haste Terrell was alive.

He had arrived at a small town, Kitchen Hills, and he had found a thriving settlement of hardware stores, a livery stable, clothing and dry goods stores, as well as several saloons. He had headed for the largest one. That would be where he'd find what he needed. He still had his fifty dollars from prison. It had been money he had earned as a "trusty." He had been reluctant to part with it; indeed, to let anyone know that he carried that much money on him.

"Howdy," the scruffy-looking barkeep had greeted him, smoke curling from his dangling cigarette.

"Howdy. Can a thirsty man git a drink round here, if he works for it?" Frank asked.

"Depends."

"On what?"

"On how bad a man wants to drink and what kindo' work he's willin' to do."

"For couple o' shots o' brandy and a glass o' whiskey, do most any kind o' work."

The bartender squinted at Frank, taking a long drag from his cigarette and exhaling slowly before speaking. "Outhouse out back needs cleanin' and a good lime treatment. Guess that would be worth couple shots o' brandy and whiskey. Do a good job, might even throw in some supper."

"Long 's I can clean up somewhere fore I eat," Frank had told him.

"Can arrange that. Shovel, bags of lime, everythin's out back." The barkeep had nodded to the rear of the saloon. "Say," he said to Frank, "what's your handle?"

"Call me Ed. Ed Mulcahy," Frank had told him, surprised at himself by the name that he had pulled from his memory, his grandfather's on his mother's side.

After the odious task of cleaning the outhouse had been completed and he had washed himself as clean as possible at the outside pump, he had presented himself for his pay.

True to his word, the saloon keeper gave him his brandy and whiskey, also one of the best grilled steaks that Frank had eaten in some time. He had relished the food and drink, and for the first time since he'd left the penitentiary, he had felt somewhat optimistic about his future.

It hadn't taken very long for the saloon to fill with men. Drifters, ranchers, miners, prospectors, and to Frank Ward's distaste and hatred, there were even one or two buffalo soldiers.

However, seated at a nearby corner was a foursome of heavy drinking, heavy smoking cardplayers whom he had decided were worth keeping an eye on. He had watched, listened, and paid close attention to the cries of alternate joy and dismay that came as the slaps of discarded cards had fallen on the table. Every action had foretold the dangerous drama that was about to take place.

It had been a high-stakes poker game. The intensity in the room had been palpable and heavy. Frank had held his breath along with everyone else in the room. Something had been about to happen, even a blind man could sense the tension. Frank had checked for a way out of the room, perhaps the back door, in case he should need to make a quick exit.

Abruptly, a chair had been scraped back and thrown to the floor as a huge, red-headed cowboy had stood up, his gun drawn. Several shots had reverberated within the saloon walls, and every man had ducked to the floor, including Frank.

"Nobody cheats John Grant, by God," the man had said, his eyes flashing angrily.

Frank Ward had been astonished that the unlucky victim lay on the floor near the spot under the table where Frank had taken refuge. With a sweep of his arm, he had scooped the gun from where it lay, dropped by the murdered man's lifeless fingers, and had slid it into his belt. Not rising, he had scooted out toward the back door. He knew no one had seen him leave; each man had been busy protecting his own hide.

Frank had no problem later that night breaking into the hardware store to get what he needed. Another gun, holster, ammunition, some tinned food, coffee, and even a feed bag and a bag of oats as a treat for the horse, Ned.

Next stop, Texas.

Chapter Twenty-three

Bethenia made her way to the stable to check on Red Chief. Al had told her that the horse was improving rapidly from his bout with the locoweed, but she wanted to find out for herself. The horse was so important to Haste. He'd be happy to see a healthy Red Chief when he came back from the mustang roundup.

She had slipped a kitchen knife into her deep apron pocket, because she planned to cut some new cabbage heads from her garden. Aunt Lacey and Cook had gone for a buggy ride to see some of the countryside and, Bethenia guessed, to have some time to get better acquainted. Bethenia planned to have ham and cabbage for supper, along with some young carrots and new potatoes. She smiled to herself. Who'd have thought an unlikely couple such as her aunt Lacey and Cook would be interested in each other?

She thought about her husband. When was he coming home? He'd been gone less than a week, but to her, it was a lifetime. She wondered, when will he truly be able to start our life together?

In the stable, she greeted the horses, Red Chief and Jasper, who both gave her friendly snickers of welcome. "Hope you've both been good boys," she told them.

"Got some apples and carrots in my apron pockets for my special friends."

She picked a currycomb and brush from the shelf and began to groom Red Chief. He started to nuzzle and nose around her apron pocket, aware that that was the place where she stored carrots, apples, and lumps of sugar.

"Oh, you're looking for the goodies, eh, old friend? Well, we'll see," she chided him as she moved to continue brushing his coat. The horse's coat and mane were looking much healthier. Uncle Al was right. Even the horse's eyes were brighter. The dull, faraway look caused by the locoweed had disappeared. Haste will be pleased to see this change, she knew.

In the next stall, she heard Jasper whinney for her attention. "Don' fret, Jasper, my old friend, I'll always save somethin' for you. I'd *never* forget you, don't worry yourself, ever," she said soothingly to him. "And we're still going for our ride soon 's I finish with Chief."

She continued to brush the reddish-brown mane of the horse. Already, she could see copper-colored highlights sparkling in his thick, luxurious mane.

"You're a handsome brute, Chief," she informed him, "but you know that, don't you?"

Jasper whinnied for the second time, and Bethenia started to scold him. "Now, Jasper, be patient, I'm . . . ." Suddenly, she felt a distinct chill as if a door had been opened. Apprehension flicked over her as she remembered the derringer. Things had been so quiet at the homestead, the all had let down their guard. She had become complacent as well. She could visualize right where she had left the derringer that Haste had warned her to keep with her at all times. It was on her bedside table. She froze in instant fear. Her hand stopped in midair, still holding the currycomb as she stood stock-still, and swallowed, aware that there was someone else in the stable.

Frank Ward watched her from the deep shadow of the stall. She was an attractive wench, he'd have to give the trooper that, even prettier than she was when he'd first seen her at the hotel. A neat little package, small-boned and slight, but as he stood there, he observed how she handled the horse. He could see she was obviously strong for her size. Her skin, creamy brown as coffee laced with cream, was suffused with blush tints from the exertion of grooming the horse. Curls of her glossy black hair clung to her moist forehead, and her feminine attractiveness caused an unexpected tightening sensation in his groin. By damn, it had been months since he'd had a woman, even if his one was a Nigra. Besides, he'd be pleased to defile something belonging to that black trooper.

"Looks like I'm 'bout to make your aquaintance, after all," he drawled. He was laughed when he saw Bethenia's startled reaction—like a rabbit about to be snared by a rabid wolf.

She whirled around to face him. Tall, gaunt, the man had the coldest, palest blue eyes she ever had seen. He was scarecrow thin: his clothes hung loosely on his body and were held together by the wide holster belt and his twin guns. She saw instantly the ragged smirk which widened his thin cheeks, but did not extend to the rest of his face, grimy and soiled from days of sweat and travel dirt.

She knew who he was at once—Frank Ward, her husband's sworn enemy. She was determined not to show fear, even though her heart was beating erratically. She was innately aware that any semblance of terror on her part would only please her attacker.

"What . . . what do you want, Frank Ward?" She hoped her voice sounded strong and calm.

"Why, the little lady remembers my name," he said, bowing low in mock curtsy.

He leveled a gun at her and commanded "Saddle up that there horse, we goin' take us a ride in the country. Never mind," he said, as he spied Jasper already saddled. Al had saddled Jasper that morning so that Bethenia could ride him for his daily exercise.

"Git on up on him" he demanded, and as soon as she had done so, he tied her hands to the pommel of the saddle, warning her that she would die where she was if she gave him any trouble. He led her out to where he'd left Ned. Holding on to Jasper's lead rein, he mounted and quickly pushed his horse to a gallop. Bethenia could do nothing but follow. She was a captive, and she had no choice.

Red Chief, suddenly aware that he had been denied the carrots, apples, and sugar that he knew were in Bethenia's apron pocket, kicked angrily at the front of the stall and broke free. With a forceful jerk of his massive head, he tore the rein from the bridle halter and freed himself.

It was early evening by the time Haste arrived back at the sod house that he and Bethenia shared. The mustang roundup had been successfully completed sooner than expected.

The quiet that greeted him was noisy in its silence. Suddenly, Haste experienced a hollowness where his stomach should have been. A precognitive shudder passed through his body. Someone walking on my grave, he knew. He dreaded what he knew he would find. From the empty kitchen, to the living room with

Aunt Lacey's sofa neatly made up, into the last room, the bedroom, where his fears were confirmed when he saw the derringer on the bedside table. Why did Bethenia go out without it?

He had expected to find Al Page at the house. At Fair Acres Ranch, Connolly had informed him that Cook had assumed responsibility for visiting his house almost every day. Gus Bellamy had checked the sod house as well, and it was he who took Haste aside that day to speak to him.

"Maybe somethin', Hat, and maybe not," he told him, "but there was a mighty thin, blue-eyed stranger here day or so ago askin' for directions to your place. Didn't see him myself, but from what the boys said, sounded like it could be Frank Ward."

Gus saw the worried look that raced across Haste's face, and he attempted to reassure his friend. "Was out to your place, myself, last night. Didn't see a thin'."

"Mighty obliged, Gus. 'Preciate it."

Now, he was almost afraid to check the stable. If the horses were gone, his worst fear would come to fruition. Bethenia must have been taken against her will!

He ran to the stable. Empty. Both Jasper and Red Chief were gone. He lit the lantern that he kept there and spotted the currycomb and brush on the floor. Then, he saw the broken stall door that Red Chief had kicked open. He searched the back of the stall, and in the corner, he noticed footprints made by a man's large cowboy boots. The prints had been made fresh that day. A man had been here. The horses were gone—and his wife was gone. Somehow, Frank Ward had found them.

A nagging feeling of self-reproach almost choked him. He should not have left his wife in the care of others. He struck his fist into the wall.

Quickly, he came to himself and realized he'd have to

act and act at once. It was almost dark, too dark to follow a trail. Besides, the horse he had ridden home was
spent, he'd really raced the animal, anxious to get home
to his wife. That meant he'd have to return the ten miles
back to Fair Acres to borrow a fresh mount. He hated
the delay. Every moment that his beloved Bethenia had
to suffer at the hands of the crazy Frank Ward made him
almost crazy. He had no sooner mounted up when two
horses and a buggy pulled into his yard.

"Al? Cook?"

"Hat, you're back!"

"And Bethenia's gone!" Haste interrupted angrily.
"Red Chief and Jasper, too—"

"Oh, my God, Al, we shouldn't have left her alone,"
Aunt Lacey keened.

"Haste, what are you goin' to do?"

"Go after her! Got to get a fresh horse and follow the
trail! A man *was* here . . . found footprints in the stable
. . . can't stand here jawin', got to go—"

"Wait," Cook interrupted, "this brace of horses we
have here been just walkin' slow like all afternoon . . .
can use them." As he spoke, he released the harnesses
and traces from the buggy, "Can track at night well as
day so don't need to wait for daylight. Didn't live with
them Utes without learnin' somethin'. All we need is
that there lantern. Let's go, we'll find her!"

Riding his own horse and holding on to Jasper's lead
rein, Frank Ward led a trussed up Bethenia into a stone
canyon. She estimated that perhaps she was twenty
miles west of her home. Since they had left her sod
house that morning, Frank Ward had not stopped. The
sun was high in the sky, but now that they had halted in
the canyon, she realized that the way their shadows fell

on the ground, they must be moving in a westerly direction.

At the end of the canyon, she noticed a cleft in the rock wall which appeared large enough for a horse and rider to get through. She had seen it as soon as her assailant had tied her feet and hands and pushed her brusquely to the ground. She saw, too, that Red Chief had broken his restraints and followed them. *Bless your heart, Chief, you don't want to be kept away from the treats I have in my pocket, do you?* She knew, too, that Frank Ward had seen the magnificent horse and coveted him. "Chief, don't let him catch you," Bethenia whispered under her breath.

But Red Chief, standing a hundred yards away, was aware of the outlaw as well as his intentions, and he eyed Ward balefully, his white eyes large and threatening.

"Goin' git that red bastard, son of a bitch," Ward said, as he tightened the ropes around her hands.

"Be back directly, then me and you have all night to git better acquainted."

Bethenia's stomach lurched as he placed his filthy face near hers. She could smell the raw, rank, sour body odor from his unwashed body. However, she would not flinch as she stared boldly into his cold eyes. Her attempt at hostility was not lost on Frank, however, who then made an obscene gesture toward his groin.

That was when she noticed that both of his hands were mutilated. On his left hand, his fourth and fifth fingers were curled uselessly against the palm, and on his right hand, his third finger was missing. They were hands capable of doing only evil things, she thought.

He left her with a malicious, cold, heartless look and went over to hobble Jasper. Then, she saw him set out with lariat and rope to try to catch Red Chief.

Don't let him get you, my friend. Head him on a wild-goose chase far away from here, she prayed. She strained to hear the pounding hooves fading in the distance.

She thought about her situation. If only she could get to the knife in her pocket. Impossible, with her hands tied behind her back. She looked around wildly, but there was nothing, only the hard packed dirt of the canyon, a few pebbles, thistle brush, and scattered twigs. She looked in vain for a sharp rock nearby. Nothing.

Her predicament angered her, and she shook her head to fling away the sudden rush of tears that scalded her eyes. Fool, dummy, she berated herself, why didn't you pick up the derringer? You would have had some chance of defendin' yourself. By the time this ordeal is over, you'll probably wish you were dead. She had no doubt as to Frank Ward's evil intentions.

As the tears fell, she bent her head forward, as for the first time in her life she felt helpless. Racking sobs shook her body, and she felt more vulnerable than any other time in her life. Sweat and tears combined as the sinking sun's rays still burned her skin. Even her long, thick black hair had become a problem. She remembered the conversation with her aunt, back in Boston, now it seemed so long ago.

Aunt Lacey had told her more than once to braid her hair tightly before she put it up in a bun, securing it with heavy, steel hairpins.

"Your hair is so silky and smooth and heavy that unless you braid it tightly to give it some body and strength, the hairpins slide right out of it, and your hair falls loose as if you'd never fixed it. Your mother's hair was like that."

"But, Aunt Lacey, sometimes I'm in a hurry . . . don't

have time for all that braiding, so I pile it up, stick a few pins in it, and I'm gone."

"That's why there's steel hairpins everywhere in the house," her aunt concluded.

This morning had been one of those hurried times. She had been anxious to take care of Red, feed and water the calves in the "nursery," exercise Jasper with a brisk ride, and pick cabbages, carrots, and potatoes from her garden for a boiled dinner. She'd pushed the pins into her hair and raced to get her chores completed. And the harrowing ride that Frank Ward had forced upon her had not helped. Her hair was loose and scraggly as she continued to sob.

She raised her head to catch her breath, and she saw a shiny steel hairpin that had fallen from her hair.

"Thank God," she murmured. She bent over and picked up the pin with her mouth. Her mouth was bothered by the dirt and stones that came along with it, but she spat them out and positioned the hairpin between her teeth and twisted her body by pulling her knees forward so she could reach the hemp rope that held her ankles tied.

She picked at the hemp fibers and began to loosen the woven strands that formed the rope. Once she dropped the pin and had to search frantically for it. Finally, she discovered it in the folds of her apron in her lap. She began again, picking and plucking desperately, hoping to be free before Ward returned. It took almost three quarters of an hour before she could rip free the bonds around her feet.

She jumped up and ran quickly to the rock wall, searched with wild frenzy until she found a jagged edge. Another half hour of frantic activity, and suddenly, she was free.

She ran to Jasper, unhobbled him, rode toward the

back of the canyon, out through the stone passageway that she had seen in the wall.

She did not know where she was, only that she had to get away. She knew that if she let Jasper have his head, like most horses he would head straight for what was familiar, his own stall.

By now, it was late afternoon, and the Texas sun would soon be hidden.

"Let's go home, Jasper, home."

The horse's ears pricked up, and he started off. Almost at once, Bethenia heard thundering hooves behind her. *Oh, god, don't let it be him!* She pressed Jasper into a gallop as the stinging dirt from the road flew into her eyes. *Don't let this be the end of my life—at the evil hands of a madman! Oh, Haste, where are you?*

She heard the whir of a lasso, felt the sting of a rope as it whizzed by her face. She leaned flat over Jasper's back and urged him to move faster.

"Please, Jasper, run! Run!"

Her hair whipped around her face. Her breath was forced from her lungs in ragged gasps. She bent as low as she could, pressing her knees closer into her mount's flanks. The terrifying sounds of the approaching pounding hoofs came closer, echoing in her ears. She could hear the hoarse exhalations as the animal bore down on her. She felt his hot breath on her leg as he drew along side of her. Incredulously, she heard the snapping curl of a lariat. She tried to steel her body against the scourging lash. It was not aimed at her but at the horse at her side.

The red blur was Red Chief, racing for home with them.

She urged Jasper on. "You saved me before, friend, I know you can do it again." In the distance, she thought she saw a light. Was someone searching? She dared not hope, and when she looked a second time, the light had disappeared. It was almost dark. If she could only make it before the sun set in the western hills behind her.

Why hadn't Ward tried to shoot her? Or the horses? He had the guns, she'd seen them. She dared not look back a second time. She could still hear him getting closer. Then, Jasper stumbled in the swiftly falling darkness.

Chapter Twenty-four

True to his word, Al Page was an excellent tracker. The Ute Indians had taught him well. For example, he had learned from them that the impression of a footprint in sand or snow could allow one to guess the probable height and weight of a man. A clump of horsehair on a bush or thistle where the horse had scraped his body as he passed by gave the direction taken by the animal. The droppings from the animal, whether fresh or dried, allowed him to gauge how long it had been since the horse had passed by on the trail.

Al got down on his knees to examine the horse's footprints.

"Yeah, that's Red Chief, all right. See that new hind shoe you put on, right there." He pointed to a distinct print in the dirt. "And Jasper's prints are here, too. But there's a strange horse. I'd say a farm animal from the looks o' them hoof prints. Wait . . ." He'd heard something. He leaned forward and put his ear down to listen intently.

"Horses comin'!" he told Haste.

He leaped up and ran for his horse.

"Double round back, Al. See if you can hit them from the rear! Here, take the lantern," Haste said.

"Don't need it. Moonlight's enough for me. Keep it, so if it's Bethie, she can find you."

The strategy was simple. The two men understood each other without further explanation. As in their military experience, Haste would finally face Ward and his guns, and Al would provide protective ammunition from the rear.

Suddenly, Bethenia and the horses burst into the circle of light. Jasper and Red Chief were racing abreast of each other as their pursuer followed, pushing his horse unmercifully.

Haste stepped out to wave down the horses, unmindful of the danger.

"Bethie!" he shouted.

It took a few hundred yards before Bethenia could rein in Jasper and bring him to a halt. Haste ran to her, and she almost fell into his arms, crying with relief. They clung to each other, oblivious to anything except one another.

"Now, ain't that a purty sight," drawled Frank Ward, as he sat on his heaving, foam-flecked horse with both guns drawn and pointed at Haste and Bethenia.

Haste instinctively pushed Bethenia behind him.

"All right, Ward," he shouted, "you got the drop on me! Got one chance . . . better make it good, or I'll . . ."

"You'll what? Ain't nuthin' you can do, Nigra, but die. You and your missus there! Nuthin! Ain't as good with my aim as I used to be since you done messed up my hands." He swung his leg over the saddle and dropped to the ground. His eyes and both guns were focused on Haste and Bethenia as he sauntered nonchalantly toward them. His swagger was apparent. He was enjoying this moment. He'd waited a long time for revenge, and he intended to savor every moment of it.

Haste made an attempt to push Bethenia into the dark fringes of the night, away from the lantern's glow.

Frank Ward's eyes narrowed as he saw the movement. He shook his head and his diabolical grin struck terror in Bethenia as she watched.

"That's no problem for me," Ward snarled, "git you first, then her! You both mine now to do what *I* wants!"

Haste knew that some action was preferable to no action, and he had to act, despite the guns that he faced. He kneeled quickly, drawing and firing his gun all in one motion. Had he hit Ward? Bethenia screamed, and a huge dark shape hurtled forward. Bethenia could only see flashing, slashing hooves in the darkness. Red Chief bore down. His whinney of triumph filled the night air as he hit Ward squarely in his forehead. Ward's head cracked open with the force of the hoofs. As if by reflex, Ward continued to fire, the bullets flying wild as they spun from his guns. Red Chief's pounding hooves then flailed Ward's inert body.

Weak from fear and fright, Bethenia clenched her fists to her mouth as Haste reached Red Chief to calm the quivering beast. Sweaty foam crested on the horse's body, and his voice rumbled throatily as he stomped his feet in continued frustration. Haste constantly tried to comfort the horse; leading him away from Ward's broken body. Red Chief's white eyes roiled with hate, but Haste, with firm urgings, attempted to quiet him.

"It's over, old man, all over," he whispered.

Bethenia walked quietly from the shadows, carefully avoiding any view of the broken body. "He has been frustrated all day, Haste. Maybe you could say he's loco, but he's been denied the treats I'd promised him. Here, Chief."

She gave the horse some of the bits of apples and carrots that had remained deep in her apron pockets all day, forgotten by all—except Red Chief. She called Jasper, who was cropping nearby. "Saved some for you, too. You're a good old boy. Saved my life again," she told him. She patted the animal on his sweaty nose as he greedily gulped his portion of the carrots.

Al Page rode up quickly, breathless and winded by what he had witnessed.

"Had him in my sights, Hat. He never would have gotten off a shot. But when I saw Chief comin' out o' the dark, man what a sight! Whew!"

"I owe everything to that animal, Al, everything."

Even Al Page didn't know, but long ago, while on a cattle drive, in his spare time, Haste had taught Red Chief to react to the sound of gunfire. He had known what such a sound would mean to the horse.

Chapter Twenty-five

Aunt Lacey and her new husband Al Page would be leaving for Boston in two days. The two couples had just completed a satisfying meal of roast pheasant, mashed potatoes, gravy, and greens, topped off by a fancy marble cake that Aunt Lacey showed Bethenia how to bake.

"Aunt Lacey, didn't dream when you came to spend the summer that you would be going back to Boston as Mrs. Page, did you?" Bethenia teased her aunt.

"The last thin' I was looking for was a husband, my dear. But you know the old sayin' from the Bible, 'The Lord works in mysterious ways. His wonders to perform. . . .' So, who am I to reject His wonders?" She looked with adoring eyes across the table at her husband.

Haste inhaled deeply from his cigarette before he spoke to his longtime friend. "So, Al, you're going to start a business of your own, is that it?"

"That's what me and Lacey talked about. Open up a restaurant. Lacey here," he reached for her hand, "says they could use a eatin' place up there that serves good food that colored people like. You know, sweet potato pie, collards, barbecued ribs, fried chicken, food like that. An thought I'd even try to interest them in my chili. Good Texas chili, think that'd go over?"

"The way you make it, Cook? Of course. Nobody makes chili the way you do."

"You still going to run your school, Aunt Lacey?"

"Oh, yes indeed, Bethenia. I have to have somethin' to keep me busy and," she smiled at Al, whose eyes had never left his wife's face, "keep me out o' my husband's affairs."

"I can't think of anything in this world that has given me more pleasure than to see my two most favorite people in the world happy together," Bethenia gushed cheerfully. "Don't you think so, Haste?"

"I sure do agree with that, Bethenia, and I'm happier still that it happened under our roof, my love. And let me tell you, by the time you folk come back to visit *next* year, we'll have a brand new wooden house!"

"I believe you will, son," Al said. He motioned to Haste as they moved back from the table.

"Hat, don't you think we should take our smokes outside, so as not to bother the ladies?"

"Good idea, Al. Right behind you."

Bethenia remarked to her aunt after the men had gone out, "Men always seem to have the need to be together, somehow."

"I guess it's instinct ... or their way of supporting each other, Bethie."

"Haste is really going to miss Uncle Al. Dreadfully, I know. They have been through so much together. Haste has told me, more than once, that he never would have made it as a trooper if it hadn't been for Cook. Haste said one time they were out on the western plains of Texas for days, suffering from the heat, no water and practically out of food. Supplies hadn't caught up with them, and the men rode nearly five-hundred miles in al-most four days without water. Got so desperate that they sacrificed the weakest horses and drank their blood. I think that was the time when Haste said he was nearly ready to desert and give up on the whole thing, but Cook said, 'No, they don't think we colored men have the stomach, the guts, to make it, but we're goin' show them. We's as good a soldier . . . maybe even better than some of them.' And, you know, Uncle Al was glad to ride the trails with Haste as cook when Haste was trail boss. Those two are closer than some fathers and sons, I guess."

Neither woman said anything for a few minutes as they put the food away and cleared the table. Finally, Aunt Lacey spoke.

"Guess it will be up to you and me, Bethie, dear, to see that they stay close and continue this friendship. We shouldn't begrudge them the time they spend together, and we shouldn't feel shut out. The main thing to re-member is that we are each mighty fortunate to have men like them to love us."

"Had to thank you, Haste, for the grand weddin' you and Bethenia gave me and Lacey." Al started his thanks as soon as he and Haste had settled on an old bench out-side. "Never in all my life thought such a wonderful thin' would come by me. A decent, upstanding, classy lady like Lacey would see fit to marry up with a cow-boy, ex-trooper, sometime camp cook, like me. Damn, sometimes I can hardly believe my luck. Some kind of miracle."

In the dark, Haste could not see the heartfelt emotions that crisscrossed his friend's face, but he could hear the depth of feelings that were reflected in the man's voice. He threw his arm around Al's shoulder.

"Miss Lacey knows a real man when she sees one, that's all. Cook, my friend, they don't come any better than you."

Haste lit another cigarette before he spoke again. Al could sense the tension in his voice. "By the way—"

"Yeah? What's on your mind, son?"

"Did you have any trouble reportin' Ward's death? Been meanin' to ask, but didn't want to bring it up in front of Bethenia."

"I knew you were curious ... one o' the reasons I brought you out here to talk. Funny thing, Hat, I went to Evan Connolly the next mornin'. Told him I had been out lookin' for a stray and that I'd found a white man, dead, out there on the road leadin' to Fair Acres, and what should I do? Told him it appeared like the man must have been thrown by his horse, who must have shied from a rattler. Told him I saw a rattler shot dead nearby. Man must have gotten off one shot and killed the varmint, but died from the fall, I guess. Told him there was blood all over a rock layin' there."

"What did Evan say?"

"Why, he told me that since so many Texans were dead set against Negroes, especially anybody who had been a trooper, and since some didn't even trust those still in the army, I'd better stay clear of the whole thin'. He'd send some o' his boys out to check fences, they'd find the body and bring it in. Said the less talk about the situation, the better. Said he always believed if a man carried himself like a man, should be treated like one—no matter his color. Course I didn't tell him that I shot the rattler and placed him right near Ward's body, and that I killed me a rabbit and poured his blood all over that rock. I agreed with him . . . the less said, the better." Al Page said with a wink.

"Didn't anyone see the hoofprints of our horses all over the place?" Haste wanted to know.

"Don't know. Didn't ask. When I left the area, only *his* horse's tracks could be seen, headin' back the way he'd come. Back to his home stall, I'd guess. Evan Connolly said the sheriff came and identified the body as Frank Ward's, an escaped criminal, a rustler, murderer, and a well-known renegade."

"That so? The sheriff didn't say what Ward was up to in these parts."

"Nope, but *you* know and *I* know that Evan Connolly knows that you and Ward had crossed paths fore."

"Guess I owe *that* white man a lot."

Al Page turned his face to look directly at Haste, their faces lit only by the glow from their cigarettes.

"Well, now, son, that's where you're wrong. I wouldn't say you owe *him,* I'd say it was equal-like. You owe each other. Remember, if it weren't for us in the Tenth Cavalry, this part o' Texas would never have been tamed. Don't forgit them days and nights we was chasin' Mexicans over the Chiricahua Mountains. Fightin' all them Indians, tryin' to git them back to their territories. Did we do all that for *us?*"

He spat out a shred of tobacco and stared through the darkness at Haste.

He heard Haste sigh and agreed, "I guess not, Cook."

"Damn straight, you guess not," he continued. "Did it cause the United States Army said that's what we *had* to do—paid us thirteen dollars a month to map out this land, find water, good grazing land, and move the Indians so that the settlers could live out here. So, no, no, son, you don't owe *nobody.* Should be the other way round. Ain't no need to be humble. Be proud knowin' you had a job to do and you did it!"

"Thanks, Cook, for reminding me."

"Thanks not needed. And one more thin', Haste, fore you start givin' up on yourself. I saw the way you stood up to Ward the other night. Him with his twin guns, and you with only one. Knew he was a mad man, but you didn't back down. Saw the whole thin' from where I was, I had the drop on him, but—"

"Sure glad you did. I was hopin' that if you were in back of him you could save Bethie. Again, thanks, old pal."

"Already told you, no thanks needed. I am the one to be thankin'. It's cause you're the kind o' man you are, a man who understands men and the right of the world. Sarge, if it hadn't been for you leadin' me, showin' me how to be a good trooper, I wouldn't have made it. Lord knows where I'd be—ex-slave knowin' nuthin' but slavery. Then, I joined the cavalry and met you. Guess we learned together, eh? Now, look at me, married up with a fine woman, and on my way up north to open my own place! Son, I'd be proud to be half the man you turned out to be! Thank *you!*"

Chapter Twenty-six

The newlyweds had returned to Boston. Bethenia and Haste settled in to start their married life in earnest. As a result of the Ward episode, Haste was even more solicitous of his wife.

"I'm so sorry, my love, that you had to live through somethin' like dealin' with that bastard, Ward. I'll never forgive myself for leavin' you alone, puttin' you through that ordeal."

"Oh, Haste, you know by now that your wife is tough—after all that we shared on the trail." She snuggled even closer to him. "And I'll tell you somethin' else, husband mine, I'm never going anywhere without that little protector you gave me. I know that Texas is far from being as civilized as we'd like—so really, part of that mess with Ward was my fault. I should have had that derringer with me."

"I'm not sure even that would have helped, as crazy as he was."

"Haste, honey, it's behind us now. Long 's we're together, everythin' is perfect."

However, Bethenia sensed a concern on her husband's part. Night after night, they enjoyed tender lovemaking. Each experience brought new delights to them, and they slept comforted in each other's arms. But it was obvious to her, deep in her heart, that Haste had a concern, or concerns, that he had not yet shared with her.

One morning, she awoke to find his place in their bed empty. She got up quickly and found him already dressed, staring out of the kitchen window, deep in thought. She had just tumbled from their warm bed and stirred by the sight of her strong, stalwart, and sensitive husband, she tiptoed behind him, resting her head against his back. It felt so reassuring to her.

She sensed a fleeting momentary resistance in his body before he relaxed and turned to greet her with a warm kiss.

"Good morning."

Bethenia stretched up on her tiptoes to receive his kiss. Haste had a way of making her feel wanted and loved. She delighted in his strong masculinity—made her feel secure and safe. But, this morning, she had the feeling her personal security and peace of mind was threatened.

"You all right, Haste?"

"Who wouldn't be all right with a beautiful woman like you in his arms first thing in the morning?" he teased her.

"You seemed so far away just now, starin' out the window. Still upset over not getting that permit, aren't you, to build the new house?"

The morning sunlight that streamed through the window brought even more loving warmth to his soft, brown eyes as he looked at her. He had pulled his dark wavy hair to the back of his head, tied it together with a leather thong, and it glistened with a rich, healthy glow. It seemed to Bethenia that the planes and contours of his rugged face were more sharply etched than ever.

Never had she seen him look more handsome. Even the deep concern he bore now only added determination and strength to his features. Bethenia could guess that it was when his men saw him like this that they trusted him to lead, whether in battle or on the trail.

She knew she would do all that was in her power to make this man happy. This one man whom she had thrust herself upon, had coerced into taking her from her dastardly fate in Oklahoma to her unrealistic dream in Denver—this man whom she had fallen in love with when she saw his face reflected in the white heat of the blacksmith's forge—this was the man she would love until death claimed her.

Haste sighed deeply before he answered.

"They said, and Bethie, I could hardly believe their reasoning, makes no sense to me, but the clerk said, 'Understand you bought the Josh Carpenter place.' I told him, 'Yes, sir, paid cash money, have the receipt right here.' "

"What did he say to that?"

"Said, 'Where did you git enough money to buy property?' Bethenia, he didn't believe me! So, when I told him who I was, Haste Allen Terrell, that I was an ex-trooper, that I had been trail boss for Evan Connolly, and that I had been rewarded for my work with the Pinkerton agency, then he smirked and said, 'Oh, yeah, your the Nigra that helped catch . . . who was it . . . the Ward brothers?' Bethie, honey, it was almost as if *I* was the criminal!"

"Then, what did you say, Haste?"

Bethenia saw her husband's face flush with anger.

"Oh, he shuffled some papers on his desk, looked me straight in the eye and said, 'Sorry, son.' I wanted to tell him so bad that my momma never had no sons who looked like *him*. Anyway, he said Josh didn't fulfill completely his homestead pact. He only lived on the place three years instead of the *five* years required by the federal law. He couldn't sell me what he didn't own. Then, he said, he can't give me a permit. But, will give me sixty days to show him I have a right."

"Do better than that, I told him. I'll bring you the law that proves I have a right to what I bought! And, Bethie, that's what I'm going to do!"

Haste rubbed his eyes wearily and turned away from the window. With his arm still around Bethenia's shoulder, they moved to the kitchen table. They each sat down, and he reached for her hands across the table.

"I know the law says that I can own this property. I'm sure of it. One day Colonel Wooster was talking to me, he always was a fair man, but one day he said how surprising it was to him that so few of the colored soldiers had deserted, in spite of the hard times they had.

"He said that day that an honorable discharge meant that the colored soldiers, like anybody else, could get in on the Homestead Act."

"And what is that, Haste?"

"Well, in 1862, the government was anxious to settle the West. So, President Lincoln signed the Act giving land to any person twenty-one years old, head of a household, provided the person lived on the land for five years and was a citizen."

"We've only lived here six months."

"Yes, but the same law said, according to Colonel Wooster, that after six months, if you wanted to take title earlier, you could do that by paying a dollar twenty-five cents an acre."

Bethenia's face lit up when she realized what her husband had said.

"Haste! I've got money in the bank in Boston! Oh, Haste . . ." She moved to his side.

Haste smiled at her, reached for her and hugged her impulsively.

"I know what you've got in Boston, my love, and that money is going to stay there. I've figured it all out. All we need is two-hundred dollars to pay for the land, and it's ours!"

"But, Haste—"

"No, no, I'd be a pretty poor husband if I couldn't come up with two-hundred dollars. I'd sell Red Chief, if I had to, fore I'd take *any* of your money. But it won't come to that. I still have a few pennies to rub against one another. What I need is a written copy of the law, and a certified copy of my discharge papers. I'm sure the colonel will help me. Something these rednecks can't dispute. They don't believe we're entitled to anything. You should have seen how red that man's face got when I first told him what I wanted. 'A building permit?' I could have been asking for the moon."

The recent experience made Haste's voice quiver with anger. He told Bethenia, "You . . . you should have seen him, Bethie! Stared at me as if by just looking at me I would disappear from his sight. Like . . . like his staring at me could melt me into a spot of grease on the floor, something he could wipe up with an old rag. Want you to know, Bethie, had all I could do to keep from reaching across that desk, pulling him to his feet, and stomping *him* into the ground. You know what makes me mad is that it was for the likes of him that we cavalrymen fought like the devil to tame this part of the country. It's the rednecks like him that try to deny us our due. Damn, I need proof! Got to get it from somewhere."

"You'll find whatever it is you need, Haste. I know you will. You've never let anything stop you. How can I help?"

His answer came with a quick smile.

"Keep loving me and believing in me, honey, that's all I ask. I've promised you a wooden house, and by damn, that's what you're going to have. We're not goin' to spend our lives in a dirt sod house."

He got up abruptly and walked over to the kitchen wall where a young twig had thrust its way through the mud. He broke it off angrily and threw it into the fire. Bethenia heard the hiss and crackle as the wood's green sap spit through the flames.

Haste slapped his sombrero on his head.

"Goin' to take care of the animals. Be back for breakfast soon."

Bethenia watched him walk toward the stable. Would they be forced to leave the property Haste had already purchased? He was so determined to make it as a rancher with cattle and horses.

She dressed and busied herself with preparing their breakfast. She put a pot of coffee on the fire to brew. Home-cured bacon plus scrambled eggs and hot grits were prepared by her capable hands. Everything would be ready when Haste came back to the house.

But she was not prepared for his announcement when he stepped inside the door. She could smell the pungent odor of his sweat mixed together with the horses' scents. She saw a dark scowl on his face, and her heart responded with a thudding pound. She could hardly believe his next words.

"I want you to go back to Boston."

His words lay like a wooden barrier suddenly raised between them. Bethenia whirled around, the mud walls of the room closing in on her.

"What did you say? Go back *where?*"

"The only way I'm going to be able to convince these people of my rights is to go to Fort Balance, get proof of the law, and . . . my papers."

"But, why do I have to go to Boston?"

"Bethie, there's no way I'm going to leave you here alone, not again, not after—"

"Well," she broke in, "if you think I'm going to run back to Boston, forget it—"

"But, I'd be worried, and if you're with your aunt Lacey and Al, then I'd know you're safe. I have to *know* that, not guess about it. Don't you see?"

"No, I don't see," she countered.

"That I . . . look, don't make this harder for me! I've put you through enough. That Ward business—"

"You make it sound like I'm a problem, Haste. I'm your wife, remember, we're in this together." Her eyes blazed in anger at him, and she stamped her foot defiantly. "Don't you know I only want to be with you!"

She slammed the plates of food on the table. It was obvious that neither of them wanted to eat. The steam curled from the food into the chilly morning air, the eggs lay like large accusing eyes on the plates. Bethenia felt a wave of nausea come over her, and she shook her head to free the angry tears that unexpectedly dimmed her eyesight.

She ran into the bedroom to fling herself on the bed. She heard Haste come in and kneel down beside the bed. He stroked her hair tenderly, his voice was low and determined. "Bethie, I beg you, try to understand. I will not be cheated. Will not! I did what the army asked me to do, fought when I was told to, spent cold nights, hot days in the field, went hungry, thirsty, and went without to do what the government said I had to do. Now, I want what I'm entitled to. And I intend to get it, or die trying. No one can fault a man for that. And, Bethie." His voice softened as he continued to caress her. "I've told you before, it was *your* determination, *your* single-mindedness that I've always seen in you that makes me love you so much. I won't back down. Deep down, I know you wouldn't want me to. So I'm going to Fort Balance. I will send for you soon 's I get back."

"You won't have to send for me," Bethenia said through her sobs. "I'm not leaving. You may think you're the only stubborn, intractable one in this family, but you've met your match, Haste Terrell, in me."

She sat up abruptly and flicked the tears from her eyes. Her voice was thick, but determined. "So, you do what you have to do, and I'll be right here waiting till you get back. And see that you come right back, or you know me, I'll be coming after you."

She gave him a brave smile.

Haste gathered her into his arms, and breathed a submissive sigh. "Don't doubt that for a moment, my love. Knowin' you as I do, don't doubt that for a minute."

Chapter Twenty-seven

Haste was still hesitant about leaving Bethenia for the second time. This time, he did not have the reassuring presence of his old dependable friend, Al Page. Charley Garcia and Gus Bellamy had been on the trail with him, and he had confidence in each of them. He approached Charley first.

He found Charley mending a bridle that needed new straps for reins. Charley had used a sharp knife to cut long strips of leather and was preparing to attach them to the headstall. He seemed at home at the Terrell place, always ready to do any and all odd jobs for Bethenia and Haste.

Garcia eyed his former trail boss and realized at once that Haste was in a serious mood. Charley knew Haste was never one to mince words. When he spoke, it was because he had something to say.

"Morning, Charley. Fine job you're doing there." Haste pointed to the beautifully cut leather strips. "You always had the knack for working with leather."

"Guess so." Charley's black hair hung in a dark forelock across his eyes, and he flicked it back with a brisk toss of his head. "Guess I got that from my pa. He always worked good with leather." He waited for Haste to continue. Haste's eyes, like twin augers, bore into Charley's face as if daring him to flinch or recoil from their direct scrutiny. Haste voiced his concern without preface.

"I'm going to ask you, Charley, to help me again. You know I'm not the kind of man who likes to ask for favors."

"I know that, Hat. What can I do for you?"

"Would you ... I have to go to Fort Balance ... would you mind staying close by for a couple of days? Keep an eye of thin's?"

"I will do whatever you want, not to worry, whatever."

"Thanks, Charley. Knew I could count on you. I'll ask Gus Bellamy to help you out."

"He's a good man, Bellamy, a good man," Charley repeated, as he picked up the strips of leather. "Don't worry, Hat, I will be here to watch over everything."

Later that night, Haste informed Bethenia of his plans. He pleaded with her, "Please, my love, stay close to the house ... and take the derringer with you if you go outside. Better yet, keep it with you, always."

He twisted his body and pulled her close to him.

"Bethenia, you know you're my life. Without you, I'd be nothing, have nothing. Never in this world did I expect a lovely young girl to come out nowhere, riding a horse like the wind and ride right into my life and my heart! But, my love, that's what *you* did!"

Bethenia responded to Haste's desire and intensity by her own need to be loved. Her eyes glowed with desire, and it seemed to her that her skin flamed hot for the want of her husband's touch upon her flesh. She moved closer to him, impatient for his advance.

"Oh, Haste, love me, please," she begged, her soft moans and whispers lost in the warmth of his chest as he leaned over her. "I never knew that love could be like this. That I could love anyone as much as I love you. Love me, Haste. God, don't preach to me . . . love me, love me. You'll be gone in the morning," she moaned. "Don't waste a minute!" She reached for his lips.

"Why, you greedy, little, impatient vixen!"

Haste grinned down at her. His lips met hers with such ferocity, such hunger, he almost robbed her of her breath. And she responded. So many untoward situations had denied them their promises of fulfillment that this night their twin ravenous cravings for each other were almost violent in their passion. Each of them sought to block out every distraction, except each other. Gone were the sod walls, the dusty, dirt trails, the stone canyons, and deceitful evil men.

At last, Haste's hungry mouth searched to savor the honeyed sweetness of the golden globes on Bethenia's rounded breasts. The erotic energy that pulsed in response from her body was matched exquisitely by his own. Her breathy gasps that feathered in his ear sounded to him as if the fluttering wings of a thousand birds beat in unison near his temple.

"Ah, Bethie, how can I leave you again? How can I tear away from your arms?"

He held her close. It was as if he were trying to memorize every part of her body with his own. He knew he would have to physically tear himself away from her in the morning. It would rip his soul to again leave the one person in the world who meant more than life to him, but he knew he had to do it, or their future would be deprived of all joy.

* * *

As Haste and Red Chief moved briskly along the trail toward Fort Balance, his thoughts turned back to the days when he first joined the cavalry. There were no wide trails then, no roads, only resistant, fighting Indians anxious to keep their land and not be returned to their territories. There were treacherous Mexicans, herds of buffalo, wild horses, long-horned steer, and hard times. He knew that it was the efforts of men like him, the buffalo soldiers of the Ninth and Tenth Cavalry, who had done their part in taming the West and made it possible for others to live here. Would his hopes for a decent life with Bethenia be denied? All because of his color?

His anxiety grew as he thought about his mission. Was Colonel Wooster still stationed at Fort Balance? Would he find what he needed there to prove his claim? Was his future bound by the dictates of others? Why wasn't he judged by what he had done, as a man, as a soldier, as a trail boss, and as a Pinkerton agent? He gritted his teeth. They'll not deny me my rights, he vowed silently. I'll get what is mine, or die trying.

As he and Red Chief moved down the trail, past wooded areas of pine and oak, scrub brush, some cacti, and rust-colored stone canyon walls, the hot Texas sun bore down on them. He looked for a place to rest, preferably a shady spot, by a stream, so that he and Red Chief could cool down. He reckoned he would be at Fort Balance before nightfall.

He had traveled another twelve miles when he spotted an abandoned camp. It was at the foot of a small hill, shaded in part by some cottonwood trees. Luckily, behind the rough shack was a small brook, apparently fed by a spring hidden in the hills.

"Good place to rest, my friend," Haste told Chief. He removed the saddle and bedroll and led the horse to the brook. For himself, he swallowed some cold coffee that Bethenia had prepared and ate a sandwich while Chief rolled in the grass and then started to crop.

Haste finished his lunch and rolled a cigarette. He took a deep, satisfying puff as he watched Red Chief feeding nearby. In the noonhour, all the earth appeared still and quiet. Few birds were about; only the insistent shrill noises of the heat bug filtered through the wavy mirage of the grass.

He signaled to Red Chief, who trotted up eagerly and was rewarded with a carrot.

"Come on, old man, got to get going, as peaceful as this spot is." He started to saddle the horse when he was startled by the sound of pounding hooves that disrupted the noon silence. Both he and the horse looked in the direction of a dust cloud coming toward them.

"Haste! Haste!"

By God, it was Bethenia! He dropped the saddle and ran to grab Jasper's reins and jerk the horse to a stop.

"Bethie, what are you doing here?"

A wide grin split Bethenia's flushed face. Her black hair, thick and tousled, framed her eager young face. Her dark eyes sparkled with mischief.

"Oh, Haste." She dropped from her horse, winded and breathless. "I couldn't stay back at the ranch, just couldn't."

"Is everything all right there?" Haste demanded. "Why couldn't you stay put like I asked you to? And how did you find me?"

"Oh, everything is fine. And I couldn't 'stay put,' as you say, because I didn't want to 'stay put,' " she said defiantly. "So, I told Gus either he'd help me track you down or I'd do it myself, alone. Look, over there." She pointed to a rider some hundred yards away who acknowledged Haste with a wave of his sombrero. Haste recognized Gus.

He turned to his wife. He was angry with her, but his anger softened when he saw the eager, fresh face of the one he adored waiting expectantly for his response. The morning desert sun was reflected in the depth of her eyes, and on the lovely sheen of her moist skin. And it outlined the desirous form of her lithe young body.

"Bethenia," Haste sighed, "what am I going to do with you! You are the most stubborn, willful, woman I've ever known! I should make you go back."

"Make me?" Bethenia mocked him. "Look, Haste Allen Terrell, I've been with you on the trail for six weeks or more. Traveled with you on the Goodnight-Loving trail from the Oklahoma Territory to Colorado. Went through all kinds of weather—rain, sleet, heat, snow— lived with twenty-five hundred head of long-horns, eleven or so cowboys, Indians, and even renegades. Slept under the chuck wagon in a cooney and ate hardtack, beans, and biscuits along with everybody else. I never asked for anything to be made easier because I was a female. So, Mr. Terrell, if you think a little three-day excursion in the wide-open spaces of Texas is going to keep me home, you don't know your wife Bethenia Cooper Terrell very well!"

She stopped for breath, her face flushed with her intensity.

"Don't you see, Hat?" she pleaded. "I've got to be with you. Always. Whatever happens to us, I've got to be with you. Don't send me back."

"Bethie." Haste's voice softened as he gathered his trembling wife in his arms. "I guess we'd better get moving." He kissed her tenderly, tasting the salt from her tears which now flowed freely down her cheeks.

"We'll go and get my certified discharge papers, as well as a copy of the law. I'm certain they'll have it at the post."

Bethenia grinned through her tears.

"You said *we,* Haste, *we.* Do you mean it? *We* are going to Fort Balance?"

She hopped eagerly up and down on one foot.

"Bethie," he sighed, "you have followed and chased me just about everywhere! What a fool I am to think that you won't find me. Like I said before, you are the most stubborn, young woman I have ever met. Yes, my love," he said sweeping her into his arms, "*we* are going to Fort Balance. Now, mount up fore I change my mind and send you back home."

"Pshaw, Haste." Bethenia sucked her teeth defiantly. "Told you long ago that it would take more than a regiment to keep me from you. I knew that the minute I laid eyes on you at the Yorke homestead."

She looked at him, slyly, her eyes twinkled in a mischievous, impish grin.

"Can't guess why *you* keep trying to get away from me!" she added.

Haste grabbed her to hold her close in his arms. In a quiet, solemn voice, he told her, "Guess it's because I like what happens when you catch me. Like right now." He kissed the top of her head and led her to her waiting horse.

"Let me help you."

He made a stirrup of his hands so that when she placed her foot on it, he could give her a light boost to help her into the saddle.

From atop Jasper's back, she looked down at her handsome husband, and the loving look he saw in her eyes was both challenging and inviting.

"Well, Mr. Haste Allen Terrell, maybe it's *your* turn to do some chasing!"

She spurred her horse into a direct run, her long black hair flying with wild freedom.

"Don't need no invitation, eh, Chief?" Haste mounted his own horse quickly.

"Heehaw!" Haste shouted. Stimulated by Jasper's fleeting advance, Red Chief laid his ears back and accepted the challenge. His huge reddish-brown body soon became a blur of pounding horseflesh as he raced after Jasper.

Red Chief thundered down the trail, and for a while, the two horses raced neck and neck, until at last, winded and laughing, Bethenia reined Jasper to a halt.

"Satisfied, Haste?" she asked, laughing at him. "You finally caught me. Still, want to send me back?"

Haste saw the warm sparkle in her eyes, her lovely face flushed and glowing from both the ride and her inner excitement. He knew there was meaning and truth in his life. It was because of the woman who was beside him, waiting for his next words.

"Send you back? Not hardly, my love. You're going to be with me forever. From now on, every trail we go down, we will travel it together."

"Learned that on the Goodnight-Loving, eh, Haste?"

"Lesson learned, course completed," he told her, as he leaned over from Red Chief to kiss her.

Both horses were well-trained and waited patiently until the couple finished.

Epilogue

Bethenia and Haste Allen Terrell received the deed to their home and land, and with Haste's farming skills and Bethenia's homemaking talents, it was a pleasant and profitable homestead. Over the years, the sound of children's voices filled the air, much to the couple's boundless joy. Never again did Haste leave Bethenia alone—they were partners in life and in love.